INFILTRATION

Two boys,
one family,
a world at war

Rosalind Minett

Rosalind Minett

Uptake Publications
Kingswood Manor Cottage
Tedworth, Surrey KT207AJ

Designer: Pradeep Premalal

A RELATIVE INVASION

A coming of age trilogy

BOOK 2

INFILTRATION

ACKNOWLEDGEMENTS

Grateful thanks to Karen Perkins (editor)
and Terry Cottle

Cover design Pradeep Premalal

DEDICATION

For Alex,
a very special person
who railed against war

CHAPTER ONE

September 7th 1940

*The German air force unleashes a wave of heavy
bombing raids on London*

The cart came to a halt. The only noise here was from
animals. Dogs were barking inside the house, chickens
clucked somewhere to the left and the horse
harrumphed beside him.

'It's this house,' Jed the carter said. 'Mr and Mrs
Pawsey's. You can jump down now.'

Billy clambered down slowly, for the horse was
swishing his tail very near his face. He didn't want to
hurry. He needed to take in the place that was his billet
before he went to meet his new foster parents.

Was it only this morning that he was standing on
the station alongside Jill's pushchair while the grown-
ups discussed how to squeeze into the packed-full
train? Was it only last night he was squashed in the
cellar with all the terrifying whistling and crashing
above?

He breathed in the country smells and turned to
look at what was waiting for him. It was very different
from last evacuation. This house was quite big. There
was a lot of muddy garden in front and not far from a
pig pen there were chicken houses. It might be nice,
nicer than the vicarage where Mother was evacuated

with baby Jill. He swallowed. He mustn't be sad to be left behind.

'Brave laddie. Chin up,' Jed encouraged him as he looped the reins to keep the horse still and safe. 'I s'pose it's a bit hard to be here on your own, when your cousin and Aunty are billeted right near your ma and sister. But they'm not having animals, like here now.'

Billy nodded. 'Yes and K-Kenneth hasn't ever been evacuated before and I know this village from last time.'

'That's right. You're nearly a local.'

That wasn't really so – the locals had always called him a 'vaccie' – but he'd certainly be very welcome at one place. Perhaps he could soon visit the tiny cottage where he'd been billeted before.

Jed was already at the gate. 'You still standing waiting? Come you on, Billy. I's'll make sure you're all right.'

Billy followed him. The path was thin with flower bushes on either side, quite untidy. A dog barked again somewhere at the back of the building and hens clucked nearby. He peered around for them, ready to step away. Chickens might peck strangers. He didn't know, he wasn't used to them.

Jed pulled a rope with a rusty bell on it. It sounded a single dong.

A man opened the door but peered out as though he was looking beyond them focusing on the far distance. Two black dogs rushed forward, barking. The man shouted 'Basket!' and pushed them back. He had whiskers right down over his ears and coming out of them but not a lot of hair on his head. A few strips covered his topknot but veins showed through and there were great veins on the back of his hand when he

2

held open the door. Billy peeped along the passage. There must be a lady somewhere.

The old man said, 'Jed – where you been about? You brought the London lad?' He smiled but he didn't seem to be looking at Billy. He pointed out a wooden box 'For your boots,' but Billy wasn't wearing boots so he left his shoes on.

The carter seemed to take charge. 'Seth, how be you, then? This chappie here be Billy. His mother'm gone to her billet at the vicarage down over. I reckon as she'll be visiting afore long to see he's settled in o'right.'

'I see, I see,' said the old man.

But he didn't see, for he was fumbling his way to the back room, touching the hall walls. It was dark except for a small lamp with a parchment shade, an open book beside it. Mr Pawsey stood opposite it and opened his hands to the room with its large wooden table and heavy chairs.

'Sit you down, lad, my Missus will brew up once she's done with the hens. She has to shut them up carefully at night against they foxes.'

He pawed around in the air, bending over a little until his hands found the table and book. A pair of glasses were underneath it. He grasped them and put the wire handles over his ears. Now he peered straight at Billy through lenses as thick as the bottoms of bottles. His eyes were big pale blotches behind them. He looked quite different now. 'Ah. So here you are, safe and sound.'

The carter put his hand on Billy's head. 'Nice lad, this'n, Seth. He'll be able to spot your specs when you lose them.' He gave a rumbling laugh and the old man joined in.

'You'm right. That'll be useful. Bane of my life, they glasses. Too heavy to wear all the time and can't see without them.'

Jed gave Billy's shoulder a friendly pat. 'I'd better be off, you folk. My supper'll be on the table. Billy, you'll settle down with Mr and Mrs Pawsey afore you know. You'll see my cart round and about these lanes and I'll give you a wave.' He winked, first at Billy, then at Mr Pawsey and stomped back to the front door.

It was now that Billy had that nasty fluttery feeling like months ago, the first time he'd been away from home. It was when he was walking round the village with the teacher trying to find him a billet, and he was the last child to be taken. Now the sight of friendly Jed going out of the door started the flutters again.

The old man sat down heavily in a chair whose leather was cracked all over, and kneaded the veins in his hands. 'Billy, eh? Hmm.' He peered at Billy. 'You a useful boy?

'I think so, sir. I'll t- try.'

There was loud cackling outside the window. The old man laughed. 'One of they hen's got out, and the Missus'll be chasing it. They lead her a dance. Perhaps you'll run fast enough to get 'em in order, they hens.'

Billy said nothing. He wasn't too sure that he wanted to get near the feathery, clucking things with their poky beaks. He sat still, hoping he wouldn't be asked to help right away. He fiddled with his suitcase wondering if Mother had put in a tin of food at the bottom or anything he should hand over.

The back door opened and the lady bustled in, brushing her hands on her muddy apron. She stopped short when she saw Billy, sitting on the edge of his chair.

'Our little lad, is it? I thought I heard the cart. Well, well, well. Now then. Welcome to your new home. That nasty bombing in London, we've got to get you out of that, eh. Got to get you a little nest, here, haven't we. A little nest.'

'Billy, his name is,' said the old man, and spat very accurately into a special bucket with brass straps sitting beside the fireplace.

'Billy, is it?' said Mrs Pawsey. Her sentences seemed to end in questions although she didn't have a questioning sort of face, more like a cushion with lines and dents pressed into it as well as two blackbird eyes. 'We'll soon make you at home, my dear. Stand yourself up, can't you, let's have a look at you.'

Billy sprang to attention, keeping his polished shoes smartly together.

'My goodness, what a fine lad, aren't you. Strong as well, I should think. Shouldn't you think, Seth?'

The old man leant forward and felt Billy's arms. 'We can put a bit more muscle on that, Missus'

'M-my uncle was trying to t-toughen me up before the bombing started. I had to do lots of r-runs and wrestling.'

Mrs Pawsey shook her head. 'Doesn't look like you enjoyed it, lovey?' She shook her head again. 'No, no.' Dry tresses of grey hair fell across her face. 'Leave him, Seth. We won't be getting you wrestling, don't you worry, my dear. You're quite tough enough for us. We shall be feeding you well and you'll be a help to us old folks, won't you just?'

Billy nodded. 'Yes.'

'So it's all fair and dandy.' She smiled in a dimply way. 'I spoke to your father on the phone. He said you'd been evacuated to this village afore.'

'Yes, I was with Mrs Y-Youldon.'

'Joan Youldon? I know her. Kitchen maid up at the Grange, straight from leaving school right up to having her first little one. She's hardly grown up herself, poor girl.'

'Hardly a woman size, she,' added the old man.

'And scarce enough room in her cott for a vaccie, I'd think.'

'There were two of us. I made friends with him. Alan, he was called.'

'Two vaccies! Well fancy be. Now how did Joan manage that in her place?'

'She was nice, really nice. We p-played with her little children and did j-jobs. I made things for them.' If only he could go over right now and see them. His voice came out quietly, 'Is her house far from here, please?'

'Bless you, no house is far from any house here, if you can call some of them houses,' said Mrs Pawsey.

The old man looked at her and chuckled.

She beckoned Billy to the scullery where the two dogs lay. Their noses lifted eagerly, and one gave a rough bark. 'Enough of that, Noah! Here, Billy, you'd better come and introduce yourself or there'll be no peace once the master moves from his chair.'

They were quite big dogs. Billy put a hand towards the head of one. Immediately, they both leapt up, barking. He started back.

'There's no need to worry. It's all noise. Not a nasty streak in either of 'em. Just stand still a minute till they get used to you being here. Here's Noah.'

One dog had a white slash across its right ear and a patch on its back. The other had a white muzzle and chest. 'And this is Japhet.'

'Are they for burglars?'

'Burglars and all sorts of things, you'll see. Working dogs, aren't they.'

She took him through the house, which seemed full of big shabby furniture, and then up the wooden staircase where there was a proper bathroom and three bedrooms just like a London house, except that the landing floorboards weren't straight and creaked dreadfully.

'Now we sleep over the landing just there, and this bedroom's for you.' Mrs Pawsey opened a door and showed Billy inside.

There was a wardrobe for his clothes and he saw toy cars inside it. The bed was plenty big enough for two, if only Alan had been here. It had a dark blue coverlet and looked very comfortable. All he needed was some of his own special things to put in the wardrobe. He placed his suitcase in it.

'Where should I keep my gas mask?'

'On top of that wardrobe, lovey, but doubt if you'll need that here.'

'Have you had bombing?'

'No, bless you. Nothing like that for you to worry about, is there. Now, do you like your room?'

'It's really nice, Mrs Pawsey.' He looked at the cars in the wardrobe and then at her.

'Yes, I put those cars there specially for you and there's a pile of comics under the bed, so you'll be all right, you see.'

'Thank you ever so much.'

'Oh, a London toff, you are, no mistake. Shan't we get on fine?'

She took him down into the garden before it got too dark to see everything.

'It's dry now, but we shall have to find you some boots for outside.'

Luckily, she had got the chickens away, safe in their hutch. He'd expected that they would be rushing around inside it, pushing each other for space but they sat in a line pressed against each other in a friendly way, only making the quietest of clucks when Mrs Pawsey opened the door a crack for Billy to peer inside.

'You might like giving them their grain. And there'll be eggs to collect.'

He might, if the chickens weren't looking. Eggs were good for exchange and who knows what they might get in return. He looked at the feathery things doubtfully. Their beaks were poky and their eyes rather mean. The ones with closed eyes looked better.

'Oh you're having a good look, aren't you, love, but now let's go over here.'

There were two pigs in a sty with a small, small yard and a low brick wall round it. They looked a lot bigger than he'd expected pigs to be. They were as big as him only their bodies were sideways on. They walked like ladies on high heels but with two points at the front of the foot instead of one and their bottoms were the size of a fat man's. The taller pig was snuffling up towards Mrs Pawsey.

'Both boy pigs,' Mrs Pawsey said proudly. 'The fattest one's Hardy. Two years old. Look at him, he knows I'm talking about him. He's smart.'

The pig lifted its snout and fixed its tiny pale eyes on Billy. They looked dangerous.

'Tell him I'm eight and he's only two. If he's smart.'

Mrs Pawsey checked the pen's door catch. 'They won't hurt, but they can get nasty if they don't get what they want.'

'Like camels?' He remembered Dad saying that camels could turn nasty, ages ago. That was at the zoo where they'd gone on his fifth birthday.

'My goodness me,' she shook with laughter. 'That'll be the day when I have camels to look after.'

'Don't under-estimate pigs,' Mr Pawsey advised, coming up behind them. 'They can't talk but they can think. It's thinking that counts. Look at old Laurel.'

The pig with the black blob on its back was pulling the peelings dish towards himself with his snout, and away from Hardy.

'See. He's worked out how to get one up on Hardy, although he's smaller.'

Billy watched. Laurel was like Cousin Kenneth, smaller then Billy but smarter at getting his own way. He put his hands on the pigs' wall, but jumped back as Laurel snorted and Hardy put his snout up high. It was time to look somewhere else.

In the field nearby was a dun brown horse with a ring of fluff round its hooves, surely the same size as a camel. Mrs Pawsey followed him as he went over to it.

'Do people ride the horse?'

'Only Mr Sinclair. That's his horse. He just uses our field. We used to have cows when we were younger, you see. Too much for us now.' She sighed and patted a squashy part of her front, which might have been tummy or bosoms, he wasn't sure. The horse looked really strong. He screwed up his eyes, trying to imagine riding it, waving Mr Durban's Cossack sabre. It would be a wondrous way of escaping Hitler, or even turning on him, scaring him to death so he couldn't do any more bombing.

'Come on. Up this way.' Mrs Pawsey led the way between the field and the side of the house. Behind, there was a small patch of garden with two wooden chairs beside some rose bushes. Then a large patch with green things growing upwards, and some more brown patches with ridges along them.

'They's our vegetables, over there, so you won't go hungry with what we grow. As long as I can keep those slugs off it all, and the rabbits. Wish we could put a wall round it to keep the blighters out.'

'My Granddad grows v-vegetables. I used to help him weed the carrots.'

'Well now you can help with ours.'

Billy felt a bit more cheerful, although the carrots reminded him of that shocking time: Uncle Ted like a scarecrow shuffling towards home after the rescue at Dunkirk. Where was Uncle now? He'd be doing more fighting somewhere foreign and not having baths or dinners or bedtimes. Billy crossed his fingers on both hands that Uncle would get home safely again. He thought of his stripy spinning top Uncle had sent him from France. If only there'd been room in his suitcase for it.

An ominous rumbling in the sky stopped the tour. It was like in London but there hadn't been an air raid warning! He spotted the formation and pointed to the sky. 'They're German, they're German. Where's the shelter?' He looked around but there was no mound with an Anderson underneath. He wanted to pull Mrs Pawsey to the cellar. She didn't seem to know she was in danger. 'We must run, Mrs Pawsey,' and he took her hand, pulling her towards the front door.

Mr Pawsey had come out. He put binoculars up to the sky. 'That's reconnaissance, that is. Wretches. Looking for the lie of the land while it's just light enough.'

He looked down at Billy. 'Not bombers, my lad. Don't you worry. There be nothing to bomb hereabouts. They's getting information, that's all what it is.'

By then the noise was louder. He crouched behind Mr Pawsey, he couldn't help it. It was too like the times at home in the cellar, and any minute the ground would shake and the house fall down.

Mr Pawsey hauled him up to his feet and took him indoors again. As the planes flew over he said, 'You'm not in London now. You'm safe here, that's as why they've sent you. We haven't a shipping port here, no big factories. Those are the sorts of thing they want to bomb, they Jerries, not pigs and chickens.'

Billy took a deep breath. He must believe Mr Pawsey knew right. Dad wouldn't have evacuated him again, if not. He stood in the hall, waiting until the plane sounds had gone.

Mrs Pawsey took her hand back where Billy had been holding it, perhaps a bit too tightly. 'See it's all right now. No bombs. You pop upstairs and unpack your case. Then you'll feel properly at home, lovey, won't you? You wash your hands after, and I'll get the food on the table, won't I?'

He went up to the bathroom and found that Dad had been right. This was a better billet than Mrs Youldon's, for there was a proper towel on the bath specially for Billy, a big bar of carbolic soap and even hot water. For all that, he still wanted to go to see Mrs Youldon and the little ones, the lane where they lived and Big Ronnie next door – even the privy in the back yard. Seeing something he already knew would be so nice.

He went into the bedroom, clicked open the suitcase latches and lifted the lid. He might put his comic by his bed ready for bedtime. But there, on top of everything was the envelope from Mr Durban. Inside, he had something precious, a secret. Although Dad had passed the letter over, he didn't know about the photograph inside, he didn't even know about Cossack sabres or this one's story and its special name, shashka. Only Billy and Mr Durban knew about this.

He had a funny shuddery feeling as he fingered the flap of the envelope, knowing that the shashka had come with him. He pulled the photograph out and laid it on the bed to look at it properly. Mr Durban had taken the sabre out of its scabbard so that both could be seen clearly. Billy could almost feel the pommel in his hand that last time when Angela had let him hold it for a moment. Remembering the fearsome swish of air that rushed past him when Mr Durban demonstrated how the Cossacks used the shashka, cut, thrust, made the little hairs down his arms stand on end. So did the wicked curve of the blade, its super sharp edge clearly picked out by the light from Mr Durban's high study window. It was almost as if Billy was there right now.

Could he ask Mr Pawsey for some see-through stuff to protect it? Then he could stick it on the wall by his bed. Perhaps not. He had only just met him, so he wasn't ready to share his secret. He'd better not put it on the wall where anyone could see it. And it would be nice to be able to hold it whenever he wanted. If aeroplanes zoomed over low or there was an air raid he'd feel brave holding the shashka, even if it was only a picture. If anyone came, when Mother visited, the shashka picture should be safely out of sight. She mustn't know about the time he'd run off to Mr Durban's and heard the wonderfully scary Cossack story. And if she brought Kenneth! It would be awful if he saw it.

For the moment, he'd keep it under his pillow, until he could find a special secret hiding place in his bedroom.

Just knowing he had the photograph made his insides feel warmer as he carried on unpacking, putting away his clothes and washing things.

When he ran downstairs Mrs Pawsey led him into a dining room, where he was very glad to see a heavy table laid up with food.

'You'll be hungry, won't you be hungry? Aren't boys always?' Mrs Pawsey asked and answered herself.

He hadn't actually thought about food since eating his sandwiches, sitting on a suitcase when they changed trains, but actually that was a very very long time ago. Perhaps he was really hungry, like Mrs Pawsey said. He sat down, staring at the brown crumbly cake on the table with currants in it while Mrs Pawsey brought in eggs, tomatoes, grated carrots, margarine or it might even be butter, and a large crusty loaf.

Did she have to queue for ages and ages to get this?

'I see his eyes brightening, Seth,' she smiled across to Mr Pawsey, little dips appearing in her folds of cheek. 'Nothing like having your own, Billy, is there? Own tomatoes, own eggs, own carrots, own cake. We don't go hungry here and we're not going to either unless the Jerries cross the Channel and steal it from us.

'Do you think they will? The seaside, that's where they're going to land. Everyone says so. They could climb over the barbed wire.'

Mr Pawsey wagged a finger. 'Too busy bombing London, aren't they? And there's lots of guns waiting for them all along the coast if they get cheeky enough to try to land, don't you worry. Now you get yourself stuck in and eat right up.' He forked a tomato on to Billy's plate, followed by a hard-boiled egg and Mrs Pawsey cut him a thick slice of squashy bread, not at all like the dry bitter loaf Mother served up.

Then he ate the best tea he'd had since Nanny and Granddad's, which was ages ago, and even those last times hadn't been so good because of the rationing. He delved into the lovely things on his plate until he'd had some of everything.

'More, lovey?'

He shook his head. He had more than he could eat and Mrs Pawsey was asking if he wanted more! It was lovely that he wasn't hungry even though he was evacuated, and that everything was so yummy. The remainder of the brown cake sat on its plate, moist with its bits of date inside. He could have asked for a second piece and saved it, perhaps. Next mealtime, should he save some and get it to Mrs Youldon? Timmy and Sally would love the cake. He'd never seen them have any.

He got up to help clear the dishes. Mrs Pawsey said there weren't any chores for him because it was his very first day with them.

'But you can find my glasses any time I need, can't you?' Mr Pawsey was half joking, but he did actually need someone to do that. 'And a strong lad like you can do lots around the yard, save me bending.'

'Yes, I will. It will be fun to help.'

He wanted to do chores, but whether it was digging or feeding animals, it wasn't like war work. In Wandsworth, he could have been helping Mr Durban in the ARP hut, by running messages, or even picking up bricks after the bombing had stopped. There'd be bombsites, and people needing someone to carry all their indoor things to wherever they were going to live next.

'Where will people live, when they've been bombed out, Mr Pawsey?'

Mr and Mrs Pawsey started up and exchanged glances before Mrs Pawsey said, 'Whatever made you suddenly think of that, Billy?'

'It's this time bombs usually start, the evening, and the nights, sometimes all night. Houses get bombed and the fire engine comes. There's no front to the house and just rubble.'

'You're safe down here in the country, now. You don't want to be worrying yourself. You're going to have a lovely time tomorrow learning all about the pigs and chickens, just concentrate on that, my love.'

He started stacking the plates. Mrs Pawsey was being very kind but she didn't know about bombing, or how Mr Durban might not get his tin hat on in time, or about Nanny and Granddad being uncomfortable in their Anderson shelter. It was a guilty feeling, being safe down in the country.

Mr Pawsey put a veiny hand, as large as Dad's, on Billy's arm. 'Leave the plates, Billy. We men can listen to the wireless before it's your bedtime. My favourite programme's on tonight.'

They went into the first room he'd been taken into where the lamp and the book were. He sat with Mr

Pawsey on a squashy chair that had straw poking out at the edges. The great brass bucket in the fireplace had lots of logs piled up in it and nearby was a thick black rug that the dogs were allowed to lie on.

Soon enough, both of them sidled round the door and lay down, their paws outstretched, Noah's on top of Mr Pawsey's slippers.

Billy steeled himself for the ominous boom that announced the news, but Mr Pawsey didn't listen to it. 'All that'll be different soon enough, so as I might as well be up to date', he said. 'And you don't want to hear that war stuff.' After stacking the wood neatly and repairing the fire, he put on Band Wagon. It was such a funny programme, and Billy laughed when he did. Sometimes, Mr Pawsey said the same funny things after the wireless men and then it sounded even funnier. Everything felt very cosy.

Billy was away from everyone he knew, but now he didn't seem to mind. He did cross his fingers that Dad and everyone in London was safe. What were Mother and Jill doing now and did they miss him? Was Jill having a tantrum because everything looked strange? Was it cosy like this for Kenneth in his billet? He might be nervy, or going to be ill, like often he was. But he wouldn't let himself worry because Kenneth had Aunty. And, of course, he didn't have to put up with Kenneth being mean.

Bandwagon ended, and then there was some jolly music. 'Guess what I've got?' Mr Pawsey groaned a bit as he bent down to get something out from under the sofa. It was a shove ha'penny board. 'We can play this while we listen. Bet you can't beat me at this, Billy.' They played two games and Billy won the shiniest of halfpennies. It could go with his Uncle Ted shilling and

Mr Durban crown, still in the little wallet ready for a special event. Treasures were good for making you feel safe.

When it was going to be the nine o'clock news Mrs Pawsey came in. 'Come along you.' She took Billy up to bed and tucked him in, which was very nice of her. 'Did you bring any special comfort, my love? A little blanket, a teddy?'

He shook his head, but thought about what was hiding under his pillow. 'I have got a special picture. I might show you one day.'

'That's right. When you're ready. A picture can be very special. Perhaps I've got one too, in a quiet place where it's safe. I might show you it, one day.'

Billy smiled. He understood. She'd want to really know and trust him before she showed him her special picture.

'You going to lie down, then? Any problems, and we're just across the landing, mind.'

Billy snuggled down. It was really comfortable but rather lonely, even with the shashka right under his head, keeping him safe. After he'd been lying down a while, he remembered his pear drops. He slid out of bed and found them safe in his pocket. It felt like the right time to eat another sweet, although Mother would've disapproved. He took one to bed and by the time he'd sucked away the last sticky bit, he was ready to go to sleep.

CHAPTER TWO

September 15th 1940

A day of heavy bombing but RAF Fighter Command causes big losses for the enemy.

Billy opened his eyes to a new morning. He'd slept all night and there hadn't been an air raid to disturb him. It was as if the war was over already but after shooting him from home. It was odd not to hear Jill's babble or whinging, or Mother's voice from down below.

He sat up. The first thing to do was to find a special place for his precious picture of the shashka. He took it warm from under his pillow and held it to his face. Mr Durban would be thinking of him and willing him to always be brave. The heroes book was in the wardrobe. He remembered the day Mr Durban had given it to him, knowing Billy was going to be evacuated when Billy hadn't known himself. He bent down and found the wooden frame of his bed had a little space between the base and the mattress. No one would know the photograph was there except him, and it was close enough for him to stretch a hand down when he was lying in bed and get it out. Perfect! He'd keep it in the envelope to keep it clean and flat. Mr Durban's letter could slide inside his book and stay with any other letters he got. Dad had his address this time to give to Nanny and Granddad.

There was sun making a warm orange patch on the carpet. He padded to the window and opened the curtains. There was no aeroplane noise, no traffic. Down below the pigs snorted, and above, the sky was empty of everything except clouds. He took a deep shuddering breath. He just had to get downstairs and smell the country.

At the back door, the dogs pressed themselves against him and rushed out alongside him. Billy took a another deep breath in and smelled the damp grass, the flowering bushes, even the manure and smiled to himself. *I love it.*

Mr Pawsey came up behind him. 'Hello young Billy. Had a good sleep? Taking in the morning air, are you?'

Billy nodded and turned to go back indoors. He'd never been outside in pyjamas before. Mother would be shocked. He could feel a little smile creeping to his mouth. There were no neighbours here to peep behind net curtains and mind whether someone was outside in their pyjamas.

Mr Pawsey put a hand on Billy's shoulder. 'I suppose it'm be a bit hard, not having your cousin to share all this with; that what you're thinking about?'

'No!' Kenneth! It would be awful to have Kenneth here. Thank goodness for Aunty going with him so that Dad didn't billet both boys together. 'No-o. We're not really friends. It's just that our fathers are brothers so we have to see each other. A lot, actually.'

'Ah. Is that how it is? A bit glad to be an only boy here, are you? Well, up you go and get yourself dressed. Our breakfast'll be ready in two shakes of a bee's knee.'

After they'd eaten, Mrs Pawsey took him to the lean-to at the back door where the messy coats hung. She put on a scabby mac with muddy marks down its front and all round its hem. Then she pulled on black wellies.

She went to a pile of old boots in the corner and turned them over and over. She pulled out a small pair, but gently, looking inside them. 'These will be about right.' She was gazing at the boots sadly, although they looked quite old. Then she passed them to him. 'Here, you'd better put these on, Billy boy,' she said. 'They can be yours now. Pull'em on. Always mud round pigs.'

He followed her round as she fed the animals, collected the eggs, cleaned out hutches and pens, brought in vegetables. It all felt very strange, but rather wonderful. Early morning was very different from mornings in Wandsworth, watching Jill whingeing and Dad striding off in his trilby hat, then running to school down the grey concrete path with a sense of trouble pending.

He couldn't help noticing that Mrs Pawsey had a lot more to do than Mother, even after Mrs Donnington, the home help, left to work on the buses. Mrs Pawsey did all this animal work as well as the washing and cooking, although she was old like Nanny.

Mr Pawsey did outside jobs too. He talked to the pigs, which he said was important, and mended bits of fence and hedge so that the hens wouldn't escape. He couldn't bend easily but he had a leather cushion that he knelt on to trowel around his vegetables and pull carrots and swedes.

Billy went over to watch.

'Here by, young Billy. I'll show you how to do this and I shall be glad of your help from now on.'

Billy bent down and helped pull the carrots. 'I've done this before, with my Granddad.'

That felt rather good until Mrs Pawsey, tramping by in her shabby mac, reminded him of Uncle Ted shuffling up the road after his rescue from Dunkirk. Billy stood up and looked at his black nails. He'd been pulling carrots when he'd seen the scarecrow-like figure in its trailing greatcoat and not known it was Uncle Ted. When the grown-ups let Billy see him, it was three days later and he wasn't Uncle Ted any more but a wordless stranger with a white lock in his hair.

He screwed up his eyes. 'Is the war still in France, Mr Pawsey?'

'The war's most everywhere, my lad. Too many places. But we're Great Britain. We always win. And look at your work on those there carrots. You're a winner, I can see that.'

Billy bent down to his work again. It was nice being on the winning side. Like in school games, the team with red bands were always beating the blue bands. He always went for the red side, and he was a good runner and good at catching and kicking balls. Perhaps there'd be games here when he started school, though teams would probably be locals against vaccies, which wasn't so nice because then there were fights later. Funny, really, to think of Germany being the same – not being friends if a country didn't want to be invaded. Last evacuation, the locals made fun of the vaccies and put out their tongues. Were the locals in France rude and unfriendly to Jerries because Germany had invaded? Was it their fault, like everyone said? Londoners had invaded this village, and it wasn't their fault because they'd been sent by the government.

'The Jerry soldiers, Mr Pawsey, they've been sent to fight by their government, haven't they, so is it their fault they're in France?'

'Don't know about that, Billy. They didn't have to support Hitler, did they now?'

Hitler. He knew it! The fighting, bombing, war – it was all Hitler's fault, nasty man with his silly moustache and arm sticking right up in the air like a wooden doll. He stamped the earth around the baby carrots, one, two, three, and pretended it was Hitler's face.

It was Sunday so after they'd all cleaned themselves up, Mr and Mrs Pawsey took him to church. They set off down the lane and out to the road that led to the places Billy remembered from last year.

It was exciting to see the people he knew when they reached the church. There were no rude faces from local children. This time, all the faces seemed friendly. Some boys actually waved and inside the church, people who'd grunted about vaccies before, now turned round and smiled. It was rather nice sitting between Mr and Mrs Pawsey.

Two women sitting in the same pew asked, 'Is this a new evacuee?'

'Yes. What a nice boy I've been sent by the billeting officer, don't you see?' she answered. 'His father phoned and there was just time to make up the spare room, and the next thing here he was, wasn't he?'

The organ began, and everyone stood to sing. Mr Pawsey pointed to the words in the hymn book, so altogether Billy felt quite easy. Even the organ sounded nicer as they walked out after the service.

'Do you think the people here are used to us now, Mr Pawsey? They weren't very nice to us last year.'

'It's more that they know what you'm suffered in London, that'll be it.'

They moved back into a hedge as a van drove by. It turned into a very large stone house, more like three houses in one. The sign outside read 'Larch Manor.' The van parked just inside its leafy drive. The doors opened, out jumped a group of girls and boys, one of whom had a very familiar freckled face.

'Alan, Alan. I'm here too!' Billy yelled.

'Oh my stars, you varmint,' said Mr Pawsey. 'That's the first time as I've heard any noise out of you. You made me jump, you did.'

'It's my friend. From last time I was here!'

Alan was looking up at the huge ivy-covered house but he turned sharply when he heard Billy shout. His hands went up and his face creased into a grin. He waved, but couldn't run over because a man was shepherding the whole group up the drive to the double door where a lady stood. She was so fat that her crossed arms stuck out far in front of her. If Alan had been near enough, Billy would have whispered that she probably ate all the vaccies' food rations.

'Well, there's a thing,' said Mrs Pawsey. 'The Manor's taking all those vaccies.'

Alan was hesitating by the door.

'You coming to school when it starts?' Billy yelled. After all, Dad was too far away to be angry about shouting across the road. Alan waved and held up his thumb, so Billy knew he'd be looking out for him. There was so much to tell him. He watched until Alan was taken inside.

Mrs Pawsey said, 'Come on, you. We need to show you the right route to school before it starts and then it's dinner-time. Won't you be hungry after your work outside this morning?'

Billy nodded hard. He certainly was very hungry. He was just a bit worried, because the nice tea might have been only for his first day. At Mrs Youldon's there had never been enough and it was usually only bread and a tomato, or soup. He and Alan had always been hungry.

Today, when they got back he found she'd done a great stew for dinner with apple and custard afterwards. He ate lots and it was lovely. It was really true what she'd said, he wasn't ever going to be hungry here. Mrs Pawsey cooked hot meals with huge portions and he was going to tell Alan all about it.

All through dinner time Mr and Mrs Pawsey told him things about the village and the people who lived there. Billy told them about Wandsworth, the shopping, the shelters, the *Run Rabbit Run* games, and Mr Hendrick banging his stick.

Sometimes they laughed at what he said, and they smiled all the time, as if they really liked him. Billy felt quite different, sort of full inside and not just with food.

In the morning, Mrs Pawsey gave him a new pencil in case there weren't enough at school and Mr Pawsey gave him three cigarette cards for swaps. 'Just to make sure they're all friends with you. I know what some of they rascals be like.'

Billy set off down the lane and cut through a farm path the Pawseys had shown him. He wasn't frightened. He'd see Miss Johnson and Mr Finlay in church, and goody, goody, Alan would be there too. It wasn't like starting a new school.

Mother would say he was lucky. Kenneth would be starting a school he'd never been to, where he didn't know anyone. That meant he wouldn't be able to give blocked ink-wells to anyone. He wouldn't be the monitor. He was worse off than Billy.

In the school yard there lots of grubby children he'd never ever seen before. They weren't locals and they certainly weren't from Wandsworth. They'd chalked a hopscotch on the playground and a queue of boys and girls waited a turn. He went forward slowly in case he could join in, but one of the boys looked over and put out his tongue. Another said, 'Who the hell are you?' No one had ever been that rude to him before. Two of the girls nudged each other and giggled nastily. Billy leant against the playground shed until he spotted Alan.

'Alan!' He ran over and clapped him on the back. They jumped up and down together. Billy nodded towards the grubby children. 'Do you know those lot?'

'Some are at the Manor with me. East Enders. Bombed out, a lot of them.'

Billy looked at their torn plimsolls and odd clothes. Their others might have been lost in the bombing. Perhaps he was lucky, he'd only had to shelter in the cellar. He nudged Alan. 'Did you get bombed round you?'

'No, but we heard it every night. All the planes fly over our street because we live between Croydon airport and Big Ben. Bombs dropped not that far off and my mother said she had to get me back here quick as quick because the Jerries might bomb houses anywhere. We got a bus to her office. It's in Piccadilly and all to do with war things. We slept in the basement with all the people who worked there. It's safe, but ever so noisy in the raids. She wanted to get me on the train at Paddington. She found out this lot of children were

25

coming to our village so she joined me up with them on the platform. Alan took a big breath.

'I came here on a cart from the station. I sat up front just behind the horse's head.'

'Smashing. I'd like that. Remember the twins riding around on that haycart?'

Billy nodded. The twins must still be here. 'Guess what? My cousin's come too. He's billeted with Aunty. They're near my mother and Baby, that same vicarage place but there wasn't room for me.'

'Goody, because now you're here with me.'

Billy grinned. 'And where I am now, there's room for two in my bedroom.'

'And do *you* know what?'

'What?'

'Buckingham Palace was bombed.'

'Blimey, the King and Queen bombed?'

'It's all right. They weren't in. Anyway, the RAF downed loads of Jerry planes yesterday. There were all these white smoky trails in the sky.'

They started kicking a big pebble between them.

Billy said, 'What's it like at that Manor house?'

'Inside is very smart but we're not supposed to go into the main rooms where the furniture's covered up. We're in the servants' quarters, quite jolly in the dormitory under the roof. Food was alright last night. There's nuns as well as children billeted, so we have to look out when we mess around. And there's two land-girls. You can come round. There's a big garden at the back. Just turn up. It doesn't matter, no one will mind 'cos there's such lots of us there.'

'And you can come to mine. Mr and Mrs Pawsey said so. That's those people you saw me with. I'm with them, up the hill from the shops and down the lane with the big mud ruts. There's dogs and pigs and chickens. They give me lovely dinners. It's nice.'

'You and me can call for each other.'

'And go down and see Mrs Youldon,' Billy said.

'Yes, let's.'

The bell went and they ran to see Mr Finlay who'd grown a moustache. He was busy cutting exercise books in half. 'Hello. Wilson and – Firbank isn't it? Welcome back, you two. You'll have to muck in. Find yourself a place.' He started giving out paper and stubs of pencils.

The classroom was already full. John was back.

Billy leant over his desk. 'Hey, John. Remember coming down on the train with me, last evacuation?'

'Hello, you two.'

Alan slid in beside him while Billy went to see Sonia who was at the front, helping several smaller girls. Her hair was down to her neck.

'You're not at the same woman's are you, Sonia? The one who shaved your head?'

She shook her head. 'I'm with these girls.'

It was quite noisy, the twins at the centre of it. Dick and Mick hadn't gone home at all. They were bigger and redder than ever. They bounced up and down and elbowed each other.

Dick said, 'Yeah, super-duper! It's Billy. Squeeze in here, you. We can copy your sums.'

Mick said, 'Wotcha, Billy. Sit by us.'

Mr Finlay gave them a little cuff over the ear each. 'Just to start the day right, twins, before you ruin my appetite. Now, new children, please be careful not to sharpen your pencils too much. We have to make them last.'

'You get into terrible trouble if you lose yours,' John leant forward and whispered.

Billy showed him the nice long pencil that Mrs Pawsey had given him.

John wrinkled his forehead. 'Look out. I bet that gets nicked. All sorts here now,' and he jerked his head towards the children with dark eyes, dirty knees and fierce expressions.

Mr Finlay settled them all down and pointed to the blackboard with the date and twenty arithmetic problems. Everyone groaned. 'Get going, class,' he said. 'I'll be coming round to see which of you can tackle the difficult problems, that's numbers seventeen to twenty. The others, try the first ones. Just do your best.'

Dick said, 'You do 'em, Billy. Show us.'

'Yeah, we'll copy yours, you're good at sums,' said Mick.

Mr Finlay noticed but didn't hear what they said. 'That's right, Wilson, sit between this pair. Keep them apart and keep them quiet for me.'

'Hey, Billy, do you still do that d-d-d-d stuff?' said Mick, but Mr Finlay wagged his finger before Dick could join in.

The day went by very slowly because the lessons were all the same as last year. Billy started to think how to get up to Mrs Youldon's with some food. He couldn't steal, but he could use his leavings. If he hadn't eaten everything at mealtime, wasn't what was on his plate still his?

There was a fruitcake for tea and a plateful of buns. 'Can I eat these later, Mrs Pawsey?' he asked after polishing off two buns, and leaving another bun and his cake on his plate.

'As long as you don't give them to those hens and pigs. Too good for them, mind.'

He skipped down the lane, where it met with the wider one which led to the village.

Alan was waiting at the corner. 'Bet you the little ones will squeal when they see us.'

'Specially when they see what I've got for them.' Billy held up a bag with his bun and piece of cake inside.

They raced down to Mrs Youldon's road together and found Timmy hopping around in front of the terrace. He stopped and stood there with an open mouth as they rushed up.

'Timmy, Tim. We're back.'

Sally's head peeped out of the open front door then ran inside. 'Oh, Mu-um.' Mrs Youldon came out to see, smiling as if they were saviours.

'My big boys! When did you get back? The billeting lady didn't tell me. Come on in, come on.' She made a space for them on the bench. 'I did hope you'd be back, lots of Londoners have come now, but rough ones, not toffs like you two. We heard about being bombed out – such awful times for city people.' She looked them up and down with her nice kind face. 'So you're all right, thank goodness. I really have missed you.'

Alan rubbed one shoe against another.

She looked at his face, and then Billy's. 'You're not coming to live at mine, then?'

Billy spurted out in a rush, 'No, Alan's at the Manor and I'm up the hill with Mr and Mrs Pawsey.' If only Mrs Youldon had proper food, a bathroom and two spare beds they'd beg to be here. He pulled held out the paper bag. 'For you and Sally and Tim. I had too much at tea-time.'

'Oh, Billy! Are you sure you're allowed?'

He nodded.

Mrs Youldon went to the scullery and found a knife. Its handle had broken long ago. The bun divided nicely but the cake had crumbled quite badly on the way. Mrs Youldon gave Sally a handful, and then Tim. She licked a finger to get out the remaining crumbs one by one from the bag.

'You'll be all right there, then, Billy. They're nice and they've got plenty, the Pawseys. They'll perhaps be glad of a boy to . . .' she broke off.

He was going to ask why but she went on quickly,

'And Alan, how posh you'll be at the Manor! I've never seen inside it, don't think any of us locals have. Even the servants came from far away. All these big houses are offering billets now there's bombing. The Grange's got seven kiddies! Funny to think of those fine rooms all run over with noisy vaccies.'

Billy remembered her Tuesday work at the Grange. 'Do you have to do all the vaccies' ironing?'

'Goodness, they haven't asked me. I just go up and look after the ladies, now the men are away at war. Perhaps they will need more help. It would mean another pound or two for me. Do they have help at the Manor, Alan?'

'No. I think the nuns do housework and things.'

'You won't get too posh to come up here, will you?'

He shook his head, 'Course not, and I'm allowed out after chores and so is Billy.'

Billy nodded. 'We're often going to come down here to see you.' Every day if he could manage it. He couldn't tell her how he'd missed her, Mother wouldn't like that. He looked around at the bench, the stove, the airer of damp clothes. His whole body felt lifted up and settled down. A sort of sigh came out of his mouth. It was good to be in this little room again where Timmy's car still had three wheels, and the pack of cards waited for someone who could really build a good home with them.

CHAPTER THREE

September 27th, 1940

Pact signed by Germany, Italy and Japan

The telephone bell jangled throughout the house. It made Billy jump because he hadn't heard it before and the dogs went wild. Japhet bounded down the hall with a red mouth and tongue hanging out. Noah woofed loud and long from the back door as Mrs Pawsey bustled in from the front.

'Goodness, dogs, anyone would think the calls were all for you. Stop that wretched noise, won't you?' She held the receiver to her ear and soon beckoned Billy over.

It was Dad telephoning to see how things were.

'Have you settled down and are you being a helpful boy?'

'Yes, I am, Dad.' It felt so special to have a phone call specially for him. Dad had never been able to do that at Mrs Youldon's because she didn't have luxuries like telephones and wirelesses, or even a table and chairs to eat at. But Dad was in London being bombed every night.

'Are the air raids still terrible, Dad?'

'I can't pretend they're not, son. But I left London for the Winchester Court two days ago with the sky full of activity. I was glad to be on a leaving train. Now there are more countries for Great Britain to fight against. As I told you, war is the worst thing. However,

Shame upon the soul, to falter on the road of life while the body still perseveres, Marcus Aurelius.'

Dad's sayings. That was like being back at home, Dad puffing on his pipe, probably looking at the sky where the sayings seemed to come from. This one sounded churchy. 'Who's Marcus – '

'Aurelius. A good Roman emperor, a philosopher. He was someone who had to drive the Germans away. An intellectual leader, whose first act was to share the leadership with his adopted brother, Verus.'

Billy turned up his nose. *Verus* was a horrid name. He wouldn't have wanted to share leadership, especially if Verus wasn't a real brother.

Dad was going on, 'You'll read Roman history when you're fourteen or so. Perhaps earlier if you show your mettle. I was thinking of asking Uncle Frank if I should introduce Kenneth to it—' His voice trailed away.

That would be flipping terrible if Kenneth started doing sayings as well as Dad. Billy didn't want him learning Roman history and quoting all sorts of people he'd never heard of.

'Well, Kenneth has settled, glad to say. No sign of the nerves now. I rang your mother yesterday. I gather she hasn't arranged to get over to see you yet with Kenneth, but I'm sure she won't be long. You are all right, aren't you?'

'I am, Dad. Really.' Better get that in quickly in case Dad decided to move him. 'Mr and Mrs Pawsey are ever so kind, and I have lots to eat.' He had been going to tell Dad that Alan was here too, and about the pigs and chickens, but Dad's hotel served the meal at a set time and it was nearly that time now, so he didn't get to tell any of his news at all. He just managed to get in,

33

'I'm glad you're in Winchester, Dad. You don't have to go back to London soon, do you?'

Dad told him not to worry himself and rang off. It was a sad feeling. Although it was good that Dad was away from the bombing, the hotel food wouldn't be nearly as good as Mrs Pawsey's, and poor Dad was living all on his own.

He mooched down the hall to where the dogs were lying. Animals never looked sad. Japhet bounded forward and licked him, so he squatted down to stroke him. 'That was my phone call, see Japhet. Dogs don't get phone calls.'

Mrs Pawsey came out. 'Will you be a bit homesick, lovey? Why don't you pop up to the Manor and get that friend of yours to come here for a bit?'

Billy jumped up. 'Can he? Thank you. He's very nice, you'll like him. He's called Alan and his face is all covered with little brown spots that are called freckles. Actually, his arms are too. And his back, come to think of it. I know because we shared a bed at Mrs Youldon's.'

Mrs Pawsey laughed. 'That's fine, my dear. He can come, and welcome. We might invite him to stop for some tea when we have ours. Off you pop, then, and get him.'

Alan was in the Manor's side garden in a line of children, all with forks. A land-girl was showing them all how to dig trench lines ready to sow vegetables. He didn't go too near, in case he had to join in? He called from the top of the drive, 'Are you allowed to stop, Alan, and come up to my place?'

Alan waved. He gave his fork to the young lady. 'It's all right, we're volunteers and I've done quite a bit. Haven't I?' he added, turning to her. She nodded.

He ran down to where Billy was waiting. 'Is it okay to come, then?'

'Yes. Mrs Pawsey said to bring you up, and you might have tea with us. And I want to show you everything. What were you doing, anyway?'

'I wanted to help her,' Alan followed Billy out into the road. Her name's Rachel. Her father's a Jew and stuck back in Austria. He couldn't get out when she left. She's worried he'll get killed.'

'Is he a soldier? Do they have Jewish soldiers? My father said Austria was against the Jews. I saw a bit about Jews in the newspaper once, the Nazis bullying them.'

'No, he's not a soldier. He was a shop-keeper but the shop was taken. It's horrible.' He linked arms with Billy. 'Rachel says the Jews are being lined up and all their things taken from them, then they're shot or driven away and then murdered.'

He gasped. It wasn't like Alan to make things up. Not like Kenneth. If it was true, what the land girl told him was really scary. It meant there were lots of real thieves and murderers in Austria. 'That's dreadful.'

'I know. It's almost as bad as being bombed.'

'No, worse. Murder's really, really bad. If you're bombed, the planes don't know who they're bombing. If it's you gets bombed, you're just unlucky to be the one that's hit. But being *murdered* is someone means it to be you. They want you to die, because they hate you.'

They kicked the muddy cart ruts until they crumbled away. These thoughts weren't right for running, and for a few moments Alan didn't answer. Then he said, 'You're thinking of that cousin of yours, aren't you?'

Billy hadn't been, but he did now. 'Kenneth wouldn't *kill* me.' He might get near it, but he couldn't imagine Kenneth looking as though he was going to murder; it would be the wrong kind of face. Kenneth had more a white, or yellow or green expression. Hate and murder was red. He started walking on again. 'Don't know whether Kenneth actually hates me . . . he likes being mean and spiteful, and coming off best always – ' Billy took a breath, 'He has really hurt me sometimes, like Chinese burns, or when he smothered me with the gas mask or trapped me in the Lloyd loom basket, but he can be nice. He made me a smashing card last Christmas that he painted himself. Hey, I wish I'd brought it. I could show you.' Then he had the happy feeling in his tummy. 'But I've got something else to show you. Something secret. Come on,' and he pulled Alan's arm until they were trotting down the lane.

They reached the horse's field and saw Mr and Mrs Pawsey near the chicken house. They waved.

'Hello and welcome to you, Alan. You can show'm round everything, Billy.'

The dogs rushed out barking like mad but Alan was used to dogs and wasn't worried. He wasn't so keen on the chickens so Billy clapped his hands at them to make them run off in their fussy way. 'We won't go into their house if you don't like chickens. I wasn't sure about them either when I first got here, but now I'm all right with them. Still, we'll just look for their eggs under the hedges.'

'We used to do that at Easter before the war, only it was for chocolate eggs. My father used to bring them home from London and they had sugar stars stuck on them.'

'Cor, I bet that was expensive.'

'Cadbury's Dairy Milk!'

'Yes, we used to have that. Yum-ee.'

'People say we won't get it till after the war, now.'

They both held their tummies and bent over groaning with the longing for it.

A patter of rain started, so they ran indoors. Billy showed Alan all the downstairs rooms, then led the way upstairs and let Alan nose around for a bit. Then he stood importantly by the bed. Alan was the right person to share his secret.

'I'm going to show you something ever so ever so special, but you mustn't tell ANYONE, not ever. My parents don't know; it's a secret between me and Mr Durban. Turn your back.' He drew out the photograph and held it up.

'Let's see.'

Alan came nearer but Billy stepped back. It was too much for anyone else to touch it. 'See?'

'What is that – golly! A curved sword.'

'Sabre. A Cossack sabre and it's called a shashka. That's a special name for the extra special sabres. It's Russian and it's Mr Durban's.'

Alan's eyes went very big. 'Is Mr Durban that man who works with your father?'

Billy felt even prouder. 'Yes. Mr Durban sent me the photograph to bring here, because he's shown me the shashka and he knows it's my favourite thing.' He looked at Alan's eyes to make sure he could trust him, but Alan's freckly face looked nice as nice, just as it always did. 'Actually, holding it keeps me safe when everything's scary. I hide it in a secret place that no one knows. You're the only person that's ever seen this!'

'Gosh! You're flipping lucky. Why is Mr Durban giving you it secretly?'

The bedroom door was safely shut. Billy sat down on the bed with the photograph and let Alan sit beside him. Then he told him about running down to Mr Durban's house to escape beastly Kenneth and Mr Durban showing him the shashka and telling him the dreadful story of the beginning of the Great War.

'He was younger than my Uncle Ted and Nanny said *he* was too young to fight a war. Mr Durban was only seventeen. He went to stay with a German school-friend in the summer holidays before going to university. . . and then war started. He was stuck! The German friends told him it wasn't safe for an English person. He had to escape all by himself – you know, in the night with no luggage!'

'Not even pyjamas?'

'Not even anything. He had coins sewn in his trousers to buy food from farmers. He kept walking through woods and fields until he was across the border into Russia. He saw Germans in the villages behaving quite awfully, so he thought he'd fight with the Russians.'

'Cor! Where did he get a gun?'

'He didn't. The Russians put him at the back of their army where the cannons were. When they got to battles, his job was to pass the shot to the cannon soldiers to feed the barrel for firing. He couldn't speak any Russian so he had no idea what was happening or who was winning. Each day fighting went on for hours. Then the brave Cossacks galloped past them riding into battle, waving their sabres. They were very fine sitting high on wonderful horses, not like the one over in our field. I wish I had a picture of a Cossack I could show you.'

'So do I!'

'Actually, I haven't seen one but Mr Durban says they're handsome with the smartest uniforms.

The trouble was, the Germans had more weapons, but the Russians fought on and on ever so bravely. After one battle, Mr Durban stood on a cart and saw fields full of dead bodies, miles of them. He saw an injured Cossack with some Germans coming near, so he ran over to pull him to safety. That was the Cossack who gave him this shashka. He was dying, and he gave it to Mr Durban saying this strange word Liko something, I can't remember it just now. I'd have to ask Mr Durban to say it again because it's a Russian word, but it's a special name for a shashka that has been in many fearsome fights and killed so many enemies.

So that's the shashka in this picture. When he owned it, all the Russian soldiers respected him. They treated Mr Durban really well and helped him back to England.'

'How?'

'When they got to the sea and there were ships. He'd been nearly a year away by then. His family thought he'd been taken by the Germans and kept as a prisoner, so were ever so excited to have him back. He didn't dare tell his mother what had really happened to him or about the battles in case she fainted or something. But,' and Billy straightened his back and put up his chin, 'Mr Durban forgot I was only eight and he told me all of the story, all the scary bits and bloody bits and everything. Then he was worried about Dad not liking me to hear that, so *that's why it's a secret*. I wasn't going to tell Dad anyway. But Mr Durban gave me half a crown after Christmas.'

Alan's eyes were still big. 'Gosh. All that happened to you. I wish I'd been there. The story is smashing and that shashka looks a really dangerous sword.'

'Sabre. It is, it's fearfully dangerous. You can't touch the blade. I had to sit right back away when Mr Durban showed me how they,' he put the photograph on the bed and jumped up to demonstrate, 'hack, slash, cut, thrust, probe' with it. All the air whistled, I was scared, AND he said that the Cossacks do it with a sabre in each hand.'

'What *two!* Cor! I wish I could tell all the boys at the Manor about that.'

Billy sat down so hard beside him that the mattress bounced them. 'Secret, deadly secret. You must promise never, ever—'

'No, I won't. I really promise. You know, we're—' and they chanted together while they clenched hands and swung them up and back, '*Best friends, best friends, never, ever break friends.*'

Billy had anxious feelings about sharing his secret, but he had to trust someone. He made Alan turn his back and stand by the wardrobe while he hid the photograph in its special place, then they ran downstairs to see whether Mrs Pawsey had buns or anything nice for tea.

The village bus ran twice a week. Soon, it brought Mother. Billy saw her turn into the top of the lane neatly belted into her checked jacket. She was watching her pointed lace-up shoes so carefully, avoiding the ruts and stones, that she didn't notice his waving arms.

40

There was no Jill with her, no Aunty, but, bother, she had brought Kenneth, who was carrying his notebook and pencils and wearing his cap although it was quite hot. He looked left and right. He'd be judging the lane, the meadow and the house and thinking of something mean to say. His nose seemed to twitch, like the corner of his mouth.

Mother stepped ahead of him and put her arm on Billy's shoulder. 'Here I am, Billy, you see, just as I promised.' She stretched a hand far out towards Mrs Pawsey, who stood with Billy by the gate. 'How nice to meet you, Mrs Pawsey. I hope Billy has been good. I didn't bring his baby sister. It's just too much while she's so young and always wanting something. It's two buses to get here, and you can never be sure of the connection. Quite a feat.' She fanned her face. 'This is my nephew, Kenneth. He and my sister-in-law are billeted very near to us. She does WVS work so I look after Kenneth. He's absolutely no trouble, a really civilized child.'

Billy watched Kenneth smile up at the grown-ups. Mother really seemed to like him now, even though she had to look after him.

'Now, aren't you very welcome, Mrs Wilson?' Mrs Pawsey said in her funny question way. 'Come on in,' and she ushered them forward.

Mother and Kenneth both stepped carefully through the yard, which was untidy with straw from the mucking out. Billy followed them.

Mother had brought a bag of sweeties. 'Some treats for you, Billy.'

Kenneth's eyes were already on the bag.

'Thank you, Mother.' Billy pushed them quickly into Mrs Pawsey's hand. 'Mrs Pawsey will keep them in the larder for me.'

'I hope Billy passed you the corned beef tins when he arrived, Mrs Pawsey? I didn't bring any more food, knowing you had a sort of farm here. You'll have your own produce. I expect you have a wonderfully peaceful life, your animals and garden, just the faint buzz of the odd aeroplane, nothing threatening.'

Mrs Pawsey didn't smile back. 'We manage to find enough excitement, being wartime, and now we have Billy for light entertainment.'

Mother took off her green hat with the feather. 'Yes. I have my work cut out with my little girl. She's only a baby, really. She's having trouble settling. She misses her familiar things so she cries a lot.'

'Tantrums,' said Billy, but no one heard him except Kenneth, who moved to the sideboard where he could stare across toward Billy.

'My sister-in-law joined the local WVS immediately she got here. She's a knitter amongst other things. She's hardly around, so it's left to me to take Kenneth to different homes on different days for schooling.'

Billy scratched his forehead. And he'd been imagining Kenneth nervous in a strange classroom! 'Aren't you going to a real school, Kenneth?'

Kenneth raised his eyebrows at him. 'Me?'

Mrs Pawsey said, 'Dearie me, a big boy like you needs school, Kenneth.'

Mother went on. 'Well – you know, Kenneth is delicate, frail. The school's too far and anyway, we were told it was full. Kenneth's receiving quite advanced tuition. He's in a group being educated by the old verger who went to University when he was young. Kenneth's a real learner. The verger thinks he could get a place at Friar's Court, the grammar school, when he's old enough. Fancy that! My husband was the same, you know, successful at all his study. So, taking Kenneth to different homes has its benefits, meeting mothers of other successful children.'

Mrs Pawsey had her hands folded across her fat front bits. 'Now isn't that nice for you? But, Billy here has been —'

Mother hurried on. 'But as well as having a baby girl who still needs just everything doing for her, taking Kenneth for education isn't the end of it. On Sundays he has to be taken to church, as well as on Wednesday evenings. The verger noticed his wonderful singing voice, so now he's a choirboy. If Doreen's tied up, I have to take him.' She sighed and ran her long fingers across her forehead. 'All go. But he has the talent, you see. Such an easy, quiet boy.'

Kenneth leaned on the sideboard and traced a pattern round the woodwork as if it was someone else they were talking about.

Mr Pawsey came in from tying the dogs up at the far end of the yard. Mrs Pawsey gave him a long look and hurried off out to the kitchen, ruffling Billy's hair on the way. Mr Pawsey stamped the worst of the mud off his boots and came forward to shake hands. 'How do, how do. We're very glad to have your young lad with us, Mrs Wilson. I think the Missus has gone to make you a nice pot of tea. This Billy of your'n is doing fine, just fine, so tell us how you're doing yourself, now.'

Mother seemed very keen to speak about her troubles. Billy eyed Kenneth up and down and saw that he was doing the same back. Mother jerked her head, which meant he was to take Kenneth up to his bedroom. Kenneth carefully placed his notebook and pencils on the parlour table, wiped the straw from the sides of his shiny shoes, and followed Billy upstairs.

'Hmm,' he said, surveying the comfy room and the half-open door of the large wardrobe as if he was going to buy them.

Bother! Kenneth would be able to see the cars and paper planes kept there. It wouldn't be long before he hauled them out.

Kenneth plumped down on the bed. His bottom made a hole where the coverlet had been beautifully smooth before.

'Phew! Pigs! You can smell them from here.' He pulled his bony knees up and put his feet on the bed. 'Where we're living, my window looks over flower beds. You can't even see the veg from it.'

Billy didn't care, didn't even answer.

Kenneth went on, 'Pigs for you, flowers for me. That's like us. Like how it's going to be. I'll be at Friar's Court Grammar next year doing Latin and Physics and Art. You'll be pigging it in that tin pot village school, still having your bit of Arithmetic and Spelling, staying ignorant.'

'I'm not ignorant. I know lots of things.'

'What do you know then? Can you name all the countries in the British Empire?'

'No-o. But I know other things.'

'Like what? The names of leeeaves and treeees?'

Actually, Billy had been about to say what he'd learned on the school Nature Walks, but now he wouldn't. If only he had the shashka, he'd show Kenneth. He circled both arms in the air imagining the shashka swishing through Kenneth's sarcasm. 'I know about Russians in the Great War.'

'You don't.'

'I do. They had to fight the Germans. Hundreds and thousands of them died. Their bodies sank into the snow.'

'How do you know that? How can you know?'

Billy tensed his shoulders. This was dangerous. 'A long ago story.'

'You never had a book on it. I know all your books.'

'Well I just know.'

The hole in the bed became a cave as Kenneth knelt up to dominate Billy from a higher position.

'How. You tell me how you know. Go on, go on, you tell me.' His hand grasped the back of Billy's neck. It was just like Mr Finlay did to the naughtiest boys when they were going to have the cane. Billy hunched forward letting his jumper ride up in the hope that Kenneth would let go. He didn't.

'Tell me now. Go on.'

'A m-man told me.'

'What man? I'm going to ask him.'

'You can't, he's not h-here.'

'At home, then? I know all the men you know. I can write to him and ask.'

'Shan't tell you. Get your hands off my neck or I'll shout to Mrs P-Pawsey.'

'Go on then. Guess what I'll tell her! I can get you into trouble, all right.'

Then there were footsteps on the stairs. Mr Pawsey's voice sounded from outside their door. 'Billy's room's just here, Mrs Wilson. I'm sure as you'd like to see it.'

'Yes, I would, thank you. He slept in something like half a cupboard at his last billet,' Mother trilled.

Kenneth quickly put his hand down and moved his feet so that he was sitting neatly by the time she came in.

'I want to make sure you have enough changes of clothes, Billy.' She began talking to him as she checked all his clothes, which left Kenneth free to wander around, examine the toys, conkers and other treasures. He was soon nosing inside the wardrobe.

Meanwhile, Mother chatted. '. . . and now Jill can be relied on to say Please and Thank you, I can take her about more and Mrs Shawditch says . . .'

When Mother stopped telling Billy things about Jill and the vicar's wife, Kenneth asked politely,

'Aunty Marcia? Apart from Daddy and Uncle Bert, what men does Billy know at home?'

'Goodness me, what a strange question. The people I know, of course.'

'Of course.' Kenneth, sat down on the bed, crossed his legs, and waved his shiny shoes, left, right, left, waiting.

Mother said idly, 'Who do we know, Billy?'

His face was hot. He was up against the enemy. He needed a weapon and he hadn't got one. 'Mr H -Hendrick?'

'That's your teacher. And it's not as if we know him socially.'

'H -He knows lots of things, though.'

Kenneth was speaking over him. 'A man who talks to Billy out of school . . .'

Mother was looking beyond them out of the window now. She was probably noticing the pig smell and waiting to go downstairs again and be brought a nice cup of tea and something home-made by Mrs Pawsey.

Billy tried jumping up and down like Jill did. It always worked for her.

'Aunty?' Kenneth pressed on.

'Well there's only a few people, Kenneth: the people next door, but they hardly chat, and we certainly don't speak to the noisy people opposite. Uncle doesn't really bring his colleagues home except, well, the only other people we know that Billy knows are the Durbans.'

Billy jumped up and down faster.

Mother flapped her hands. 'Stop it, stop it, noisy thing.'

'Durbans,' said Kenneth deliberately.

Billy whizzed around so fast and close that Mother's collar blew up round her chin.

'Enough! I shall get really cross, Billy.'

'Can I meet Mr Durban, Aunty, when we get back to London? Daddy will like to meet him, too.'

'I'm sure you can, if only we could get back there.'

Kenneth smiled across to Billy, one half of his face looking friendly for Mother, the other leering a threat to Billy.

It would be terrible having Kenneth in Mr Durban's house and doubly terrible having Uncle Frank there too. Uncle Frank might teach Mr Durban how to bully. Like all the other grown-ups, Mr Durban would think Kenneth a dear little boy and he might even show Kenneth the shashka. Then Billy would be left with nothing special for himself. He pushed in front of Kenneth so that Mother could only see one boy, her own boy, bobbing up and down so she'd be sure to notice him.

'Now, Billy,' Mother put her hands on his shoulders. 'I expect you're dying to show me around, but be a dear boy and let me have a nice little sit down with Mrs Pawsey and enjoy my tea. You and Kenneth must have such a lot of news to exchange.'

'Lots,' said Kenneth.

Billy turned round to glare at him then clattered downstairs after Mother, never mind that Kenneth would get his hands on all his bedroom treasures. He kept very close to Mother, almost treading on her heels so that Kenneth couldn't possibly come between them.

'Oh, Bill-y!' Mother was saying, but Mrs Pawsey came into the hall with the tray of tea.

She smiled. 'Isn't he thrilled to have his mother here, bless him? Doesn't he just want to stand beside you as you have your tea?'

Billy nodded his head hard enough for Mother to notice. She sipped her tea and asked him some questions, but when he told her about seeing Alan, the lessons and the naughty twins and nature walks, she looked blank. She hadn't been to his school so she didn't know anyone he talked about. She'd even forgotten all about Alan. He sighed, but none of this really mattered if he could keep Kenneth from learning about the shashka. As he heard Kenneth tripping downstairs, he said quickly, 'There's chickens here, Mother. They sit in a line in their hut, you know. We could go and see if there's eggs.'

'A fresh egg.' She finished her tea and stood up. 'That would be a treat. I swear the vicar gives any we get to the refugees.'

Kenneth came in, holding a pair of cars from the wardrobe.

Mother went on, 'The vicar has to share our food out between so many people. So nice for you to have things all to yourselves, Mrs Pawsey. You are lucky.'

Mrs Pawsey said, 'We meet our quota, of course, but we are blessed in a number of ways, that's true enough. You'd better take your mother and Kenneth to see the chickens then, Billy. They may let you take an egg from them.'

Kenneth followed Mother out towards the chicken house, but turned round and gave Billy a long look, his mouth pursed. Billy knew what that meant. Kenneth wasn't going to forget about Mr Durban.

As soon as Mother took Kenneth home, Billy was going round to see Alan. He was the one person he could tell about Kenneth. They would have to put their heads together and think up a plan. If Alan came round next time Kenneth visited that might fix things. Meantime, Billy had a bad feeling in his tummy.

Mother said she would be coming on her own next time because Aunty was taking Kenneth to help at the WVS centre. So Billy felt a little bit better. When no one was looking he put his tongue out hard at Kenneth, then quickly turned away before Kenneth could tell on him.

CHAPTER FOUR

14th October 1940

Bomb penetrates tube station and explodes between the two platforms.

When he was first billeted, Billy was a bit afraid of Laurel and Hardy. He hadn't seen pigs for real before. He remembered how Hardy had peered at him with tiny blue eyes and he'd been scared. Mrs Pawsey had warned him, 'Just don't let them out, will you, my dear? Be careful to keep the catch on their gate.' He was very careful especially as his morning and evening job was to throw the scraps over Laurel and Hardy's pen wall.

He was about to collect the scraps bucket when Mrs Pawsey made a shocking announcement. 'Leave the bucket, Billy, and get your mac on. Those pigs'll be off this morning and be meat by afternoon, so we better get their ear rings on before you get off to school.'

'Earrings? M-meat?'

She nodded hard enough for her chins to wobble but he still couldn't believe it.

'They'se come to their time, my dear.'

'What time?'

'Off to the butcher, my love. We've done out bit getting 'em fat enough.'

Billy swallowed and then gasped. 'You're going to kill Laurel and Hardy?'

Mr Pawsey was pulling his boots on. He chortled, 'They's pork. That's what they're for.'

'But, Mrs Pawsey, they're your pets.'

She laughed and laughed, holding her stomach and having to sit down with the awful effort of it. 'Bless you, lad. We've all got to eat. No one's got money for pets. It's like Dig for Victory. You do that, you know all about that. It's the same. We have to give the butcher our pigs so there's a bit of meat for folks, just like the farmers who send their cows and lambs.'

He knew about meat, of course he did, but he hadn't thought of animals he *knew* being meat. It felt horribly wrong. Laurel and Hardy were family.

'Isn't it the way of the world, Billy?' Mrs Pawsey said in her questioning way. 'And without our meat lots of people would be without their ration, see.'

He tried to be brave as she was. Sending her pigs off to the butcher must be really awful.

'Come on, Billy,' said Mr Pawsey. 'Here's the staples. You come and help me put them on.' He held out two metal things and picked up a heavy thing which was a stapler. They went out to the pigs together. Billy's feet seemed too heavy to move forward. As they got to the pen, Laurel lifted his snout hopefully, then turned his black spot towards them.

'Can't staple your rear, silly pig, you. Turn around, let's have you.' Mr Pawsey stood with his back against the gate, ready to slide out of it if either pig got nasty. Because they did get nasty, Billy remembered, which is why he took so long to feel happy about feeding them. But now it would be awful not to have to feed them, to see an empty pen.

'Doesn't it hurt?' he asked. After all, it was a metal thing going right through the ear and out the other side. Poor pigs. First this, then being killed and then being eaten. It was worse than being sent to war.

Mr Pawsey gave a sort of humph which might have meant 'No'. He was pressing his backside against the gate and holding the stapler thing ready over Hardy's ear. 'Grab it lad, hold on hard.'

Billy could have said 'No', he could have run off, but he didn't. He held on hard to Hardy's ear and screwed his eyes shut. There was a loud squeal, and a spurt of hot air against his hand as Hardy kicked his way free, but the ring was in. Hardy stomped around the pen while Laurel pointed his little blue eyes towards them.

'Now you, Laurel. Let's have you, my beauty. Oho, you know what's coming, do you? Be brave then, my hearty.' And as Laurel squelched over the mud on his high heels, Mr Pawsey grasped his ear. 'Again, lad, again. Quick sharp.'

Billy held on to the hairy ear, but stroked it with his thumb. Laurel's squeal was much louder and longer than Hardy's. It was really hard to bear it. It must be like that at war, being a soldier and having to hurt an enemy, to hear him scream, even to kill him, because that's what soldiers were for. He didn't want to do that to the pigs, or to let anyone else hurt them. He had helped, just like Mr Durban had helped the Russians put shot in the cannons.

He clasped his hands round the end post of their pen gate, peering at Laurel and Hardy to see if either of them had painful ears, but by now they both had their noses down snuffling about in the mud. They didn't know what was going to happen to them. They were like prisoners who hadn't even joined in with a war. Poor things, it was *we have no choice.*

Mr Pawsey clapped a hand on Billy's shoulder then moved off toward the barn, pitchfork at the ready.

It was nearly time to go to school. Billy spent a long time leaning over the pig pen saying a tearful Goodbye. For a moment he thought about lifting the latch of the gate and letting them escape, but Mr Pawsey would get someone to catch them and it would cause lots of extra work. He would be in dreadful trouble too. He took his hand off the latch and mooched slowly to the barn. 'Do the pigs really have to go, Mr Pawsey?'

The old man spat into the fire bucket by the gates. 'We don't want folks to go hungry, do we, my lad? The pigs have had a fine life, you feeding them so well. Now their time's come. That's what they're for, pigs; eating, and being eaten. What you're for is school, so off you go and don't worry yourself.'

Perhaps Mr Pawsey might change his mind later. After all, he was the one who was going to have to walk them down the road.

Billy turned away and scuffed his feet down the path, casting a last look at the pigs. Then he turned away quickly in case he caught their eye. Laurel had poked his nose upwards as Billy turned into the lane. Perhaps he was praying.

All the way up the lane he could hear their grunts. It was truly dreadful. The sky was dark and he buttoned up his mac. He knew what was coming.

Inside the small, dusty school, Billy forced the loop of his mac on to one of the pegs. They all held five or six already.

Other boys jostled him into the classroom where Miss Johnson had pinned a large chart on the board. He didn't even feel like looking at it.

'What's up?' Alan came alongside.

'The pigs. They're going to the butcher's this morning.'

He couldn't say any more because his voice was choky, but Alan understood.

'I say, poor things. Rotten luck, Billy.'

'Silence!' Miss Johnson was taking them for History. 'Look at the board and start work.' When the class had their heads down writing out all the kings and queens of England in the right order, Billy thought of Laurel and Hardy being walked up the road. Was it happening right now? Mr Pawsey would lurch behind them with a stick, tapping their pink hairy behinds, not too hard, saying 'Come on you hairy pig, come on my beauty,' and the pigs would trot onward as long as food was in front of them, not knowing what lay ahead. And that would be the back yard of Mr Churn the butcher with his shiny knives. The pigs would have no choice. He knew what that felt like.

All day at school he felt a sense of doom. It felt worse than a rainy day – more as if the heavens were going to fall in. There was a downpour by playtime, so everyone had to stay in the hall. The school was hot and stuffy, everyone was noisy and bad-tempered and the pelting rain against the windows felt like an attack.

At the end of the day he pulled on his wellingtons and trudged home under the heavy sky. He tried to think of cheery things. It wasn't really raining much now. He hadn't got properly wet. When he got home perhaps there'd be a letter for him, perhaps a postcard. He stamped in a couple of puddles. As Dad had taught him, he didn't count on good fortune.

Mrs Pawsey was standing at the gate, her hand to her eyes, as he sloshed through the muddy ruts in his leaky boots, uncaring. It wasn't worth hoping that she was waiting to tell him the pigs were still there, for there was none of the usual snorting and honking as he approached.

Why was she standing there and not in the kitchen?

'Billy, my dear. You come along in straightaway, you come and sit down right here.'

His tummy tightened up. Mrs Pawsey's special welcome was as sinister as the lumpy black clouds had been that morning. Something awful had already happened when Mr Pawsey took the pigs? Or was Jill poorly so that Mother couldn't visit him for a whole month? He sat down in the squashy chair where Mrs Pawsey pointed and gazed at her, ready for disappointment.

'Your mother telephoned, my dear. I'm afraid I've got some very bad news. They've asked me to tell you.'

'She's not coming this month?'

'She is coming. Quite soon and with Kenneth. Because she and your Aunty need you to cheer him up.'

'Me cheer him up?'

'Yes, dear. Isn't it cheerful company he'll need? His father – I'm sorry this is awful news for you. There was a bomb landed on Balham tube station. It killed lots of people, and your Uncle Frank was there. Be brave, now.'

'Killed?'

She bit her lip and nodded.

He looked at the window, the door. They still looked the same as when he'd gone to school that morning. No more Uncle Frank? How could that be, the size of him? So he wouldn't be there ever again? He'd never come and strip Billy's jumper off ready for a freezing run to the park? He'd never pound Billy's arm muscles and put his fists up to 'make a man' of him? He'd never be there for Kenneth to sidle up to.

There'd just be Dad – and was he in Balham? He gasped, 'Dad – was he there too?'

'No, dearie. Your father is fine. He's the one who phoned and told your mother the dreadful news. Now your poor Aunty has to go to London in all that bombing for the funeral and your mother's going too. They don't think Kenneth should go. I've said I'll have him here for a day or so.

'Oh! But their billet's only down the road from that vicarage. He could go to the vicar's.'

'Yes, perhaps, but perhaps the vicar's wife can't manage him as well as the caring for your little sister. And your mother thought Kenneth would want to be with you. You'll be a good support to your cousin, that's for sure. Now you stay sitting there and I'll get you a mug of sweet tea for the shock. I've got a bit of extra sugar this week. Stay put there, won't you.'

Billy did stay put for his legs wouldn't seem to move. Bombs were awful, and he remembered that bomb site where he'd played and all the furniture showing with the front of the house blown away. And the people had been blown apart, and Uncle Frank was at the tube station when the bomb came and now he was in bits. It was the worst kind of scary. And it was surely terribly sad. He should be crying or something. He looked at his knees, which were quivering. It was a shocking thing that had happened –– but he wasn't sad. He felt a sort of lightness, then he felt bad, really bad because he hadn't felt sad when he heard there was no Uncle Frank, and he still didn't. Kenneth would. He thought about Kenneth and how Uncle Frank had always fussed over him, made sure he had the best of things. Now Kenneth's Daddy had gone. He would mind dreadfully.

Mrs Pawsey brought his tea and a special biscuit. He shouldn't have eaten it, but it was terribly nice. Afterwards, he went upstairs and sat on his bed. Not having Uncle Frank was all right for him, but not for Kenneth, and not for Aunty. She liked her husband a lot. It would be very awful when he had to see her now. And Kenneth – he'd really punish Billy if he knew he wasn't sad.

He wasn't sure what to do. He knelt down by his bed and tried to think of a prayer. That seemed to be the right thing. But the only one he knew by heart was what he'd learned at school – Our Father – and he didn't know if there was any bit about people dying. Trespassing wasn't dying, was it? He said it all the way through in case. Then he told God that he was sorry Aunty didn't have a husband any more and Kenneth didn't have a father any more. That was true. If he'd said he was sorry Uncle had gone, it would have been a lie. The Sunday school teacher once said that whatever words they used, God would hear them if they prayed. That was much better than God hearing them when they weren't praying.

He stood up and leant on his windowsill. There were the empty pens. He remembered with a lurch to his stomach that the pigs were gone, dead, cut in bits by Mr Churn's cleaver. Then he began crying. Soon Mrs Pawsey came in and put an arm round him. She smelled like the inside of a musty wardrobe, quite comforting. She said it was very, very sad to lose an uncle. Then he cried harder, for no one was thinking about the pigs.

CHAPTER FIVE

October 19th 1940

Very heavy night bombing in London, Bristol,
Liverpool, Manchester and Coventry.

Mr Pawsey was quiet at breakfast and just put a large
hairy hand over Billy's before pouring the Sunny Jim
flakes into his bowl.

It wasn't easy to swallow the food but Mrs Pawsey
just took his half-finished plates without a murmur. It
felt like a special time but not in a nice way.

After breakfast, she came up with him and took him
into her bedroom. He hadn't really been in there
before, except to just put his head round the door. She
sat him on the green silky quilt with its puffed up
squares and said, 'I think now's the right time to show
you that special picture I told you about. Do you
remember, on your first night here?'

He did, and he remembered thinking he'd show her
the shashka one day. Not now. They couldn't look at
weapons on such a day.

She was moving to her window-sill to bring a silver-
framed photograph across. She sat down by him and
held it between them. The picture showed a nice boy or
man, he was between the two, with a crisp shirt and
dark tie. His eyes were kind.

'That's my son, Gordon, a very special person. I
keep this picture where I can see him every day.'

Billy swallowed. 'Is he lost?'

'Yes, lovey, lost is right. He was going for his first job, an important interview, but before he could get there, a thunderstorm started. He ran for cover, probably thinking he shouldn't spoil his new jacket. His father bought it special for the interview, see. He didn't think about traffic and the bus couldn't stop. I'm afraid that's how he was lost.'

'That same bus Mother comes on?'

'The very one. But it wasn't the driver's fault. That was gone into, and it was found he wasn't to blame.'

Now it was sadder than ever. His secret picture was a dangerous weapon: Mrs Pawsey's was of a good son that she'd lost. He couldn't show her his picture, he'd be ashamed to act as if it was even, his secret with hers.

'Was Gordon your only son?'

'He was.' She sighed in a gulpy way. 'And that's why we told the billeting officer we'd take a bigger boy for evacuation, while Gordon's ways were still fresh in our minds, so we'd know how to look after a boy properly.'

'You look after boys very well.'

She hugged him. 'You came as though you were a gift, different from dear Gordon of course, but lovely in your way. Now you've seen my special picture, Mr Pawsey's special picture too. It seemed the right time to show you, after you'd lost someone in your family.'

'It's very sad,' he muttered. It was another sad thing. People he cared about, Aunty, Dad, even Kenneth, losing someone they loved and now the Pawseys too.

'We look on the bright side. Our Gordon never got to that first interview, or any interview, but he was saved from going to war. War started the September after he died, so he'd have been called up as one of the first. We may well have lost him by now and in a more dreadful way, see.'

She put the photograph back and sent him to his bedroom to get ready for what was to come.

The black car rolled into the front yard.

The vicar came to the doorway as Mrs Pawsey hurried forward, bringing Billy by the hand.

'Ah, Mrs Pawsey. I've come to be a support to Kenneth, and to Billy at this tragic time.' He looked at Billy with a solemn face.

Billy coughed. Should he say 'Thank you?' What did 'support' really mean? Anyway he didn't know the vicar, apart from being looked at by him, twice. He just said, 'Hallo' because he didn't know what he should do.

'Your Mother has gone with your Aunty, Billy. That's some comfort for her, God willing. And she'll be needed by your father who has sadly lost his brother.'

Yes! Dad was Uncle Frank's brother. Now Dad didn't have one, just like Billy didn't have a brother.

Mrs Pawsey took Kenneth's hand and led both boys into the sitting room, saying 'Vicar, so good of you to bring Kenneth. You must need a nice cup of tea and my husband's bringing you one right in a moment.'

Kenneth sat in his camel coat and cap on the hardest chair without speaking. He looked at the carpet and didn't bother speaking.

'Just about the arrangements, Vicar,' Mrs Pawsey started. 'You put me in the picture and I shall do what's best, so no one needs to worry.'

When Mr Pawsey brought in the vicar's tea it was just a cup for him because it wasn't like a proper visit.

'Do you want orange squash, Kenneth?' He put his hand on Kenneth's shoulder.

Kenneth shook his head.

'You boys pop upstairs, then, while we folk work out the comings and goings.'

Upstairs, Kenneth sat on the bed not looking anywhere.

Billy brought out his cigarette cards and put them in Kenneth's lap. 'You can play with these, if you like.'

Kenneth shook his head and left them lying there. It was very quiet. Billy looked around for ideas of what to give Kenneth to do. The window was shut, and none of the normal sounds were there to make Billy feel easier. Without the pigs snorting or the dogs barking, things didn't seem right. The dogs had been tied up at the end of the yard before the vicar arrived, the hens were at their feed behind their henhouse. Even the wardrobe door stayed shut, the toy cars inside.

Billy walked round to the side of his bed where Mr Pawsey had put up a camp bed for Kenneth. He was going to point to it, but Kenneth wasn't looking. It was very very difficult to know what was best to do.

Eventually Kenneth spoke. 'We're not going home any more. Mummy doesn't want to be there without Daddy.'

'Not go home to Balham? Where will you go?'

He shrugged. 'Don't know. Don't care.'

'Is Aunty – all right?'

'No. Daddy should have been evacuated, like us. She says there's no end to this war.'

'But it will have to end one day. It can't just go on and on. Even the Great War ended.'

Kenneth gave a little snort. 'That was then.' He sounded like Dad.

A plane flew overhead, quite low. Billy could tell it was German.

They heard the door latch click. The vicar had gone. Mrs Pawsey came upstairs 'Wouldn't it be nice for Kenneth to walk round with me as I feed the animals?'

Kenneth didn't answer, so she took his hand and started down the stairs.

Billy didn't tell her what Kenneth thought of animals as he trudged after them and out of the back door.

Kenneth wouldn't be able to say anything about the pig smell now that the pen was horribly empty. He didn't even seem to notice. Mrs Pawsey gave him a basket to collect the eggs in. Billy trailed behind, while she chatted all the time to Kenneth, one arm around him. He found an egg in the hedge and put it in Kenneth's basket. Mrs Pawsey started bending down, but Kenneth stayed where he was, not looking at anything.

They went towards the horse, who had his head over the fence. Mrs Pawsey stroked him, but Kenneth didn't bother. He didn't like horses either, even when things were normal.

'Shall we see if the carrots are ready?' Billy tried.

But a black cloud had come over just like yesterday's and they hurried inside quickly before the rain came down.

'My goodness, aren't we lucky we escaped that?' Mrs Pawsey said cheerily. 'Best if you play cards in the sitting room, boys.'

The rain came down and down as if each splash was chasing the next, hundreds and thousands of splashes making great puddles where the dogs had dug for bones and where the pigs had once stood with their noses up, waiting for their swill. The heavy rain was like crying and crying from the sky.

The cards were already in a pile on the table. 'Shall I deal?' Billy tried again.

Kenneth told him to play Patience and he'd watch. But he didn't.

That night, as he'd dreaded, they were both to sleep in his room. Mrs Pawsey made up the camp bed with sheets and cosy blankets. She ran Kenneth a nice, warm bath which she said would help settle him in a strange house.

Billy got into bed, put his head in his book and read about knights in armour. Kenneth came back from his bath without talking. Mrs Pawsey came in to say Goodnight. Then they listened to her footsteps all the way downstairs and into the parlour. The door shut.

Perhaps Kenneth would read a long time to take his mind off. Billy had put his comic and annual by his bed.

'Kenneth, you can put the light out whenever you like. I won't mind.'

Kenneth turned it off straight away.

The knights had been riding to battle, protected by their armour. Billy had been right in the middle of a sentence.

Everything but the rain was quiet.

Billy lay still, trying to sleep but was horribly uneasy. The rain slashed against the window. He didn't like someone else in the room who'd had something terrible happen. There was just him and Kenneth. It felt as if he'd been left in charge and he didn't feel old enough. He ought not to be silent. Kenneth had his back turned. What words should he say? He tried to remember words he'd heard grown-ups say. He practised a few.

Sleepiness was slow coming and just after he had managed to nod off, or perhaps much later, Billy was kept awake by an awful sobbing and muffled moaning from Kenneth's bed. He kept quiet because what should he do? He waited for Mrs Pawsey to come and see to the trouble. But it wasn't loud enough for her to hear and it was too late at night for him to go and fetch her. All he could think of was getting his precious shashka photo to help. He pulled it out of its hiding place and waved it to and fro opposite the hunched lump that was Kenneth. 'Be brave, be brave,' he mouthed silently.

Eventually the crying died down and stopped. Only the rain spattering the windows kept on and on.

In the morning, Billy came back from the bathroom with his words ready but Kenneth didn't sit up. Mrs Pawsey put her head round the door and said it was time to get up, so then Kenneth did. His eyes were sore-looking and dark. She put an arm round him and pushed him towards the bathroom.

'Nice egg for you when you're dressed and downstairs, my dear.'

Billy had to wait until they were at the breakfast table before he could say the words he'd rehearsed. 'Kenneth, you'll feel better soon about – Uncle.'

'You don't know what happened.' Kenneth pulled viciously at the table cloth so that the dishes jerked. That was shocking.

'Don't!' whispered Billy. 'I know it was a bomb at the tube.' He didn't want Kenneth to talk about Uncle being blown to bits.

'Daddy wasn't down the tube.'

'Wasn't he?'

Kenneth pushed his head towards Billy, his eyes glittering like a madman. 'He was on a bus, going to visit Uncle Bert. The bus fell down into a great hole where the bomb hit.'

Billy swallowed. That did seem better than being blown up. 'Fell down? A whole bus?'

'Yes. And Daddy shouldn't have been on it, visiting. Why couldn't Uncle have come to Balham? It's always us visiting you.'

Mrs Pawsey bustled in with the teapot and the eggs.

Mr Pawsey followed her. 'A good breakfast, you boys. That's as what you need.'

There was a steely silence. Mrs Pawsey shook her head slightly at him and continued passing dishes and serving things out. She took the top off Kenneth's egg. 'Try to eat that up, dear. From our chickens. Do you good.'

Billy struggled with his breakfast, toast crumbs sticking in his throat. It hadn't been his idea for Kenneth to always visit, or usually. He'd have been happy if they didn't visit at all, or perhaps just Aunty. But he couldn't say that. He shouldn't. It was hard to imagine a hole by Balham tube and a whole bus fallen into it; harder even than hundreds and thousands of dead and dying Russian soldiers.

He'd have to say something soon. He was the one with a father still alive. All he could think of was the same words he'd rehearsed upstairs. 'Aunty will come quite soon, Kenneth. Then you'll feel better. And you don't have to go to school when I do.'

Kenneth looked at him bleakly across the table. 'She's going to come after the funeral's over.'

Mrs Pawsey said that Kenneth would probably feel happier going with Billy to school than staying behind on his own.

'No. I don't think he'd like that. He doesn't know anyone. He could feed the chickens,' Billy suggested. It would be awful taking Kenneth to school.

'I'd thought he might like to be with your friends. I've written a note for your teacher.'

The sky was still grey after the day of drenching rain before.

'I'll stay here,' said Kenneth. 'I want to sit and draw, please. I've got my pencils and book. I always have them.'

'Yes. He's ever such a good drawer,' Billy said to Mrs Pawsey. 'You should see his drawings.'

She looked at both of them and nodded. 'All right, dear. You draw us a lovely big picture.'

'Can't do big. Paper shortage,' Kenneth muttered miserably.

'That's all right, just so happens I can find some big paper. And when Billy's back from school and Mr Pawsey from the market, perhaps there'll be something come here to cheer you up.'

He didn't answer, and Billy didn't know what to say next to make things better. It was a relief when Mrs Pawsey came back with some huge sheets of paper which had wrapped up some documents long ago. They weren't very grubby. Kenneth was dusting them off as Billy left for school.

When he got home, expecting the parlour to be decorated with drawings like at Uncle Frank's house, Kenneth was just putting the rubber band round his pencils.

'I'm not showing you, so don't ask,' he said. He used the largest piece of paper to wrap up a sheaf of drawings.

Mrs Pawsey called them to the front garden and told them to look out for Mr Pawsey, who was expected back any minute.

Soon enough, he came ambling along, his trouser bottoms tied up over his boots because some of the lanes were very muddy after the heavy rain. He was drawing a cart behind him and as he got close there were unmistakable sounds coming from it. Billy rushed into the road.

'Mr Pawsey, Mr Pawsey. I know what you've got in there. I know.'

Mr Pawsey grinned. 'And I knew as you'd be pleased. You come and help, then. What about your cousin? Something to cheer him up. Kenneth, laddie, come and see.'

Kenneth moved forward slowly. Billy ran to the pig pen and opened its gate, then ran to the back of the cart as Mr Pawsey leaned inside and carried out a piglet like a baby in his arms.

'Shut the pen gate, lad. I'll lift each one over, that's easiest.'

There were four: one pink, one pink with black blobs, one black with pink blobs and one pink with a black bottom. They were really smashing.

Kenneth stayed at the front of the cart, watching. It was best not to tell Mr Pawsey that Kenneth didn't like pigs. Or any animals, really. He didn't even draw them.

Billy hung over the pen for ages watching the piglets. They were such fun, all wriggly and squeaky that he almost forgot what had happened, until he thought about Aunty coming to collect Kenneth.

Perhaps when he saw the car, Billy would be too busy helping with the animals to come indoors. The vicar would hurry Kenneth and Aunty back to the Vicarage. That would be best.

He ran into the kitchen to tell Mrs Pawsey about the piglets, to tell the dogs. He sat stroking Noah, because Kenneth wouldn't come near dogs. It was tea-time. Mrs Pawsey would sort Kenneth out. She had nice biscuits in her red *East West Home's Best* biscuit tin. It had a jolly picture of houses with red roofs, a neat circle of front garden in front that just made you ache to open it and see whether there were custard creams or pink wafers inside. His first day there, a chocolate digestive had been on top of the wafers. If Kenneth had one of those, he could sit and nibble it until he felt better.

It was all a great worry. However much he hated having Kenneth here, so sad and odd, it would even worse when the grown-ups returned with their misery. It would be truly dreadful if they cried. Aunty would likely cry and that would be really embarrassing. Perhaps she'd get it over with before they got here. When people died, did the grown-ups feel all right again once the funeral was over? It was four 'o'clock now. It must be long over. They'd have to hurry to catch the train before the night-time bombing started.

He saw Kenneth trailing indoors with Mr Pawsey, so Billy pulled Noah into the back lobby and filled his water bowl. There were some large jam jars on the shelf above the sink. That gave him an idea. He hurried into the garden to find something cheery. In October there weren't many flowers. He checked round the bushes for ideas, until he saw some lavender. It wasn't very blue now, but it smelled nice. The grown-ups would all like that. He picked a big bunch and took it inside. He half-filled the jam jar with water and separated the lavender stalks so that they looked good. Best to put it in the front room where grown-ups would go.

At tea-time everyone was quiet, and there were buns left over. It wouldn't be right to take left-overs down to Mrs Youldon's today, so he just watched as they were cleared away. It would be toasted buns tomorrow, because grownups wouldn't eat buns after a funeral.

It was growing dark when, kneeling by the front window, he saw the vicar's car draw up in the front yard. Mrs Pawsey had said it was best if Billy didn't work outside after tea.

The car shuddered and stopped. In the back, Aunty's head and Mother's showed clearly. The back car door opened and Mother started to get out. He could see that they were both in black and Aunty's hat had a little net veil which was rolled upwards. He ran to the parlour before he saw any more, his insides fluttering and panicky. 'Mrs Pawsey, Mrs Pawsey. They're here!'

She went to the door, bringing Kenneth by the hand. Lingering in the background, Billy started, as he saw that Dad was with them! He hadn't expected that. Dad was holding Aunty firmly round her upper arm, while Mother carried both their handbags.

Dad said 'Good evening, Mrs Pawsey.' then murmured more things. Billy only caught the end '. . . compassionate leave.'

She said in a low voice, 'So I should think, Mr Wilson. We're very, very sorry to hear of your loss.'

Billy tried to remember those words because other people he knew might die soon. Dad wouldn't cry of course, but he would be thinking about Uncle Frank and his being in a bus crashing right down into a hole, and being his brother, so it was best not to look at him. Dad nodded to Mr Pawsey, then greyly to Billy, hardly seeming to notice things.

Aunty threw her arms round Kenneth and stroked his face, her eyes watering already. 'Poor little fatherless boy.' Kenneth hung into her, his knees weak and bendy.

Mrs Pawsey supported them both into the front room where the chair cushions had been plumped up, ready.

Mother stepped forward, putting the handbags on the hall dresser. 'Hello, Billy,' she said very quietly and he said 'Hello, Mother.' Then he stood to one side, out of the way, but Mother put a hand at his back pressing him forward into the front room, and the vicar followed with Dad.

Mrs Pawsey said, 'So good of you to collect them from the station, Vicar.'

The vicar's face looked long and sad, although he didn't even know Uncle Frank. He waited while the grown-ups thanked Mrs Pawsey for looking after Kenneth who was hanging limply on Aunty's arm. Then he leaned forward and shook Billy's hand. 'You must be a strength to everyone.' He turned to shake Kenneth's hand and clapped one shoulder very firmly as if he was holding him together, 'My boy.'

Mother turned to Mrs Pawsey, 'I hope they've been no trouble to you. Well, Billy, really.'

Mrs Pawsey said in a low voice, 'No, no. He was so upset when I had to break the news.'

No one else was listening, hunched into their coats, but Mother put her head on one side and raised her eyebrows at Billy. He looked down quickly.

Mrs Pawsey told them all to sit down. 'I shall get you a nice tray of tea.'

Billy started forward, 'I can help.'

'No dear, best to stay with your family.'

Billy sat on the extra chair behind the vicar's.

Mother perched on a high chair, crossing her legs at the ankle. Aunty tucked a piece of curl under her hat and sat on the sofa. There were lines round her mouth and her skirt was badly creased. Kenneth sat beside her, leaning against her. He looked ill. Dad hitched up his trousers and sat heavily in the wide low chair, clearing his throat. He'd be making one of his sayings soon.

Billy kept his eyes on the jam jar where he'd put the lavender and breathed in the smell. It was too difficult to look at anyone's face.

The vicar said, 'I will lead you all in a little prayer for this very sad time.' He started off with the groaning words, *Ohs* and *Los* and *Dear Father* and *Beseech*. It seemed a very long prayer.

Billy had his eyes screwed tight but he could squint at bits of people while they had their heads down and eyes shut, praying with the vicar. He kept taking huge breaths of lavender smell, he couldn't help it, although he was scared the breaths would sound throughout the room once the praying stopped and then everyone would look at him.

They didn't, because just then Kenneth threw up all over Mrs Pawsey's best rug. There just wasn't time to get a bucket. And now Billy couldn't smell the lavender at all. In the fuss, he was able to run to the kitchen to get rags and water and Mrs Pawsey. She had to do the cleaning up because Aunty was seeing to Kenneth, and Mother had good clothes on. A bit had splashed on to her skirt and shoe, so she went outside to get it off. Billy left the cleaning things and quickly disappeared into the parlour where Mr Pawsey was just reaching a hand around for his glasses, a long way wide of the mark.

'I've got them, Mr Pawsey, I've got them.' He put them into Mr Pawsey's groping paw. 'Kenneth's been sick and it smells awful. Don't go into the front room.'

'I won't, Boy. And you stay here and keep me company. They've got my good lady and the vicar to help. I was just going to do my crossword and couldn't find those glasses for the life of me. If only Billy was here, I thought, he'd find 'em for me, and here you are.'

Billy sat on the arm of his chair. 'You'll need me to fill in your crossword letters, won't you?'

'I will.' He scratched his forehead with the end of his pencil. 'Now two across, seven letters. How about 'thunder'? Do you reckon that fits in?'

Billy counted across carefully, then nodded.

'So put in just the T and the R, till we're sure. Now then, eight down. Will that start with a T? Trouble, that's what I think it is.'

'I think it is, too,' said Billy.

It was some time before the tray of tea got to everyone. Now that the front room was spoiled, it was put in the dining room and everyone moved in there. Kenneth was lying down upstairs for a little while, a bucket beside him just in case. It would be awful if he was sick again and made Billy's room smell.

From his vantage point beside Mr Pawsey and his crossword, Billy heard the vicar say they would drink the tea Mrs Pawsey had kindly provided and then have their little prayer again. He sat tight, hoping he wouldn't be called in. After all, the table wasn't laid for his supper. He always had his supper there with Mr and Mrs Pawsey, and because they hadn't eaten much tea, it was going to be ham and tomatoes and chutney and chunks of bread and dark fruit loaf.

After a while, he heard Kenneth come downstairs, saying he felt better, he just wanted to go back to his own bed. Billy hoped he only meant his billet bed. If Aunty had decided never to go back to Balham again, Kenneth would never have his own bed. Aunty fussed round him and then said he should join in their prayer before they got his coat on.

If they were going, Billy thought he'd better come to the front door. He'd wait until he heard them saying their Goodbyes. He left the crossword and hovered at the doorway, then looked back at Mr Pawsey whose glasses were off again, his head slightly bowed.

He waited to hear the prayer begin in the dining room, and soon the rhythmic, sighing words came. He frowned. It would make no difference the vicar doing all that. Uncle would still be dead.

There was a little silence, shuffling, then a chorus of muttering from everyone together. They were all murmuring the same prayer words. Then it ended. Phew. Billy felt his breath shoot upwards over his nose. A chair grated as the vicar said he would take a brief turn around the garden before driving them home.

Mr Pawsey stood up. 'Go and join your family now, Billy. I'll be needed to show the vicar round.' He went to the front door and ushered the vicar out.

Billy followed slowly and slid into the spare seat by the dining room door. The women were softly talking with Mrs Pawsey who was tutting and sympathising '. . . we did worry whether you'd get a train before any air raid.'

'Yes, it was an added worry. And do you know,' Aunty was saying in a shaky voice, 'the very worst thing, when we got on to the train to go to the funeral, there was a notice right in front of us, *Is your journey really necessary?* It was the last straw, I can tell you.'

Mrs Pawsey patted her arm, 'There, it's a terrible time, that's for sure. You're taking it all so bravely. Now, you sit awhile, sort yourselves out, no hurry, before Vicar takes you all off backalong. I'll just see to the dishes if you'll excuse me,' and she bustled back to the kitchen.

Dad stood up and came towards Kenneth who was leaning against Aunty's arm. 'You look a bit better, Kenneth. Are you?'

'I'm all right now.'

Dad beckoned to Billy to stand by him. Was this a father's prayer? Billy obeyed. The vicar came back in, but only as far as the doorway. Dad cleared his throat, then looked at Mother and Aunty as if to see that they were paying attention. He put a hand on Kenneth's shoulder and another on Billy's. 'Frank and I had an arrangement,' he said to everyone. 'We promised each other when war was declared that if anything happened to the one of us, the other would look after his boy.'

Mother's eyes widened, but she didn't say anything. She held one of her prettiest hankies between clenched hands. There was a long pause. The piglets were squealing their loudest. Mr Pawsey was doing the feed without Billy.

Dad went on, 'My brother Frank did a wonderful job as a father. Now he's gone, I will try my level best to do the same. So now I've got two sons. Billy and Kenneth.'

The room went black for a while. Then Billy realised his gaze was fixed on the vicar's coat on the chair in front of him and he wasn't looking beyond it. What was it Dad had said? He couldn't really have said *two sons*. He only had one son.

Aunty said with a sniffle, 'Thank you, thank you, Herbert. That is a comfort, I must say.'

Kenneth looked up at Dad, his face still whitish, one curl smeared across his forehead. 'What do I call you, then? Aren't you Uncle any more?'

Dad put his large hand on Kenneth's shoulder and softly closed it round. 'I am uncle and now I'm father too. If you'd like to, you can call me Dad.'

Billy stared hard at the vicar's black coat. Kenneth couldn't call him *Dad*. Could he? They couldn't *both* have him as Dad, surely. He looked up at Dad, confused.

'So, sh- should I call you *Uncle*?' he asked.

Dad answered with a cuff round his ear. 'None of that. Especially at such a time. Be a bit Christian.'

The cuff didn't hurt much but something did, low down in his throat and lower still. Billy ran out to the sanctuary of the parlour. It had been jolly bad having Uncle Frank but it was even worse not having him. Mr Pawsey's glasses were glinting on the side table. Billy plucked them up and shoved them on his face. Now he couldn't see anything but pale splodges. He staggered round the room knocking into things, his hands in front of him, blinded to all that was happening. He heard them come in after him, the women exclaiming, his father saying his name in an irritated voice. It didn't matter, he'd be a pale foggy splodge to them, not Billy any more.

His father began speaking angrily, the black patches of his trousers coming dangerously near, but then the more fanned-out black of the vicar's robe swam near the doorway.

'A confusing time, a very confusing time for a young boy away from his home.'

Dad went quiet, and the wide black shape came near and a pale pink one grasped Billy's arm, firmly but kindly. It was a safe hold but Billy's own hand shot up protectively to his glasses. It seemed important to keep them on his nose, the only thing between him and all of them.

The vicar spoke softly to him. 'Time to take those off now, my son.'

So was the vicar going to be Billy's father, now? He cowered backward. No! He just wanted to stay here, with Mr and Mrs Pawsey, without Kenneth, feeding the piglets and collecting the swill from the village and being talked to at teatimes.

Mother's voice came from a distance. 'Billy! Take the glasses off. This is no time to be clowning around.'

Aunty said, sniffing, 'Oh, Billy, stop messing around. Isn't it bad enough? Let's get back and settled down as best we can, the few days your father is with us.'

The vicar's hand swam forwards and gently removed the glasses. 'I think Mr Pawsey will be looking for these in a minute.'

'You should come to the Vicarage for a few days, Billy,' said Mother.

'If you can avoid making things worse for poor Kenneth than they already are,' Dad added.

'Vicarage' sounded like *Vicar cage*. He didn't want to be trapped in it.

Mrs Pawsey came from the kitchen to see them off. She didn't know Billy had done anything wrong. She hadn't known Uncle Frank so she couldn't be sad about him. All the dark figures in front of him, the whole blackness of it made Billy suddenly turn and hide his head in Mrs Pawsey's bulges. She smelled of flour and disinfectant.

Mother tutted and said, 'Stand straight, child. We're going now. Last chance to join us if you're going to stop being silly.'

Stop being Billy, he thought she'd said at first, because his ears were well into Mrs Pawsey's apron.

Aunty said, 'It's all a bit much, Billy, isn't it? Perhaps you'd rather come to see us a bit later on?'

Kind Aunty. He kept his face hidden so he couldn't hear or see what the adults said or did. Perhaps Aunty had saved him. Mrs Pawsey gently turned him around.

'I have to get Kenneth's things, dear. See your family off nicely, now.'

Dad looked down at Billy. 'Disappointed in you, Billy. Buck your ideas up and do better when I see you next.' He ushered everyone towards the vicar's car.

When their backs were safely turned and disappearing through the front door, Billy rushed into the front room stepping over the newspaper where the sick had been and grabbed the lavender out of the jam jar. He ran to the car just as they were getting in. He thrust the lavender at Aunty.

'This is for you. Because . . . I like you.'

Aunty started. She blushed and her eyes watered as she took the lavender gently from him and held it close. She looked really pleased. Mother didn't.

Kenneth glanced at the lavender at Aunty's chest, then unfolded the large paper with all the drawings he'd done while Billy had been at school.

He put the top one on his mother's lap.

There was a choked gasp, then Aunty's wail began. It was a really detailed likeness of Uncle Frank.

CHAPTER SIX

October 20th 1940

*Long range bombers in Belgium ready for operations
against England.*

Billy couldn't get to sleep that night for thinking of the
terrible day just past He kept remembering the round,
black bottom of the vicar's car crunching slowly away
down the lane with Mother's small white handkerchief
waving from the window, the sounds of Aunty's light
wailing and the perfume of lavender masking the
rancid smell in the front room. However hard he
screwed his eyes shut, he still saw Kenneth's drawing
of Uncle Frank and his pile of sick on Mrs Pawsey's
nice rug.

'Look at those dark rings round your eyes!' Mrs
Pawsey remarked in the morning. 'We shall keep you
home from school. What you need is a quiet, ordinary
day.'

He mooched around for a while and overheard
them discussing the terrible incident that had killed
Uncle Frank and so many others. He didn't want to
hear anything about it, yet found himself creeping
below the kitchen window to hear more. Something
about water gushing and no chance of escape and a
bus driver who couldn't stop in time. And if only Uncle
hadn't decided to visit Dad. It was just like Gordon. If
only he hadn't gone for the interview, or if only the
thunderstorm hadn't started.

Then he heard Mrs Pawsey say, 'That little lad's face, I'll never forget. Tragic, bless him. Beautiful features. Wasn't that face like one of those porcelain ornaments in the county museum?'

'Tragedy for him, yes. I should watch him, though,' said Mr Pawsey. 'Bain't porcelain right the way through.'

Billy crept away miserably. Porcelain or not, whatever that was, Kenneth was bound to come again. This was Billy's billet, but now *his* Mr and Mrs Pawsey would be looking at Kenneth. Like an ornament.

Later they called him to help with the chores.

'Nothing like work to show you that life goes on,' said Mr Pawsey.

After they'd seen to the chickens, the piglets, the fences and the yard, they had a dinner of Mrs Pawsey's vegetable soup with hunks of fresh warm bread.

Mr Pawsey put his jacket on afterwards and said they'd take the dogs for a walk. There was a lot of barking and rushing around and panting and wet tongues. Mrs Pawsey almost pushed them out of the door, saying she needed an empty house to do a good clean-up.

Mr Pawsey winked at Billy, his eyes all little and wrinkly without his glasses, and they set off down the lane, the dogs setting a fast pace. Mr Pawsey could keep up with them better than Billy, much better than Granddad would. Mr Pawsey didn't seem so very old to Billy now. He could do all sorts of strong things. He might even be able to swing a shashka if someone taught him right.

'Are you along-a-me, Billy, or what? Do you want to try taking a dog?'

Billy ran up alongside him. Japhet came up to his waist. He was the slightly larger dog so he tried holding Noah's lead but his arm was pulled straight and his body nearly followed.

Mr Pawsey put a bear-like paw on top of Billy's grasp. 'You've got to be firm, you know. Show who's master. If a dog thinks he can rule the day, he will. Same with people, you know.' He demonstrated how to jerk the lead so that Noah had to stop. Japhet was padding along in a superior way as if he never barked or rushed away. 'Look at this one. He's only behaving because he knows I'm top dog. We'll do the same with Noah.'

Noah looked top dog, lips pulled back, eyes bulging, raring to go, but Mr Pawsey with his screwed up eyes and shuffling feet, he was the one in charge.

They got to the village outskirts and the lanes were fairly dry so the dogs were let off their leads. Billy let out a little laugh as they whizzed off so fast that little hairs from their necks blew up into the air.

'How will we ever get them back?'

'One whistle. They know. You have to have a sign, you know. A noise for an animal. For a person it can be a look on the face.'

'I know that! Mother has a 'No' face sometimes and I stop doing whatever it is.'

'There you are, you see. Your mother's top dog with you.'

'Dad's top dog of everyone, though, isn't he?' and suddenly he remembered with a thump in his tummy that Dad was top dog of more people now. Kenneth. Would he stop being nasty if there was a look on Dad's face? Would Aunty?

'Mr Pawsey?'

'Mmm.'

'If a man can have two sons, can he have two wives?'

'Oho, no. Not at the same time. Not in our country. Only one after the other, sometimes.'

At that moment there was loud barking and when they rounded the corner, a small lady was stroking the dogs.

'Mrs Youldon!' He rushed up to her.

'Down!' Mr Pawsey said, some way behind him, but it was the dogs he was shouting to. They were jumping up and that wasn't allowed.

Mrs Youldon was in a blue dress with a dark blue cardigan. She might be going to a party except for her shoes, same as before, brown, baggy and lace-up. He'd never seen her prettied up before. Nice, stroky. Like Angela.

'I like your dress and everything. It's pretty.'

Mrs Youldon twizzled round, then smiled bashfully. 'Nice? It's from The Grange. They gave me these when they were turning stuff out for the war effort and I only had to alter it a bit. Guess what I've got it on for?'

Billy shook his head.

Mr Pawsey came up to them. 'Good morning, Joan. How are you managing these days?'

'Oh not so bad, Mr Pawsey. I think there's some more work coming up for me. They need women at the tinning factory, and they're going to collect everyone by van in the morning and bring them back at the end of the day. The church have started a nursery and that's where my little ones are now. So I'm feeling quite excited.'

'And you're looking very smart.'

'Thank you.' She blushed. 'I thought I'd try it on to show Billy, really. I was just on my way to your house to see him.'

'Me?'

'I haven't forgotten. Your birthday.'

He looked up at Mr Pawsey with a gasp. The last days had been so terrible that he'd actually forgotten. 'I'm nine!'

'My goodness me. A birthday. We didn't know that, the wife and I.'

Mrs Youldon smiled. 'And last year I didn't know and all we could do was sing the birthday song, but this year is different. Here's a little present from all of us.' She handed over a parcel wrapped up in brown paper. It was a good shape, all knobbly and interesting.

'Thank you.' He opened the parcel and found a set of aeroplane cards and three large pine cones painted mainly red.

'They're topping! I wanted these ever so! I'll know all the planes now.' He looked at the cones.

'The little ones did those at the nursery,' she said. 'They wanted to give you something too.' She looked up at Mr Pawsey. 'They think the world of Billy, my little ones', she said. 'I'll get back to them now I've bumped into you, Billy. Saved me a walk. I'll go and show them my dress. Make sure you come up ours, soon.' She turned back down the lane with a wave.

Billy hugged the things to him. He would go again soon, and he'd have to tell her about Uncle Frank, but he'd never take Kenneth there.

They walked on and on, the dogs speeding away and then back again.

'We're going far!'

'We are that.' Mr Pawsey's face had folds around his mouth, and just now they looked longer. 'Haven't done this route since-- '

And suddenly Billy guessed that Mr Pawsey was thinking about Gordon. He probably walked the dogs with Gordon, and now he couldn't. He'd gone for ever, like Uncle Frank. It was horrible that one person dying made everyone think of other people they'd known dying, so the sadness spread across all sorts of people. He put his hand into Mr Pawsey's hairy one. It was like having another Granddad. You *could* have two Granddads. It was only Mother who had a father alive. Would Dad mind that Billy had Mr and Mrs Pawsey instead? That they weren't just a billet?

Mr Pawsey was saying, 'It's a day for a good long walk, especially now as it's your birthday. Exercise. Do you good.'

The dogs ran ahead with cheerfully wagging tails until they came to a stream.

Billy ran to see. 'Cor. Super!'

Japhet barked once, and both dogs went to charge down the bank, but Mr Pawsey was too quick. He'd already grasped their collars, one in each hand.

'Now we put their leads on,' he said.

'But they want to swim.'

'They do. Oh, they do that. But look here. The bank's high and straight up so once they're in they can't get out, and the water's deep because the river's near. Look how it's swirling around. Water going two ways. Dangerous for them. And if you're ever here, don't ever try to swim or even paddle. There's a much better place a bit further on where it makes a pool.'

He yanked the leads as the dogs strained to get near the water and led the way through a dark woody path until they came out into the sun again. They clambered over the stile and down a slope until a flat, grassy patch was in front of them and a stony-edged pool at one side of the main flow. The dogs were let off their leads and rushed in, making crystal drops fly in all directions.

Billy laughed. 'Can I paddle?'

'Now why do you think I've walked this far?'

Billy tore off his shoes and socks. He paddled out to the dogs and splashed around them. There were a few flat stones in the middle of the pool. He looked around for more and placed them down so that he'd made crude stepping stones. 'Look – a path, Mr Pawsey. You'll be able to walk across.'

'I'd better not risk it. I used to. You'll not be the first one who's thought of making one of those, young Billy. Do you like this place then?'

'It's top-hole. Did you really know it was my birthday? Is this a birthday treat? Did my mother tell you it was?'

Then he fell silent, there certainly hadn't been any cards or packages left for him. It was like last year. They'd forgotten.

'No. But if you think about it, your family have been tied up with other things, haven't they?'

Other things. The misery came back like a huge thump. He kicked at the water a few times, but the sun of the day had gone. Mr Pawsey was putting the leads back on the dogs.

'Come on now. It's nearly four. Must get back before it's dark. I shall need you to find my glasses back home, and we left that crossword at eleven across, remember? L- it began with.'

Billy was stamping the water off his feet on the longer grass.

When they got back, Mrs Pawsey already had the tea on the table, so Billy ran upstairs to get washed. He could hear Mr Pawsey muttering to her but he stopped when Billy ran down again.

It was not until they'd finished their tea that Mrs Pawsey said, 'We didn't know it was your birthday, Billy, but we're going to celebrate it properly. We shall take you to the pictures on Saturday.'

He leapt up. 'The pictures! Really, truly? I haven't been for ages and ages.'

'Yes. *Pinocchio*'s on, all about a naughty puppet boy. Isn't that just right for making boys laugh?'

Mr Pawsey was holding a brown cardboard box. 'And this. Open this 'un. The Missus gave it to me around twelve years ago, but my eyesight's not good enough to use it now. I think I can teach you to use it properly.'

Billy opened the box and a huge gasp escaped. Inside was a camera, a real one. He took it out and held it tightly. He could feel the metal under its soft black covering. It folded up, click, and you could put it in your pocket.

'It's a Kodak', said Mrs Pawsey proudly.

Mr Pawsey took the camera from Billy and removed the entire back. 'This is how you load your film, but you must do it somewhere dark. Never, never outside in the daylight.'

He took Billy by the arm and they went in the cupboard under the stairs. It was pretty dark there. Billy giggled, it seemed such a funny thing to do. Mr Pawsey took a film out of his pocket, unwrapped it and slid the edges into a slot on the metal winder.

'See that? Think you can do it?'

He took it off and gave it to Billy who could do it easily. Then they shut the back of the camera and came out of the cupboard again. It was fun; mysterious and important, like a secret.

'That was a bit like hiding in an air raid,' Billy said.

Mrs Pawsey pressed her lips into her teeth. 'We're very lucky we don't have all that,' she said. 'I try not to forget it.'

It was nearly reminding Billy of the bomb at Balham so he pressed the camera into his chest until it hurt. Then he could think about the camera and how wonderful it was. He jumped up and down a bit then asked,

'Can I take a photo right away please?'

'A bit of a lesson, first, I think. Each snap you take uses up some film and when it's finished, we have to go and have it developed and printed, which costs money.'

'I've got a shilling, Uncle Ted gave me last year. It was for something special, and this is.'

'I think it's going to cost more than that. But I'll teach you how to take 'em tomorrow.'

Early the next day, before Billy had to set off for school, Mr Pawsey showed him the adjustable range finder. 'It'm worked by this small thumb screw, see, on the right side.'

He put his hands up as if they were a picture frame. 'That's how you choose your shot. You must hold the camera very steady. Best to rest it on a post or sommat.'

Billy listened very hard as Mr Pawsey explained about the light, the composition, and the shutter speed. Kenneth didn't know anything about these things.

The camera was so exciting Billy could ignore his heavy inside places where memories of Uncle Frank and the after-funeral visit were fluttering about like horse-flies.

They all flew back into his mind once he got to school. Alan was waiting for him on the lane leading to the school. 'I heard. Rotten luck, but it was the bully uncle died not your special one, wasn't it?'

'Mm. Uncle Frank, Kenneth's father, and Kenneth had to come to stay with me. It was awful.' That was as far as he got for once they got to the playground, everyone crowded round him, shoving Alan out of the way. They'd all heard about the Balham bombing and wanted to know the details.

Mick said, 'Cor, Billy. Your uncle got blitzed in that bus outside United Dairies. Our Mum shops there.'

Dick said, 'United Dairies has got a great socking hole outside it and the bus tipped right in. Everyone dead.'

'Lumme,' one of the East Enders joined in. 'Wish I'd seen it. Did your uncle die straight away?'

'Was your uncle burned up?'

'Was he drowned when the water gushed up?'

'Burned or drowned or blown up?'

Billy whirled his shashka arm round and round, saying 'I dunno, dunno, dunno.' He ran the length of the playground whirling and chanting, the others following with their 'Tell us, then. Tell us'.

Alan pushed forward, 'Shut up, you lot. Leave him alone.'

But they didn't. It was like a swarm after Billy and around him, buzzing and fussing until the bell went.

The teachers had been telephoned with the news, probably by the vicar. They were extra kind to Billy and let him off his spellings, but he just wanted things to be ordinary. At home time, the buzzing around him started again but he folded his arms and said loudly, 'I've got a camera. It was for my birthday.'

'Yaw. I bet!'

'Well, I have.'

'All right. What make is it?'

'It's a Kodak.' That stopped the sneering.

'Real truth, Billy? Bring it to show. Photograph all of us? What's it do?'

Then he stood still and told them about his present, the shutter speed, putting in the film in the dark and everyone stopped asking about Uncle Frank.

Alan walked home with him. 'You will let me have a go with it when I come round, won't you?'

'The film's very expensive and I'm not to waste snaps.'

'Swap you, then.'

'What for?'

If only Alan could go to Mother's vicarage instead of having to go himself. That was no good. Alan ran into the Manor and Billy mooched off down the lane alone.

All days end. That was one of Dad's sayings, usually when Mother complained of a bad day. Billy thought of this as the red roof of the Pawseys' house showed behind the trees. This normally gave him a cheery feeling. The curving front path looked like a smile and he was sure the dogs were grinning at him as they rushed to him with their tongues hanging out. There was a bit of barking, but it was only to welcome him, or perhaps to tell Mrs Pawsey he was home. He would ask

Mrs Pawsey if Alan could come over on Saturday for the whole day. Then they could do exploring and forget all about horrible things.

As he came to the back door, Mrs Pawsey put an arm round him and pulled him into her bulgy middle.

'Was it all right at school today?'

'No, it was rotten. They all kept asking horrible questions.'

'Never you mind, lovey. Let's go and have some tea then why not go and show Mrs Youldon your camera? I've put some of my fairy cakes in a bag for you to take.'

His mouth stopped feeling so tight. He did want to show the Youldons his camera and it was nice to have the cakes to take them.

After tea, he put the camera round his neck and ran off down the lane. He'd take three photos: one of Mrs Youldon, Tim and Sally together, one of just the children, and if big Ronnie next door and the usual crowd were playing on the street, he'd photograph them too. He was around the corner and into the main village before Mrs Pawsey had had a chance to tell him what time to be home.

He saw Mrs Youldon before she saw him. She wasn't in her nice blue dress now. She was back to the baggy thing with threads at the hem and a great apron round her. She was at the doorway looking hassled, for there were no big children in the street to mind the little ones.

Timmy and Sally jumped up and down when they saw who was coming. 'Billy! Billy!'

He ran up to them. 'Thank you for the fir cones. You painted them jolly well. Look at what I've got! It's all mine, my camera!' He turned round, 'Mrs Youldon, look what I've got. Mr Pawsey gave it to me and I'm going to take photos of you.'

'Well I never. It's a proper one, too.' She felt the top reverently as he let it concertina open. 'My little ones have never had their photo took.'

'I'm going to take it.' He put Timmy and Sally side by side outside the front of the cottage. They nudged each other and started to giggle. There was no gatepost to balance his camera on, but he held it very still while he examined them through his viewfinder. 'Keep still now.' He pressed the shutter as soon as they'd stopped fidgeting. It would be a picture of them giggling together. That'd be nice. 'Can I take one of you, Mrs Youldon?'

'Ooh dear, I don't know. I'm in the middle of some extra washing for the Grange.' But she took her apron off, and stood stiffly.

'Smile.' He took one of her on her own, and another one of her standing shyly behind her children. 'Finished.'

Sally ran to peer into the camera. 'Where are we, where are we, Billy?'

He laughed. 'Not inside the camera! I have to finish the film and then take it to get prints. Then I'll show you them, and you'll see yourselves in a picture.'

Mrs Youldon put her apron back on again. 'It'll be lovely to have photos of the little ones so I'll always know what they looked like, young. It'll be nice for them, too. I don't know how I looked as a child. Just no idea.'

'Didn't your parents get you photographed?'

She smiled in a way that showed him it was a silly question. She was poor. She hadn't lived the sort of life where you went to a town and got photographed.

Billy knew exactly how he looked when he was young, flat-haired, clean and ordinary in new clothes. There was a photo on the mantelpiece in the lounge at home: he stood on a stool wearing a pale blue buster suit, Mother on one side and Dad on the other, all very serious.

He clipped the camera shut, the little ones watching closely as the inside concertina'd flat again.

Mrs Youldon looked at him proudly. 'You do look grown-up with your camera, Billy. I hope you're very careful with it.'

'I am,' he said as he followed all of them indoors. Steam from the copper at the back belched into the small room. 'I'm not going to let Kenneth even touch it.' He swallowed. He knew he must tell her what had happened. 'I ought to let him, because his father died, my Uncle Frank.'

She gasped. 'What – just died?'

'A bomb in London.'

She gave him a hug. 'That's dreadful, really, really dreadful.'

He thought he wouldn't tell her the whole story. Like Mr Durban protecting his mother when he got back from Russia, Billy didn't want bad stuff going into Mrs Youldon's head; she was only a small mother.

'Your cousin, poor young boy with no father now. And you, losing your uncle, Billy. You must be very sad.'

Billy remembered that he should be, and hung his head. Then he said, 'It was Aunty's sad loss. I picked her some lavender.'

'Lavender? That was nice. You are a good boy.' Mrs Youldon picked up the damp clothes ready to iron. It was a huge pile. So was the dirty pile waiting for the copper. She must be taking in extra work because she had no evacuee money.

He picked up a pair of sheets that had fallen off the load of dirty washing and took the whole pile towards the copper.

'Thank you, Billy, such a help. I wish you'd come over more often, you and Alan. You could earn tuppence an afternoon if you'd look after Tim and Sally safely so that I can go to work. When you're not at school, of course.'

He nodded. 'Righto, I will. I like looking after them. Not for the money. You can buy more food to put on your shelves instead.' He smiled down at them as Sally tugged at his jumper and Tim measured his height against him. His insides already felt better. He did so like being here. He pointed to his paper bag. 'Guess what I've got in here? It's fairy cakes for all of you.'

CHAPTER SEVEN

October 21st 1940

*New Zealand cruiser drives Italian destroyers away
in Red Sea.*

When he got home, Mrs Pawsey was in the kitchen
peeling a huge pile of carrots. He opened his mouth to
ask if Alan could come over on Saturday but Mrs
Pawsey was already speaking.

'Here, Billy. Can you cut these heads off and sit
them in this tray of water? Then they'll be ready for
you to plant out in a couple of days?'

He rolled up his jumper sleeves and took up the
knife.

'Your father telephoned.'

He put the knife down. What now? His chest
thudded and he crossed his arms over it, hard.

'He wants you over there for two days, before he
has to go back to London. Jed'll take you and the
vicar'll bring you back the following evening.'

'Then I'll have to stay the night! Can't I come back
with Jed? Couldn't he wait for me and have his dinner
there?'

'Oh no, no. It's what's been arranged, dear, and it's
for your parents to decide. At such a time as this, you'll
want to be with your father.'

He wouldn't, not with this happening. It would be
awful. They'd all still be cross with him as well as being
sad as sad. He wouldn't know what to say. Two whole
days! What would they do all that time? There'd be

grown-ups with funeral faces, and they'd make him be with Kenneth, who was all quiet and strange.

Mrs Pawsey broke into his thoughts, 'Your little sister will be glad to see you. It's been several weeks since you were together.'

Jill. It was ages ago since that night at the station when he'd last seen her. She might still have that little bear he'd put into her baby hand. She would be glad to see him. She hadn't had him to play with her and perhaps she'd cried when Mother came here, leaving her behind. He brightened. 'I bet she'll jump up and down and say her words over and over again. That's what she does. And she'll want me to read to her.'

'That's right, my love. Won't that be nice?'

Yes. He could play with Jill, and not look at the others much at all. He might ask Mr Pawsey if he could take his camera. He could snap Jill, then he could show Mr and Mrs Pawsey what she looked like.

At the sound of Jed's horse next morning, Billy leant out of his bedroom window. It would be good to have a photo of Jed on his cart with the nice brown horse, bright red on his harness. He put his hands up like a frame. He called down.

'Jed! Stay there, please. I got a camera for my birthday. I'm going to take your picture.'

He rested his elbows on the windowsill and adjusted the distance. The photo would look smashing.

Jed sat like a statue. 'Well I'll be blowed. No one's never taken my picture afore.'

Then Billy ran down to clamber aboard, the camera around his neck.

'You'se be very, very careful with it, Billy. There'm be no chance you'se'll get another camera if you break that, or let anyone else break it.' He knew Mr Pawsey had only let him take it with him because of how it was going to be for him at the vicarage.

'I know. I'm not going to let anyone else TOUCH it.' If anyone tried, he'd make the 'Don't' face. Anything else they could take or make him give to poor Kenneth, but not the camera.

The jogging journey was quite nice, all through the red and gold trees, the horses kicking up the thick layer of fallen leaves. Soon the branches would be bare.

Jed dropped him off by the vicarage. He stood where the cart had left him and watched Jed disappear over a browny-green bank and down into the distance.

What would the vicarage be like? He'd never been in one before. He held his overnight case in one hand, the camera still strung round his neck. He wasn't going to put it down if he could help it.

The vicarage was a grey stone house with a tiled roof. It was near to the church, which was very like the one in his village. The gate was green like Nanny's and there were flowers at the sides of a path running to the front door where a pale woman stood, a duster bunched in her hand.

'Are you Billy? I'm Mrs Shawditch.'

She wasn't as smart as Mother and Aunty. He'd have expected her to be smarter – a vicar's wife – but her cardigan bagged around her waist, there was no little white collar on her blouse and her shoes were clumpy. He wouldn't have been looking at clothes, only her face had nothing on it, no smile, no expression, as if that sort of thing had all been worn off.

'Come in. I'm sure it will cheer everyone up to have your visit.' He saw that she had green eyes and pale hair, but she didn't look cheered up herself. She turned to call his mother. 'Billy's here!'

Billy held out his hand, ready to shake hers. She started, as if she'd been dreaming and now had to return to work. Her hand was moist, limp. 'Well. Your father's busy for a while with the vicar but I think your mother's still in the kitchen. She's helping me prepare the vegetables. Quite a lot of us for dinner today.'

He stepped inside. There was no dog to bark. He could smell soap and old clothes. A box of them waited in the hall for giving away. They looked faded and very old. Who was going to want any of those?

A set of wooden picture frames all along the hall wall frowned down on him with different texts: *Behold, I waited for thy words, I listened for thy wise sayings*. That one had a pretty border round the words in green. *Lo, My Redeemer cometh* had sun rays around it. And *He forgave them their Sins* was on plain grey. *Jesus Loves You* was in thick coloured block capitals. The coir mat said *Wipe Your Feet*, so he did.

'Marcia! Your son!' the vicar's wife called again, running a hand through slightly messy fine hair. 'She won't be a moment, Billy. I just have to see to a – a gentleman who needs a set of new clothes and something to eat.'

He peered down the hall after her as she opened a back room door. He caught a glimpse of a long-haired tramp standing in rumpled grey trousers, everything else bare. Mother was just passing him, whisking aside her skirt as she did so. She wouldn't have wanted to accidentally touch him. She closed the door behind her. Clip. Her eyes lighted upon Billy.

'Hello. You get bigger each time I see you, I do declare. It's all that football I suppose, that and your farm food.'

'Hello Mother.' It had only been a few days since she'd seen him. Could he have grown in that time? He looked down at his legs. It must be his trousers, which had got so short lately. His boots were a long way from the trouser hems. He stood behind the hallstand where only his top half showed, his big legs hidden by the bottom of several coats hanging from the curly hooks.

Mother didn't seem to be sad. Perhaps it was all right about Uncle Frank now. He wasn't her brother, after all.

'Now. Your father's only got two more days with us. So you will be a good boy, won't you?'

He nodded. 'I didn't m-mean not to be the other day.'

'No, perhaps not. Very well, we'll pass over it.' She took a couple of steps towards him, her arm outstretched. Perhaps she was going to pat his face.

'What's that round your neck?'

'My c-camera.' He stepped back. 'Mr and Mrs Pawsey gave it to me.'

'Really!'

'Now that I'm n-nine.' He would have looked straight into her eyes if it hadn't been for the other day, his behaviour, and Uncle Frank dying. When someone died you didn't look at people, at least, not at their faces. He looked at her waist where a checked apron was tied round her tweed skirt.

Mother twitched and her hand shot up to her mouth. 'Nine? Oh, my goodness! We've missed your birthday, haven't we? And I think that happened last year. It's too bad.'

He felt guilty, as though he always made his birthday come at the wrong time. 'It's all right, Mother. Mr and Mrs Pawsey are taking me to the pictures on Saturday.'

'How kind. Well, you do know we would have sent you cards. I mean, you've even had a party in the past. With a clown, games and everything. That was before the War, of course.'

She looked back at the door she'd just closed and bustled him back out of the front door. 'We'll go this way, and I can show you round the garden at the same time. I've been busy in the kitchen, peeling vegetables. There are —— people here. The vicarage helps them with food and clothes. I feel I must help out in some way, not that I'm any cook. I sorted out a whole cupboard of old clothes for the WVS. Aunty's busy down there now, packing food parcels. She says it takes her mind off her tragedy. Some other women there have lost their menfolk, too.'

Outside the front door they turned right and through a gate into a large but shabby garden where Mother spread her arms wide as if she might be taken in flight. 'Here we are!'

It was not as if there were swings and slides or anything. He could see it was farmers' fields beyond the garden and when he hopped up on a pile of wood he could see a horse dragging a plough in the distance, neat rows churned up behind. A flurry of birds surrounded the plough as if to help it move along. 'So free, away from the noise and everything. This is the best place.'

She moved on. They passed a vegetable patch and a border of flowers with dead blooms flopping forward. 'So much to do,' said Mother. 'Anyway, we must make you a cake. Oh dear. I hardly like to trouble Aunty, and Mrs Shawditch has all these extra people to worry about.'

'It doesn't matter. I don't mind.' Mrs Pawsey's cakes were super anyway.

They moved down the garden, Mother turned her head from side to side as if troublesome people were about to come at her or even the Jerries. 'Well, hmm. Good boy.' Her eyes moved back to the door. She must be thinking about the man with a bare top, or all the things she had to do.

After a minute, Billy said, 'Is Jill looking forward to seeing me? It's been ages.'

'Jill? She's at nursery. Better for her to be occupied. But Kenneth's here. We'll go and find him.'

'It doesn't matter.'

'I think we should.' She pushed a tall gate open and pointed. 'That's the church. See the tower? Quite high, isn't it? And look through the hedge. Those are grouse padding around.'

He bent down to watch them. 'Grouse. Funny name. All hunched backs and spotty. They look like their name.'

Mother wasn't listening. She led him back towards the house and round to the far side. They stood on a knobbly path where the borders were filled with weeds. 'Not sure where he'll be. Probably drawing somewhere. It's not good for him to be on his own for too long.'

She looked at an upstairs window with a metal bar across it and lifted her chin so that her hair fell backwards towards her waist. 'Ken-neth?'

A pale face appeared at the window. A pale hand followed, just the one, and it had a pencil in it.

'Yes, he's in his bedroom.' Mother beckoned him down.

Billy frowned. '*His* bedroom? I thought K- Kenneth and Aunty were living with that other lady, d-down the road?'

'Yes, but because of what's happened, Mrs Shawditch thought it best for them to be with us, not fretting on their own up there. We've popped Kenneth into Jill's little room for comfort.'

'Oh.' It hadn't been much comfort when they'd popped him into Billy's room at the Pawseys.

While they were waiting for Kenneth to come down she said, 'I think a bit of fresh air will be good. You two can go for a walk while Mrs Shawditch and I finish the dinner. Kenneth can show you the village.' She took his overnight bag and led him back to the front gate. 'Do you want to leave your camera with me?'

'No thank you.'

She looked at him, so he tried a No face for her to see.

'Oh, all right then. Snapping the countryside, are you?'

He didn't need to answer because by then Kenneth had appeared, long socks and polished shoes as if he hadn't been evacuated. Or perhaps he had to go to church all over again because of Uncle Frank.

Mother looked relieved to see Kenneth carrying a jacket. 'All ready to go for a walk, Kenneth, dear? You must have read our minds,' and her laugh trailed amongst the faded flower heads and grass stumps. 'I'll leave you boys to have fun together.' She pulled the front door open, then sidled past the box of old clothes and Jesus texts.

Billy looked at the weeds peeping between the flagstones at his feet. Fun? What was he supposed to do? What sort of things?

Kenneth shrugged into his jacket although it wasn't cold. He looked at Billy as if he was the tramp in the back room. 'They thought you'd cheer me up.'

'Oh.' Billy hesitated, looking around. It would be better to be near the house than out on a walk alone with Kenneth.

Kenneth said, 'No good waiting. Dad's in the study with the vicar.'

Billy jerked around. Could dead people come alive?

Kenneth saw the jerk and snorted. 'I said *Dad*, not Daddy. We all know where *he* is – dead and buried under the ground. Gone. All that's left is your Dad. But now it's our dad, isn't it?'

His voice was horrible, mean and bitter like a witch. That awful night-time crying had been better than that. Even the sick. Billy stood still. Should he say, 'I'm sorry for your loss' right now?

But Kenneth was pointing at him and saying, 'And what's that supposed to be?'

Billy stepped further away. 'My c-camera. No one's supposed to touch it. Mr P-pawsey gave it to me.'

'All right. Why would *I* want to take photos? I can draw. You can't draw. You have to use a camera to get pictures. It's like cheating, really.'

Kenneth stomped off, heaving his arm up into a beckon as if it weighed a ton. Billy followed slowly.

They went out of the gate and down the lane, the opposite direction from the one Jed had gone in. Billy didn't rush to keep up. If he was behind, he wouldn't have to speak or even to listen. They went downhill, one behind the other, between two high hedges and round a corner. Now the vicarage was out of sight. It was rather scary with no one else there. He kept his eyes on the church tower. He'd be able to follow that if Kenneth meant to run ahead and lose him.

He followed Kenneth down lanes where the houses were set well back with green patches in front of them, then along an avenue of large trees whose few golden leaves allowed the day's sun to glint between the branches. They went past a little pond where some small children were fishing. One of them smiled. He smiled back. It would have been nice to join in, filling jars with minnows. Kenneth had already passed by without looking.

Eventually Billy said, 'Are we going to the p-place where you're staying?'

Kenneth said, 'No,' and didn't turn round.

'The village?'

Kenneth didn't answer.

'Where are we going?'

'Just don't talk, Right?' He kept on, three paces ahead, kicking a little pebble before him.

They passed the village school, squat and stony. The playground wasn't concrete. It had grass and two trees. A teacher with a big smile was helping a few children who were digging up some potatoes. It looked fun. He searched for words. If he was supposed to cheer Kenneth up, he ought to say kind things.

'Are you sorry the school was too full for you, Kenneth?'

Kenneth stopped, looked over to the school and then to Billy. 'Huh. Place for peasants. Sums and spellings. I think I'm a bit beyond that now. Mr Robyns-Curtis is doing Shakespeare with us older ones.'

'Shakespeare! I know. Angela does that!'

Kenneth whipped round, pushing his face forward. 'Who's Angela?'

Billy took a step back. 'A-a girl.'

'Where? Not here?'

'Mmm, not really.'

'At home, then? I don't know her. Does Aunty Marcia know her?'

'Y-yes.'

'Where? Where is this Angela who does Shakespeare?'

Billy turned round and started running. 'I'm going back now. I'm going to see Dad.'

Kenneth caught him up. 'Stop. You'll be in trouble if I say you ran off without me.'

Billy stopped.

Kenneth drew a breath. He didn't usually run fast. 'There's no Angela in our school back home. There's no Shakespeare.'

'No. Somewhere else.'

'Where?'

'Just people we know. You don't know them.'

'So now I will. When we go back, I'll be going where you're going. I'll see this Angela. We'll talk Shakespeare to each other. But you won't understand it.'

Billy stopped, pressing his feet into the ground, staring at Kenneth. This wasn't just a story. When they went home Kenneth *would* be there, being petted, nosing into everything, going where they went, coming everywhere with them. Even when they went to the Durbans.

Kenneth stared back making goggle eyes. 'Bluh! Look at you, stare cat. Soppy and stupid.' Then he turned away as if he felt sick again.

'I want to go back,' Billy said, and moved off again at a slower pace..

Kenneth said nothing but walked the same way, this time behind Billy. Now it was uphill so it took much longer. A dark cloud was following them. Billy didn't want it to catch them.

He said, 'Rain might come. Let's run.'

'No.'

Billy compromised with a fast walk, just the occasional hop run. He could hear Kenneth's stomping feet behind him.

Dad was standing at the vicarage gate as they came near.

'Billy! Why don't you wait for Kenneth? Don't walk ahead like that, walk together. What did I tell you about being a bit Christian?'

Billy tried to remember the texts in the vicarage hall so that he could sound a bit Christian, 'Lo . . . something', 'Jesus . . . something,' but all he could remember clearly was 'Wipe your feet.'

'Lo . . .' he began.

'Hello? Is that all you can say to me? I've only got today and tomorrow, then I have to be back. Your behaviour the other day meant you've lost several days with me.'

'Sorry.' Billy looked down at the knobbly stones at his feet. Wartime could be ever so sad.

Kenneth passed Billy and stood beside Dad, his eyes alive now. He leant against Dad, who looked down and put a hand very softly on his head.

'Are you all right, Kenneth? Take it easy, now. Go indoors and see if Mrs Shawditch can find you a glass of milk to go with your malt and cod liver oil. Build your strength up.'

Kenneth flicked a curly lock from his eyebrow and looked up at Dad with a Christian face. And Dad smiled sadly through his beard.

When Kenneth reached the door, Dad walked back down the path with Billy.

'It is good we could get you brought here. He'll need you, your strength, as he adapts to the changes. If only I could be here more often. Travelling through London is a nightmare at the moment. Raids every day, hopping between shelters, transport chaotic. He looked at the sky. *If we don't end war, war will end us* – as H.G. Wells says.

Uncle Frank had been travelling through London when the war had ended him. He wanted to ask if there would be bombs when Dad would be travelling back, but it was best not to say 'Bomb'. It was a *No* word, now, like Bum.

Instead, he said, 'Will you get back home before dark?'

'I'll be sure to, don't worry.' He put his large hand on Billy's shoulder. 'It's a bad thing, war. Boys play at it, spotting the aeroplanes, cheering the flames when an enemy one's hit. It seems exciting. But it's not.'

Dad was thinking about the games Billy played with his friends. Or perhaps about Uncle Frank. It hadn't been exciting to be blown up. It was a bad thing, even if it was good that the bomb had ended Uncle Frank and not Uncle Ted or Dad. 'Dad, do you have to go on buses in London?'

But Dad was going on without listening, 'As you grow up, you must do your best to keep the peace.'

'I shall,' said Billy fervently.

'At home, as well as in the wider world. Keeping the peace means not being selfish.'

He looked hard at Billy. He must mean something. At home. Billy thought back. There were Jill's tantrums, but he didn't shout back at her. He'd played with her to stop her tantrums, so he did help keep the peace. But Kenneth's visits, every Saturday. It was Kenneth who was selfish. Would he be able to keep that peace? Is that what Dad meant?

Dad took his hand off Billy's shoulder and stretched his arms out wide as if to relieve a load on his back. He put his hand in his pocket for his pipe and lit it. He leant on the vicarage gate, looking outward down the little lane towards the church. And then he said it.

'Things will be different when we get home, Billy. They have to be. I'm responsible for two boys now, and Aunty won't have much money. It doesn't make sense for there to be two houses. She doesn't want to go back to Balham. And she needs us for company.'

There was silence in the lane. The autumn light fell dark red on the hedge tops and the clouds hovered lower, threatening to cover the last of the day's sun. Next week it was going to be November, all grey outside and readying for winter.

Dad took another breath, 'So . . . we shall all live together. We don't use the front room much. We've decided that it will be Aunty's room. She'll need some of her own things round her as well as somewhere to sleep.'

Billy didn't have to tilt his head upwards to look at the sky for it seemed to be getting lower and lower. Soon it would land on his head.

Somewhere for Aunty to sleep. His back teeth hurt as he clamped them harder and harder together. He didn't need to ask.

'As for Kenneth, well, your room's quite big enough for another bed. You can share a room, boys much the same age. You can be best pals. Kenneth will like that.'

Best pals! 'No! I w-won't.'

'You *will* share. Now that's what I mean when I say don't be selfish.'

'No, I meant, I w-won't be – being b-best pals. I can't.'

'Billy! Of course you can. You are.'

It was too much to bear. He wanted to shout out into the silence, tell the whole ruddy world, *I don't like Kenneth. He's mean and hurts me and takes my things and pretends everything's my fault.* But he didn't. He just looked down at his boots. The lace of one was untied and it trailed over his foot like a line of snot.

'Now then,' said Dad. 'I know these are difficult days, being away from family on your own, and the shock of – poor Uncle Frank passing away. But think. How would you feel if that had happened to me and you had no father? Wouldn't it help if Kenneth was a real pal to you?'

And Uncle Frank had been his new father! 'No! It would make it worse!'

'Take that back!'

Billy didn't answer. He kept his eyes on his bootlace. Dad just didn't know. He didn't even know Billy as well as Mrs Donnington, or as Mrs Youldon and Mr and Mrs Pawsey did. He really didn't know Kenneth, what he was like. He never heard what went on upstairs. It wasn't Dad's fault. He had to work away from home lots of the time. And now his brother had died. It was only Billy that Uncle Frank had been nasty to. Everyone else probably liked him. Kenneth did. Aunty did and Dad did. He was sad. So Billy ought to say something kind right now.

'Sorry.' It caught a bit in his throat because he wasn't sorry for what he'd said about Kenneth. He swallowed and lifted his camera. 'If I t-take your photograph with Mother, you'll be able to l-look at it when you're away at work.'

'Yes, that would be nice. Mother told me you'd been given a camera. Lucky chap, aren't you? I expect Kenneth must think you get all the luck.'

Billy paused. 'I've g-got two p-pictures left on the film. I saved them for you, Dad.'

'That's nice of you, Billy. Yes, take a picture, one of us all. I'd like to have a family photo on my desk at Chambers.' He tapped his pipe out on the top of the gate and moved down the path. 'Come on, let's go in. Jill will be back in a moment from nursery.'

They wiped their feet, then passed the other messages. Billy looked up at the *Jesus Loves You* text. The children in the picture didn't look at all like Billy. He looked away. Not worth looking at Him.

Mrs Shawditch came out of the back room in her white girls' socks and her men's lace up shoes. 'Billy!'

He lifted up his eyes. 'Yes, Mrs Shawditch.'

'You haven't seen around yet. We must see to that later. You'll need to wash your hands before lunch. Up the stairs, second door on the right, and then you can go and see Kenneth in Jill's room.'

Billy plodded upstairs and used the bathroom as ordered. He came out but didn't know where to go next. Jill's room? There were three more doors and then the stairs went up again. It was a big house.

One door was slightly open. He stepped towards it. Kenneth was sitting on a pink bed, postcards of fat children with dimpled knees on the wall behind him. He had his feet on a camp bed covered by a travel rug. He was like an invalid but busy drawing. He looked up.

'It's squashed in here. No room for you. They're putting you in a niche on the upstairs landing.' He went on drawing.

'A niche? What's that?'

Kenneth tutted and lifted his eyes to heaven. 'You just don't know anything. It's a bit where the wall goes in, room enough for a shelf or chest of drawers. Or a camp bed.'

The front door opened and closed below them and Jill's jabber started immediately. Billy hurried to the stairs. Jill would be excited to see him.

'Ji-ill. Ji-ill!'

The curly head lifted up towards him. The same plump cheeks and a bit of a dimple. Her knees were a bit like those in the postcards. She stared at him as she struggled to her feet.

Mother, folding the pushchair, said, 'It's Billy, pet. Billy.'

Jill went on staring.

There was a footstep behind him. Kenneth squeezed past and padded down the stairs. Jill toddled towards him and hugged his legs.

Mother hesitated, then said to Billy, 'Kenneth's been teaching her to draw. She loves it. You could try doing that with her. Both of you, perhaps.' She hurried towards the kitchen.

Jill looked after her with a little scowl.

Kenneth's face had no expression. He placed delicate fingers on her head and moved past towards the nearest door. 'I'll lay the table for Mrs Shawditch first,' he called after Mother.

'Thank you, dear,' Mother's voice wafted from the kitchen with the boiled meat smell.

'Draw,' Jill moaned as she trailed after Kenneth into the dining room, making a large detour around Billy.

Billy stayed where he was, in the hall, alone. Aunty came in shortly afterwards. She looked tired. She patted Billy on the cheek. 'Billy. Hello dear. Nice ride over on the cart?'

But her eyes were dull and her stockings wrinkly. 'Time for dinner now, isn't it, and I'm too late to help. We've been so busy today, packing food parcels for the prisoners of war. Does your school collect?'

He nodded, not sure what to say. Their collection was for people who'd been bombed out in London. She'd cry about Uncle Frank if he told her.

Mother saved him for once, scuttling into the hall. 'There you are, Doreen. Good. I think you need something to eat. Come and sit down, Billy. It's dinner time.'

As Aunty went upstairs to wash, Billy moved into the big room where Kenneth had gone to lay the table. Jill was on a throne of cushions beside him at the far end of the room. An old but muscly man was coming through another door from outside. He didn't look at anyone; he didn't say anything.

Mother and Mrs Shawditch brought plates of gristly stew to sit on a large table with no tablecloth. Several men were already sitting round. They looked the right age to be soldiers. One was the tramp, now in a clean checked shirt, his hand hovering over a plate of bread. People nodded to each other and took their seats, plates steaming in front of them. There was a big dish of potatoes and another one of carrots.

Kenneth leaned over and whispered in Billy's ear. 'They're prisoners-of-war but we're not supposed to know. They don't even speak English.'

Everyone just sat there until suddenly the vicar came in like an actor on to the stage. He lifted one hand and said his prayer so that everyone could mutter 'Our Men'. Billy always thought of Uncle Ted when he had to say this. Today he should think of Uncle Frank too. Did *Our Men* mean dead ones too? He couldn't ask now. Or at all really. He might ask Mr Pawsey later.

The vicar sat and lifted his knife and fork. Everyone began. The tramp's chewing sounded above any clinking or muttering from the others.

After dinner, the other people went out of the side door behind the table nodding thanks to Mrs Shawditch. The vicar explained that they were land workers and people who couldn't manage by themselves. Kenneth looked over at Billy and twisted his mouth. So wasn't the vicar telling the truth? The vicar!

It was a very odd sight to see Dad start to pack the dishes. Mrs Shawditch told him that he was just to enjoy his family while he could, so Mother, Billy and Jill all went outside under the lowering sky. Dad turned towards Aunty and Kenneth, bringing them out too. Jill started jumping up and down, seeing how loudly she could make her shoes sound on the tiled porch floor.

Kenneth raised his eyebrows at Mother and said, 'I'll take her off, shall I?'

'Thank you, dear. You are such a help.'

Billy watched the two figures disappear past *Wipe your Feet* and *Jesus Loves You*, hand in hand.

Jill didn't look back.

'Such friends,' said Mother.

Aunty walked beside the flower beds filled with weeds and rusty rose petals. 'I told Mrs Shawditch I'd help in the garden. This all needs attention. So much to do.'

Dad said, 'Doreen, you do enough, especially now you've put your name down for war work. No point wearing yourself out.' He turned to Mother, shaking his head as Aunty moved off down the path.

Mother said, 'Are you hinting that I should help? What do I know about gardening? Anyway I am the one taking Kenneth to and fro, as well as Jill, and helping in the kitchen. None of it exactly my forte.'

'*Rich gifts wax poor when givers prove unkind,*' Dad said softly, staring into space. 'Shakespeare.'

'Shakespeare!' Billy said. 'Angela . . .' Then he stopped and checked behind him, but it was all right. Kenneth was upstairs with Jill.

'Oh you've heard of Shakespeare, have you?' Dad asked.

It was risky to put the Durbans into Dad's head, so he said, 'Kenneth's doing it with his teacher.'

'Is he indeed? Good. Glad to see you're talking to each other about such things. You'll be able to learn about Shakespeare from Kenneth, then.'

'From Angela,' Billy muttered softly to himself. 'Shall I take your photo now, Dad? While it's still light enough?'

'Ooh, you are sounding professional,' said Mother coming up behind him. 'I'll just run and comb my hair. My bag's still in the hall.'

She came back looking brighter. He rested his camera on the gatepost. Just as Dad put an arm on to Mother's shoulder, Billy pressed the shutter before she had time to set her mouth. The sun was low behind him so that his parents were framed in a backdrop of shaded trees. It should look good.

Dad said, 'That was quick, Billy.' He removed his arm from Mother's shoulder where it had looked so friendly. He was putting the hand into his pocket. He pulled out some coins and put them into Billy's hand. 'This is to help with developing and printing. It can be an expensive hobby, photography.'

It was three half-crowns! Billy paused, making sure they were for him. 'Thank you, Dad. Thank you very much.'

'It was your birthday. Your mother and I are sorry we missed it.'

'It doesn't matter. I can get my photos done now.'

'How many photos have you got left on that film?'

'Only one, now. I want to take Jill, if she'll let me.'

'You go and take one of Kenneth,' said Dad. 'If Jill's around she can sit with him.'

Billy twiddled the cord loop on his camera, but he knew it was no good. He turned and went back into the house. He plodded upstairs. Only one photo left and now he must waste it on Kenneth. Even if Jill was there, he wouldn't want a photo of her with Kenneth. He'd just take one of Kenneth alone. When the prints were done he'd give it to him. He jolly well wouldn't want it himself.

In the bedroom there were pieces of recent art pressed on to the far wall with parcel tape, a parrot, two aeroplanes in a dogfight, a castle, really smashing pictures. Kenneth was ever so clever. He had his head bent over a drawing of something. He didn't hear Billy. Jill was lying on the floor on her front doing her scribbles with a fat red crayon.

Billy slid in, his back to the wide-open window and lifted his camera. Just as he put his finger on the shutter, Kenneth noticed him and put up both hands saying, 'Don't snap me. I don't want a picture of me now.' But it was too late, the shutter clicked.

'Kenneth! You've spoiled it! Your hands were in the way. Now you've wasted my very last photo.'

'I didn't ask you to take it, Dimwit.'

Billy flung himself through the door and stomped on to the landing. If only he hadn't snapped quickly he could've told Dad that Kenneth didn't want a picture, and then taken a nice one of Jill. He'd have let her stand on the porch ledge.

He went downstairs slowly. He'd finished his whole film. What was he supposed to do now? There were no toys in sight, no football. They all thought Kenneth wanted to play with him, but he didn't. And Jill wouldn't even look at him. He reached the hall again.

'Not playing with the others?' Mrs Shawditch asked softly, bringing a pile of clean cutlery back into the dining room.

'They don't want to.'

Aunty was lying down, but Mother and Dad were in the front room. Mrs Shawditch took Billy to join them. She suggested they all play a nice card game. She picked up a pack of Happy Families from the sideboard. She called up to Kenneth, but he said he was busy drawing.

'A real artist,' said Dad. 'We'll leave him to it.'

Dad, Mother, Mrs Shawditch and Billy sat on the hard chairs round a card table. There was no room for anyone's elbows.

'Let's enjoy this.' Mother said very firmly. 'It's going to be a very long time before we have the chance to play games again.'

Again? Billy couldn't remember Mother ever playing games with him.

Dad looked over at Billy. 'I've said, haven't I, that it's really not easy to travel these days. And now I've got Aunty's house to sell. It may be some time before I can visit everyone again. So we must make the best of these times as a family.' His face was grey, and he didn't look as if he was having the best time at all.

The vicar's wife dealt the cards. 'We must trust in the Lord.'

Billy looked at her dull eyes. She had to, married to the vicar. But all that Billy trusted was that he could collect all of the Bun the baker family because they looked the jolliest.

He concentrated on their fat red faces with the deep dimples and adopted them as his own. He was Master Billy Bun. He would spend his life running in and out of the bakery while Mr Bun in his white apron shouted 'Oh Ho Ho' and dusted flour on to cake trays. Billy would be giving Mrs Bun a hand, stirring things, licking the bowls she passed to him and eating the tasty bits which crumbled off her sugary cakes and the fresh crusty loaves.

CHAPTER EIGHT

October 25th 1940

French leader Petain meets Hitler

It wasn't late, but the sun had long gone down when the vicar's car stopped outside the Pawseys' house. The tiled roof was outlined by a sliver of moon and Billy could just make out the two trees near the pig pen. The dogs barked in anticipation. They'd be all round his feet when he got in. The house was in darkness, of course, but inside the fire would be crackling and Mr Pawsey would be feeling around for his glasses.

If he hadn't known, if he could pretend he didn't know, then everything could be just the same as it was before the horrible times with Kenneth staying and the adults coming for him. The funeral had sickened all the days following, and now it was hardly worth wishing to go home again, or for the war to be over, with how things in Wandsworth were going to be.

The vicar cleared his throat. 'Well, here we are, young man. Please give my regards to your foster parents. I won't stop.'

'Thank you for the lift, sir.'

'Possibly the last one, I fear. Petrol's getting more and more expensive, over three shillings a gallon now. Rationing is going to get worse too. So I may not be able . . .' His voice trailed off as he turned to lift a set of Red Cross parcels on to the passenger seat, hovering them in the air ready to put them where Billy had been sitting. 'I've slipped a prayer book into each of these packages,' he said. 'I like to think of our boys having an hour of quiet reflection before they go into – conflict.'

'Does that help, sir?'

'I like to think so, my boy. Yes, of course it must help. And here's a prayer book for you.'

Billy looked at the scratchy red cover. 'Thank you. Is it a birthday present?'

'Ah – for reflection.'

Billy slid out of the vicar's car and shut the door carefully. An hour for reflection? Uncle Ted had three days and nights for that, standing in the sea while his boots went green. A prayer book wouldn't have helped.

He bent to the window and thanked the vicar for letting him stay, then ran quickly indoors, putting the prayer book on the hall table. He might meet a soldier who'd want it.

The dogs rushed to meet him and he bent his head over them as they barked and licked alternately. Mr and Mrs Pawsey gave him a quick look. They didn't ask him if he'd had a nice time but set him to work straight away. Mr Pawsey said he had terrible difficulty with the crossword. Billy could help him just as soon as he'd fed the piglets. Mrs Pawsey put a torch and the slop bucket into his hands.

Out by the pig pen, he ran the torch over the piglets. They lifted up their snouts and came running. They must have missed him. Billy hadn't been away quite three days but they seemed to be bigger already. He hoped they'd take their time becoming pork.

Mrs Pawsey had nearly finished making a cake when he came back indoors. She needed him to scrape the bowl because she couldn't bear anything to go to waste and somehow she couldn't seem to scrape as cleanly as she used to. He would be like Sonia, whose mother allowed her to scrape the bowl.

Once he'd washed the pig mash off his hands, Billy was able to help Mrs Pawsey very well and she reckoned he had more mixture round his mouth than she'd left in the bowl. She found that very funny and laughed just as if she'd been Mrs Bun the Baker's wife.

He put his hand in his pocket and pulled out his half crowns. He ran to find Mr Pawsey. 'Look! My father gave me all this for getting my photos done. I've finished my film. Now I can take it to get photos, can't I? When we go into town to the pictures?'

He looked at him quickly. He wouldn't have forgotten, would he?

'Yes, Billy boy. We'll see to all that on Saturday,' Mr Pawsey said, holding up a page of newspaper. 'Now. My crossword . . .'

Billy ran out of the door on Saturday, a wonderful Saturday, the Pawseys both behind him. He wanted to be the one who put out a STOP arm at the bus stop.

The village bus trundled up around eleven. It was quite full but they got seats together up at the back. He sat down with a big bounce.

'You excited, Billy?'

'Rath-er. I've only been to town once before, Mrs Pawsey, except for the very first day we got here, all of us from my school who were being evacuated. That time we got straight off the train on to the coach and then to the village, so we didn't see town. Then when it was winter-time, the Grange lady got a coach and took all the vaccies to see the Christmas tree and we all got two sweeties, a balloon and sang songs. There was a piano and ...'

'Oh my goodness me, haven't you a lot of chatter? I reckon as you are excited. Yes, I do.'

It was lovely travelling through tree-lined roads and past grassy mounds instead of the dirty high buildings and brick walls of London. There were winding lanes through trees with golden and brown leaves. They reminded Billy of Dad leaving home in Wandsworth for a month's work at Court, Mother saying crossly the trees would be bare before he got home. And they were.

Now the trees looked lovely to him with hills behind them. They passed a field with a land girl pushing a plough. An old man in a torn jacket walked slowly behind her, and a crowd of black birds followed. 'Look!'

Mr Pawsey knew him. 'That be Mr Jackson, still hard at it. Four good sons, he has, all soldiers doing their bit, God rest 'em. Reckon it'll be a while till that young lady gets her furrows straight.'

As the bus passed the first houses of the town, a lot of people pressed their faces to the window. A row of ladies were lined up outside a big building. They were in their ordinary clothes, jackets, headscarves, pleated skirts, but each held a long pole pretending they were guns. A man in uniform was shouting at them so that they stood straight, shouldered their poles, then pointed them at the enemy, all keeping together in line. He giggled, and some grown-ups laughed too. It was quite funny, but Mrs Pawsey said it was important for women to join in the Home Guard so that there weren't just old men looking after the country. Billy looked at the floor. He should be in the Home Guard, at least when he was twelve. Would the war last that long, three whole years more?

The bus reached the market place, where there was a little tower with a big clock at the top under a pointy pink roof. Shops surrounded it on three sides, and another road went uphill. Most people stood up and Mr Pawsey moved to the gangway. 'We get off here, Billy. Come along, you.'

It had been a long time since Billy had been in a town, and he'd only been in this one once before, when all the vaccies were taken there to see the Christmas tree. It was a very different town from Wandsworth, much cosier and not so crowded.

Mr Pawsey was helping Mrs Pawsey up saying, 'You going to shop, Missus?'

'I am that. I'll see if they've got any biscuits or currants.'

'Then I'll take the boy, while you queue.'

Mr Pawsey led the way up the hilly road to the chemist's but Billy soon overtook him. They passed the blacksmith's, an exciting place that he'd always wanted to see. In London, he hadn't even known that horses had shoes or a man to put them on. He peeped inside but there was no horse inside being shoed. He made a disappointed face at Mr Pawsey.

'The blacksmith has gone to war, leaving his old father to work on small jobs.'

Gaps showed all over the black wall where big tools had hung. Billy pointed to the spaces. 'The walls are all empty,' Mr Pawsey.

'All the metal's been taken away for weapons, lad. Not much for a blacksmith to work on.'

There was a new poster on the outside wall. Billy stopped to read *If you can't go to the factory, help someone who can.* There was a little boy and girl going into a kind lady's house while their mother, holding a little suitcase, waved Goodbye. 'That's like what Mother's doing, isn't it, Mr Pawsey? Looking after Kenneth while Aunty works at WVS?'

'I suppose so, laddie.' Billy looked at the picture again. Aunty was too sad to look like the happy lady waving Goodbye, and Mother wasn't a smiley lady bending down to a little child. She definitely would not want to look after other children, but Kenneth was older and did his drawing all the time, so was never a nuisance to her.

The hill was quite steep. Mr Pawsey was panting a bit with the effort so Billy slowed down. They passed a shop with knitting wools and cotton reels in a small window and then came the chemist's.

'Here we are, see the sign.'

The shop was painted black with Mr E. Winthrop, Chemist, Druggist, painted in curly white letters over the door. As Mr Pawsey opened it, a wonderful smell filtered towards them. Billy recognised lavender and the stuff you sniffed when you had a heavy cold. The shelves had row after row of old-fashioned bottles with funny words on them. The chemist was smarter than Dad in his three-piece suit with a fob watch showing on his middle. He stopped arranging the bottles of cough medicine and came to serve them.

Billy handed over his film to be developed and watched the five pale fingers close over it. When it was placed in its envelope and the order form filled in, Billy used some of Dad's birthday money to pay. There was some over. He looked at the handful of change. 'Sir, please may I buy another film?'

'Just about. I've only got two 120s left,' the chemist said, passing one over.

'Tight is it?' Mr Pawsey asked.

'Like anything and everything. The supplier's just told me I'm not getting any more. All film's needed for aerial reconnaissance, now. They're going to let us have that Tint rubbish to sell. We must warn your young man. It'll be no good for his camera.'

'No? We shan't risk it then. Thank'm kindly for the warning.'

As they made their way out of the shop, Mr Pawsey put one hand on Billy's shoulder and the other on the precious film. 'You be careful not to waste any snaps, now. Probably no more films for us folks until the war's over, not unless you have friends in high places.'

Billy looked at the sky, but no one up there would give him any special favours. He started counting in his head the photos he really must take before the new film ran out.

The hilly street led out into the country soon after the chemist's. Mr Pawsey said his 'How do's' to two old men who were sitting outside their small houses on hard chairs. Then they turned downhill again towards the picture palace.

Billy started skipping. 'Mr Pawsey, I've been to the pictures before but not for ages. I went to the pictures in Wandsworth. It's the Gaumont, and I saw Robin Hood. Some of my friends go to Saturday pictures, but I'm not allowed because of the bad behaviour. Some of the locals come here on Saturdays but none of my friends have seen Pinocchio yet, I'm the first one.'

'That'll keep the varmints wanting to friend you then, won't it?'

The picture palace was quite grubby down its front wall and paint was crumbling off. Billy looked up high to see where it said *Pinocchio*. Above that it said ABC not Gaumont. They went to join the queue where Mrs

Pawsey was saving them places. Two girls in front of them were jumping up and down, so he couldn't see the poster of Pinocchio properly. A bigger boy was showing off with his yo-yo, making it whizz round in a circle as well as up and down. There were a lot of grown-ups too, and some grizzling small children.

When the usherette opened the heavy black door there was a squeal from the girls. The first people pushed in to pay, the queue pressed forward and Billy felt worried. 'Will we get in before the picture palace is full?'

'Don't fuss yourself, we will.'

Billy started counting the people in front. How many seats did a picture house have?

He'd counted to thirty four before they reached the front.

'Here we are, Billy. All in nice time, see.' Mrs Pawsey showed the tickets, and the usherette beamed her torch in front of them to three seats right near the aisle.

Mr Pawsey turned to help Mrs Pawsey who had to tuck her shopping under the seat.

The velvety seats tipped up so that small people could perch high. They'd only just sat down on them when the lights went down. The news came first. It was quite scary and thunderous, lots of grey tanks rolling through dust, soldiers mostly with dirty faces, but smiling widely at the camera while a horrible serious voice told what was happening. He searched for Uncle Ted's face amongst the ranks of soldiers marching and in trucks.

Afterwards there was a film about sparrows which was boring. Then it was the interval with a crowd at the toilets, and the worry about finding the right seat again afterwards. All the children there seemed to be chatting or squealing or jumping up and down. It was very noisy and exciting. The usherettes took their torches away, the lights went down. When it went dark, everyone was quiet straight away.

The moment soft music began and a picture of a big old brown book with its fancy lettering came on to the screen, Billy sit still as sill. The spotlight fell on this tiny, weeny figure and you saw it was Jiminy Cricket starting the wonderful tale in his big book. A lovely song about wishing on a star helped things come true. A nice old man, a bit like Granddad, had a coloured wooden puppet and it was Pinocchio. He so wanted a boy and then a fairy came and made Pinocchio live, but not a real boy until he deserved it. Was it like that for Mr Durban, wanting a boy of his own and then meeting Billy – although really Billy belonged to Dad. But then, so did Kenneth now.

Pinocchio had little red shorts with straps and the sun shone round him. He made a lot of mistakes and got into all sorts of trouble. He told whopping lies so that his nose grew and grew. All sorts of funny and scary people led him into bad things. There was even a smarmy one cheating at the billiards table who was quite like Kenneth. Pinocchio was a bit bad, but he got better, and at the very end he was a real boy. Gepetto was sort of his father and was so happy. It would be wonderful to be a boy that made a Dad laugh with joy.

When the lights went up, Billy could hardly bring himself to leave the picture house. The super songs that the characters had sung went round and round in his head. All the children were chattering and begging to see the film all over again. It would be smashing to just sit back on the velvet seat and see the whole thing right through as if it was new.

Mr and Mrs Pawsey were smiling because Billy was so happy. 'Reckon as you'm enjoyed that thorough,' said Mr Pawsey.

'I did, I did. I wanted it all again!'

As they got on to the dark and chilly street outside, Billy started hopping and skipping, 'Hi Diddle de dee,' he sang, 'an actor's life for me.' He would forget the dreadful things that had happened and were going to happen. He skipped all the way to the bus stop singing. Perhaps this would be a magic song that would come true for him, like wishing on a star, even though he had no blue fairy to wave her wand.

That night, he lay in bed late going through the whole story in his mind and humming the tunes.

In the morning, after breakfast and chores, he ran off to the Manor to tell Alan all about Pinocchio. Two boys were working on their own in the vegetable patch.

'Where's the lady – the land girl?'

'They're all up at Barfell Farm, digging the potatoes.'

Alan was inside, which meant going past all the nuns at their prayers in the hall, to get to the dormitories upstairs. This made him tread so quietly that Alan didn't even hear him coming. He was deep in a book but when he saw Billy's head round the door, he grinned in welcome.

'I've come to tell you all about Pinocchio.'

They sat on his bed for ages being all the characters and trying out some of the songs.

'The best part was when he told lies. His nose kept growing with each one, until it was as long as a sausage.'

'Wait.' Alan went to his box. All the Manor children had a box for keeping their own things and some treasures, like letters or comics or a sweet. He rummaged around for a moment and brought out a piece of brown plasticine. 'This was stuck to my shoe after Craft at school, so I kept it.' He rolled it into a sausage and pressed it on to the end of his nose – 'Pinocchio, see!'

Billy's giggling sent Alan to the mirror on the back of the door to see how he looked. They took it in turns to put it on their noses and make up whopping lies, just like Pinocchio.

'I can jump twenty feet high.'

'I can spell all the words in the dictionary.'

'I've got a gun and they're sending me to war.'

'I've got a shashka that is the most powerful weapon on earth and can kill a hundred Hitlers.'

They were laughing and rolling about on the floor making a noise loud enough for a nun to come in and shoo them away downstairs. She was on house-cleaning duties so they'd be in her way even if they were quiet.

They ran into the rough ground at the back of the Manor where before the vaccies came it had been lawn and flower beds. It was quiet there, because there were no trees for people to climb up or anything else to do.

Alan said, 'Was it all right when you went to the vicarage, and all that?'

Billy's stomach went thump as if all the potatoes the land girl was digging had fallen out of his insides. He sat down on the grass and told Alan all the serious news about Kenneth.

'And now Dad is going to be his dad too. It's silly, because he's Kenneth's uncle. You can't have two dads even if one is dead.'

'If he's Kenneth's dad, that makes him your brother.'

'No! He's never going to be my brother. They can't make me.'

'Bet they'll say he is. If you live in the same house with the same father, people will think he's your brother, anyway.'

Billy thumped the grass beside him. 'No. No. No. It's flipping awful.'

Alan was quiet for a bit. 'It is rather rotten, but at least you aren't sharing your mother.'

There was no point answering. Alan didn't understand. Having Kenneth as a cousin *was* like sharing his mother. Although Kenneth had his own mother who thought he was perfect, Mother was always nicer to Kenneth too, because Kenneth was quiet and pretended to be good. And now he would always be a boy whose father had died, so everyone had to be nice to him.

Alan stood up and whirled around a couple of times. 'Come on,' he said. 'Cheer up. Tell me about your camera. Have you taken any snaps yet?'

CHAPTER NINE

November 14th 1940

German bombers devastate Coventry and its cathedral

It seemed like weeks and weeks, waiting for Mr Pawsey to take him to the town again. Would his photographs come out? How good would they be? He knew that going to town wasn't something that happened at all often, but eventually there was a slight accident.

'I've gone and sat on these wretched glasses, all while I was looking for 'em too! You'se 'll be glad about it, Billy, for I shall have to be off to town again to get 'em mended. So we can collect your photographs, see.'

The glasses had broken where the metal bit sat over Mr Pawsey's nose. He hadn't been able to fix them himself, for he had to do that with them off his face. When he was wearing them, he couldn't see anything.

'You'll have to find the bus stop, I reckon, Billy, or I s'll land up in the next village, the amount I can't see without my glasses.'

Billy held Mr Pawsey's arm all the way to the bus stop.

'At least I can see the bus,' Mr Pawsey joked as it pulled up beside them.

The bus was crowded and when they got to the town, the queue outside the grocer's was very long.

'I suppose as we'll have to join it, lad. Not that I've a ha'porth of an idea what they're queuing for.'

It was a long wait and when they got to the front it was only suet. Mrs Pawsey would be pleased, but it wasn't a very exciting buy, like chocolate biscuits would have been.

After they'd dealt with Mr Pawsey's glasses, which took a long time, they went up to the chemist's. Billy started hopping and skipping, chanting, *I've got no strings to hold me down.'*

'Let's see what sort of job you've done on those photos, young Billy my lad, before you get too chirpy.'

'Chirpy! That's what I am, just like Jiminy Cricket.' Billy reached the black shop front first and pulled the handle down. He opened the door for Mr Pawsey, just as Dad would have liked.

'Good morning, and to you, young man.' The chemist found the folder of photos and checked the contents.

'Did you take some of these, then, Mr Pawsey?'

'No, no. The lad did the lot.'

The chemist put his hand on the packet. 'Well. Some of them are remarkable. Beginner's luck?' He slid them over to Mr Pawsey, who left them for Billy to pick up.

Billy pulled them out one by one. How amazing to see things exactly as he'd seen them weeks before! Everyone was held just in that moment for ever. He gazed down at Jed sitting on his cart looking up at the bedroom window, the horse's mane lifted and his nostrils slightly flared.

Mr Pawsey looked over his shoulder. 'Goodness me, you've as done a grand old job with that, young Billy. Looks just like something out of the picture papers.'

Billy pressed his lips together, almost holding his breath.

He looked carefully at each snap before passing it on for Mr Pawsey's judgement, all except one.

'Ha, the little Youldons. Well done, well done. Now this of the chickens, should have waited a bit for better light. This one – you needed to put your parents more in the foreground, but still a good job.'

'And that one's rather something, isn't it?' said the chemist.

He pointed to the one Billy was putting quickly to the back of the pile. It was Kenneth, his glaring eyes just showing over the top of his hands. 'Indoor snap, sideways light. Daring. And he's captured that as good as a professional, hasn't he?'

'Hmm. Seems as Billy doesn't like'm much,' Mr Pawsey said as Billy put the photo back in the envelope. 'Thank you very much, Mr Winthrop. I suppose it'll be a while before we're back with the next film. Billy's making it last, aren't you, lad?'

'Yes, I am. But when the war ends, I can have another film, can't I?'

He saw the men grimace at each other as though they'd forgotten Great Britain always won wars.

'Can I have an extra print of these three?' Billy passed the chemist the negatives of Mrs Youldon and the children. He turned to Mr Pawsey. 'Mrs Youldon will want them, and I want copies. I've still got lots of Dad's birthday money left.'

'Aha. You're angling for another visit to town, I see.'

They left the chemist's and made their way down the hill. 'Reckon as you've got a special talent for photography. Fancy that, being as a coincidence that you had the camera as a birthday present. It's a good thing to have a skill outside of book learning. Something to develop for your future.'

'If I don't have to be a soldier, you mean?'

Mr Pawsey sighed and put a hand on Billy's shoulder. 'Even at its worst, the war shouldn't last that long,' he said.

A thundering of aeroplanes in the sky suggested he was wrong. Billy hunched his shoulders. When he became a man, he must serve his country. If only he wouldn't be cannon fodder, which had been what Uncle Frank had told him.

When they got home, Billy showed his photos to Mrs Pawsey. She held up her hands in amazement. 'You've taken your first photos and they're like a – I don't rightly know – a studio's. I reckon we've chanced on a real talent in you.'

'Can I take them to show Mrs Youldon?'

'In the morning.'

He was up early and after breakfast and chores, he cantered down Mrs Youldon's lane. She was outside cleaning the front windows. He waved the envelope at her. 'They've come!' and they went indoors to look at the photos.

She took each one carefully by the top two corners and peered closely each time. 'Coo, Billy! They're clear as daylight. Look at my youngsters, bless them. And look at me.' She giggled. She looked at each one and then at Billy. 'They're all ever so good. You are a clever stick.'

He held out the three photos of her and the children. 'These are for you to keep. I'm having extra prints done for me.'

'Really? Ooh, Billy, I've never had true pictures of anything, let alone my own face. And it's a wonder to have them of my little ones, and all. You wait till I show them to Mary! She won't be able to stop talking about it.'

Her face was so happy it made Billy's insides tickle and a strong and important feeling spread through him.

Mrs Youldon called the little ones in. 'Look what Billy's got, look what he's done!'

They ran up to him and he held each photo up for them to see. Their eyes went huge.

'It's Mummy! Look, in that picture!' Sally squealed.

'Is that us? Is that what we look like?' said Timmy.

What a funny thing to ask! Billy wrinkled his eyebrows. Then he remembered that the only mirror in the cottage was the little broken bit Mrs Youldon used to comb her hair, and that was too high for the children to see in. They hadn't really seen themselves before. Both of them peered a long time at each photo.

'Your Mummy's going to keep those photos. You can look at them every day now.'

Mrs Youldon glowed. 'I'm ever so proud of them, Billy. Of you. Really'.

Mrs Youldon was smiling and nodding. Her face looked really pleased. But she wasn't as pleased as Billy was. He'd done something right. He was good at something.

CHAPTER TEN

March 24th 1941

Hitler says there will be war with the United States

Billy put his toes on the underside of the ball and lobbed it high into the air. It was his last kick before he had to go back to the Pawseys' for Mother's visit.

Now that Mr Finlay was organising football games two afternoons a week, all the boys were practising everywhere, up and down the lanes, in the field by the school and at home there was enough space beyond the chicken coops for practising goals. There was even more in the back field of the Manor and, like most days, Billy went there after school.

Alan, at the other end of the field, lobbed it back, straight as a die.

'Super. You're quite a good player,' he said as Alan ran up with the ball.

'Okay, we all know you're the star.'

Billy turned his mouth down at him. At this very moment, he had to leave the others to play without him. 'Got to go. Tell me what happens later.' He pulled his socks up, then turned the tops of them down. His knees were filthy.

Alan turned towards the group of boys a little way off, waiting to go on with the game. 'Shame, but it'll look bad to be late when your mother's come on the bus to see you.'

'I know. It won't be just Mother, though. And football's my favourite thing. Kenneth coming is my worst. He's always trying to make me look stupid. I wish you were my cousin and not Kenneth.'

Alan screwed his face up. He'd played round at the Pawseys' a couple of times when Kenneth had been there. 'He's all right, I suppose. You just like doing different things, and he gets at you because you're stronger although he's older.'

'He's nastier! You haven't been up against it. He's always nice when you're there, when anyone else is there.'

'Well I won't be this time. I'll be goalie for once. Go on, shove off, you.' Alan was only joking. It was his way of showing Billy he was on his side.

Billy jogged down the lane, in time to wash his knees and change his socks before Mother's bus arrived. Mrs Pawsey was putting cups and saucers on the dining room table. 'I thought we'd have a nice sit-down tea this time, not just a cup of tea on a tray. I've made scones and ginger cake, something to put a bit of brightness in your poor cousin's cheeks, isn't that so? I hear he's been poorly again.'

Billy nodded. It hadn't been serious, just a chesty cold. He went to the gate to wait for Mother. Perhaps she'd bring Jill. Perhaps she wouldn't bring Kenneth if he was recovering. But as she came into sight around the horse's field fence, he saw that she had brought both of them. The sun was bright behind the three of them and shone right in Billy's eyes. It made him squint to keep his eyes on them. A strong light shone on Kenneth's forehead and knees as he moved between the brief shadows of trees, and then he became just a silhouette, the brilliant sun rays making him a golden child from another world. Close to the fence, Jill trotted beside Mother as they came up the lane. Billy waved, but she didn't.

Mrs Pawsey came to the door to welcome them. 'Come along in, Mrs Wilson, Kenneth, and the little one too. Isn't it a treat for us to meet Billy's sister at last? Isn't that nice?'

Then they were in the hall and Mother was giving a long account of happenings at the vicarage that went on right until she had her hat off and they'd all gone into the sitting room. He glanced at Kenneth, who was unsmiling as ever these last months, but not too terribly sad, and then at Jill, who put her head in Mother's skirt. It wasn't worth saying anything. None of them wanted to know about the goals Billy had scored, or the time the pigs escaped and he'd had to chase them all the way to the Blackstop milestone.

Mother's account ended with Kenneth's news. 'He's studied so well with the verger, that he's been given a place at the Friar's Court Grammar, although his age group don't normally start until September.'

Mrs Pawsey nodded at Kenneth. 'Well, my dear. Isn't it good that you're going to be at a proper school at last? That's what you need; other boys, the noisy playground and sitting in a classroom.'

The left side of Kenneth's mouth lifted in a small smile or something like it.

Mother wasn't listening. 'Such an honour to be taken. It's not just his written work, it's more about his art. The Senior Master was so impressed. He told Kenneth to prepare a portfolio. A portfolio! And he's scarcely eleven, mind you! Think of that. He started there a fortnight ago. He loves it.'

Kenneth lounged against Mrs Pawsey's dresser fingering the worn runner.

Billy said, 'Does it feel funny to be back at school, Kenneth? Do you like it better there than our old school?'

Kenneth flicked his hair off his eyes. It had grown long at the front. 'The Friars Court boys are very civilised.'

'What does "civilised" mean?'

Kenneth gave a soft laugh and exchanged glances with Mother as though he was an adult with her, rather than a boy with Billy. 'We don't spend our time kicking muddy balls around to amuse ourselves.'

Mother was pulling Jill's hair into neater bunches where the ribbons had slipped. 'He comes home as clean as when he leaves! When I rang my husband about Friar's Court, Mrs Pawsey, he was over the moon. They have a superb art room and even though it's wartime, they haven't run out of paints or brushes. Kenneth will have ideal opportunities. Herbert was always pleased to have an artist in the family and the good thing is, Jill's getting so much from drawing with Kenneth.'

'Will you do me a drawing, Jill?' Billy scrabbled in the drawer for paper and a pencil with a good point.

She hung her head.

'She's shy,' Kenneth said. 'Only used to me, nowadays, old thing.'

Billy was just about to shout, 'She's *my* sister, remember,' even with Mother there, when he did remember. Now, she was Kenneth's sister too. He bit his lip hard. And he didn't like being Kenneth's old thing at all.

Mrs Pawsey set the paper and pencil on the table for Jill. 'There, dearie.'

She put an arm round Billy. 'I'm going to take your cousin into the kitchen. I've got some malt extract to help top up his vitamins.'

Mother made herself comfortable in the pink damask armchair. 'Thank you, Mrs Pawsey. So kind. Kenneth needs all the boosts he can get.' She put her elbows on the padded scroll arms and said, 'Now, Billy, I'm all ears.'

Once Mrs Pawsey had taken Kenneth out, Billy said, 'I miss Aunty, Mother. Why can't she come with all of you?'

Jill hadn't even touched the pencil. She stepped in front of Mother, one step, two steps.

Mother leant round her. 'Aunty Doreen's always busy nowadays. We hardly see her. In the evenings they're up the road, where they're living. She devotes herself to Kenneth. They read together and listen to the wireless. She works all day every day at the WVS while I'm left to fetch and carry, collect and deliver. That's my lot, Billy!'

'I could help you, Mother, if I was there with you.'

'I've explained already, haven't I? You've seen for yourself. The vicarage is full.'

Jill started jumping up and down as Mother spoke, blocking Billy's view.

'She's probably bored, Mother. Jill, Jill, let's play with your little ball.'

She stopped jumping and hid her face in Mother's skirt.

Mother called out, 'Kenneth – can you take Jill upstairs to play, please. Let's have your bits of news, Billy, then I'll have a chat with Mrs Pawsey.'

What would hold Mother's attention? He knew not to mention the Youldons. He gave her his latest school marks, then started talking about Alan at the Manor, the many rooms, the land girls and the nuns but, with his mind on the game being played right this moment at the Manor, he soon got on to football. Because Mother wasn't interested in that, his news didn't last long. She was ready for her women's chat. Football was something Billy was really good at and if only he could tell Uncle Ted, because he'd be pleased. Dad wasn't interested in games, neither was Mother and even if he'd been alive, Uncle Frank, who was really, really good at games, wouldn't have liked for Billy to be good at them too.

As she moved to the kitchen, Billy started up the stairs to join the others. He heard a slight scuffle, a giggle from Jill, a whisper from Kenneth:

'Quick, Billy's coming, he might be nasty to you. Hold on to me, I'll save you.'

'What did you say?' Billy challenged, as he reached the top of the stairs.

'Nothing,' said Kenneth, eyes large and precious, like barley sugar. 'Did I?' he added, turning to Jill.

Her little plump face peeped out from behind his corduroy shorts. She shook her head.

Billy clenched his fists. He could feel how very cross he was all over, and sad inside. It was like when they'd been told about war at school and why countries got into it. Jill was Kenneth's *collaborator*. That was the word. Letting him do nasty things and helping him, really.

Billy used the bathroom while he listened to Kenneth helping Jill to explore all around his home. *His* billet, he reminded himself. He was the one who should be showing Jill around it all. His eyes traced the pea-green paint of the dado rail and imagined the shashka hanging there. He saw himself lifting it down, turning and standing proud at the bathroom door holding it aloft at Kenneth. That would make him shake and stand away from Jill. Then Jill would admire Billy again and she'd know she was much safer with him. He would be the one in power.

He moved to the landing and called, 'Let's go outside and play all together.'

'No thanks, old thing. We're happy as we are, aren't we, Jill?'

Billy plodded downstairs to Mother, who was trying to avoid the snuffling and lickings from Noah and Japhet. They didn't know she wasn't keen on animals.

'Mother, I used to play with Jill all the time when we were in Wandsworth. Now she doesn't even speak to me. You said that teacher that Mrs Shawditch gave a room to has gone to her new job, so why aren't I at the vicarage with you?'

Mother moved her head from side to side so that her hair swung over one eye and then the other. She was a bit like a film star, the one on the newsreel that came on before *Pinocchio* started. He'd be so proud if she came to his school, if the other children could see her and say breathily, 'Is that your mum?' But she never visited him on a school day.

She spoke in a sensible voice. 'It's the responsibility, Billy. There's only so much I can manage. You know I have to help Mrs Shawditch with the housework and cooking. I might as well be Mrs Donnington! Wartime, all these changes, it's very difficult. Nothing's as it should be, and then . . .' she dropped her voice to a shadow, '. . . with what happened to Uncle Frank. You know. We told Jill that Kenneth would be very sad and she must be nice to him. She follows him everywhere. I think she's a comfort, dear little thing, keeping him company. Whereas you would be – more of a challenge. Boys can't comfort, can they?'

Billy thought back to the awful death day last October, Kenneth's white face in the bedroom, the playing cards loose in his lap. The not speaking, the not playing with anything. But Billy had helped find the drawing paper, and saved Kenneth from having to go to school. At bedtime, he'd said Kenneth could turn the light off whenever he wanted. His shoulders hunched as he remembered the terrible crying in the middle of the night. 'I did try.'

'His art,' Mother went on, talking over him. 'He's so talented and makes so little mess. Either a pencil or a tiny box of water colours, that's all. He only uses a spot of each. Now he's helping Jill along that path too. Aunty thinks all of it's helping Kenneth to get over everything. The new school will help too. Dad's so glad.'

'Dad said I should go to the village school. But Kenneth's going to a grammar school.'

'He's eleven, you're not yet ten. You're fine where you are. Your father was so pleased with your marks. All ten out of tens.'

'But that's b-because I keep doing the same work over and over. Each time we get new children from London, we have to go over the old things all over again. And some of them c-can't even do hundreds, tens and thousands and I have to help them.'

Mother sighed and swung her scarf over her shoulders. 'I'm sure I don't know what to do about it. And now your father can't. I came to tell you today. He's being called up.'

Billy's breath came out in a whoosh. 'He s-said he wouldn't be! He's in a – a reserved occupation. He's – exempt.' That word suddenly whisked his thoughts back to the day he'd first heard it, and thought it was X-M-ed. Uncle Ted was his proper self then, making jokes and explaining what 'exempt' meant, saying Billy might be exempt from dinner. That lovely roast that they ate nearly every Sunday at Nanny and Granddad's. Nanny! Granddad! It was so long since he'd seen them that he scarcely knew what they looked like now. And Uncle Ted – his favourite person. It was no good pretending the white lock at the front of his hair would have gone back to black even if he wasn't fighting in the trenches.

He put a clenched fist into each of his pockets. 'Will Dad have to go in the t-trenches?'

'I really don't know, dear. I thought you'd lost that stutter at last. Hands out of pockets, please.'

'It's not fair. He was exempt.'

Mother looked down at her shoes, the brown ones with the pattern of dots. She looked sad. Perhaps it was because she hadn't got enough rations to buy new ones. 'The war needs men his age now, even in his job.'

'But Mr Durban's not going to war and he works at Dad's Chambers. He's still in the Home Guard. I know, because Angela's been writing to me.'

'He's training others in the ARP. Otherwise he might be called up. We need all the fighting men we can get.'

Billy swallowed. 'Has England run out of soldiers?' Were they nearly all lost? In the Great War, Mr Durban had seen hundreds and thousands of dead bodies in Russia several times, and that was just the first year of the war. He screwed his eyes up to imagine it. If this war had run out of soldiers, was there field upon field of English soldiers dead? They'd be lying on top of the earth because there was no snow for them to melt into. He put a hand up to his face. If only Uncle Ted wasn't one of them.

Mother gave a hard smile. 'Of course there are more soldiers. Just no more young ones.'

'Couldn't they send Scottish ones, and – um – vicars?'

'Oh they have, don't worry. My vicar has a murmur on his heart, so he can't serve.'

'Would Uncle Frank have been . . .' his voice tailed off as he looked around to check that Kenneth was still far enough away not to overhear the upsetting name.

'Called up? Yes, perhaps he would. But what happened to him was surely worse than being a soldier. Poor Aunty. Now your father going away. We women have to manage without the men – we just have to get on with it. We all have to. That's war for you.'

She tip-tapped hurriedly away, saying she must help Mrs Pawsey with the tea things.

It was 'We have no choice' again. Billy mooched off towards the chicken houses. Dad was far too old to fight. He'd never even seen Dad run. How would he escape the guns? It wasn't right. Look at the state Uncle Ted had come back in, and he was quite young. Now he wasn't a jolly uncle who did handstands, but a scarecrow with a white streak in his hair. If he was there at all.

In the morning, when they had done all the outside chores, Billy and Mr Pawsey tackled the pile of paper bags in the scullery. They all had to be folded into neat squares for re-use.

Billy slid another square on to the enamel table. 'You know my father's been called up?'

'I know, lad. It's hard.'

'He doesn't know where he'll have to serve. We're sending more and more soldiers. Mother says we haven't run out of them yet but Des Seabright is only five foot two and he's gone to war, and big Ronnie says sixteen-year-olds will have to go next. He'll be sixteen in 1943. Do you think the war will last that long?'

'If that's what it needs to win it.'

'Suppose we lose –– will all our soldiers be left in foreign lands?'

'They'll be brought back. Let's not have those worries or that long face, Billy my lad,' said Mr Pawsey. 'We shall win this war, just like we did the last. Look what Mr Churchill is doing. He's not going to let Hitler get away with all this evil, you'll see.'

Mrs Pawsey called out that their dinner was on the table. 'It's only Homity Pie, I'm afraid. We've used our meat ration up until Monday.'

Mr Pawsey groaned as he led Billy into the dining room. He loved his meat. 'Tell you what, Billy. We'll delve into those tins of corned beef you brought when you came. The Missus has had them at the back of the larder all this time. I reckon as now we need 'em to cheer ourselves up.'

Mrs Pawsey nodded. 'Well perhaps as we should. Tomorrow. But instead of fretting about the rabbits getting our lettuces, it's about time you lay in wait for the blighters and get me some customers for rabbit pie.'

Billy shuddered. He loved leaning out of his bedroom window, watching the fluffy tails bouncing around the fields.

She cut into the pastry and served out a large slice on to Mr Pawsey's plate, and another on to Billy's. The leeks and potatoes slid out of their pastry case but they looked pale.

'Sorry there wasn't cheese to put in the pie but I've made bubble and squeak shed to go on the side, so we'll have something tasty.' She took the lid off the vegetable dish. 'At least we'll never be short of cabbage or carrots. Come to think of it, why don't you run down to the Youldons, Billy, and take a couple of carrot lollipops for those kiddies. I've scrubbed a couple of nice straight ones ready. That'll put the smile back on your face. And look, sun's coming out.'

He did feel more cheerful when he saw the carrots stuck on to sticks ready for Timmy and Sally. He put them into a paper bag and went to the back door. There was a glimmer of sun, although it wasn't really nice spring weather yet. He had a plan.

'Can I be out until tea, if Mrs Youldon lets me stay?' He searched around for some jam jars. 'These are for tiddlers, in case I find any.'

Mrs Pawsey smiled. 'You be back well before dark, then.'

As he cantered down Mrs Youldon's lane, he saw her outside cleaning the front window. He waved the bag at her and they went indoors to the children.

Sally and Timmy peeped in the paper bag and started sucking their carrots straight away.

'Look at my youngsters, bless them. Nice of Mrs Pawsey. You thank her from me.'

It was a good time to ask if they could go to that stream where he'd walked with Mr Pawsey and the pool where he'd paddled.

'Can I take them?'

They both stopped their sucking immediately. 'Yes, yes, yes!'

Mrs Youldon hesitated, but he saw she couldn't bring herself to say 'No' with both of them dancing up and down in front of her.

'All right then, it'll be a treat for them. Don't lose sight of them, Billy. Right?' She wrapped a pack of sandwiches in greaseproof paper. 'There's their dinner. You had yours? Go careful now, it'll be muddy on the banks. No mischief, mind, you two. You're in charge, Billy. It's half past one now, and you be back at five at the very latest.'

His jam jars bounced around his middle on some string Mr Pawsey had given him as he went off, one little one on either side. Sally danced down the road in front of Billy. Tim trotted beside him trying to make his footsteps the same length.

When they got to the big road beyond the shops, the boundary of Tim and Sally's everyday world, they saw the signpost was damaged. The village names had been scraped off, especially the capital letters. Now no one could read them. Someone had painted an arrow and 'To Hell' and underneath in brackets 'France'. He thought of Uncle Ted there, the green boots and dirty hairiness when he came down the street back from Dunkirk. Was he any better off in the trenches?

The baker trundled up in his van, interrupting the thought. 'Off down to the stream, are you, kiddies? I might be down later myself for bit of fishing while there's a touch of sun to see. We must have some fun, even in war.'

They moved off the road and on to the lanes, last year's leaves flying up around the kicking feet of the children. Tim was in high spirits, whooping and turning while Sally ran in front. Billy had been worried the walk would be too far for her and he'd end up having to give her a piggy back all the way back, but so far she was just as fast as Timmy. He looked at her little body in a rough green dress cut from something Mrs Youldon had brought back from the church's bring-and-buy. Mrs Youldon wasn't very clever with her needle, not like Aunty Doreen.

Tim was racing Sally now and they were squealing loudly as one touched the other. He steered them past a muddy section of track and then they were into the snatch of trees and the grassy track up to the small hill. Tim lay sideways and rolled down, laughing. Sally watched, hesitating.

'I'll show you, how. I'll show you,' Timmy called.

But she was dancing on, daring him to catch her. 'Don't go too far!' Billy found a fallen tree and was just climbing it to call down to them when he spotted a bike juddering along the track between tree stumps.

'Alan! Yippee!'

The freckled face looked around bewildered until Billy leaped down beside him. 'Hello!' They'd only seen each other two days ago, but there was so much to say.

'Wait on. I've Tim and Sally.' They'd run out of sight so he started after them. 'C'mon Alan, we're going down to this nice place with stepping stones.'

He ran down the path, calling the children, Alan followed on his bike as best he could.

There were little squeals ahead as Billy rounded the bank where the overhanging trees began. He could see Sally getting ready to roll downhill with Tim instructing. They were on the steep bank leading down to the deep water.

'Stop!'

Tim started and obediently stood still, looking round for Billy, but Sally had already begun her roll forward. Her breathy giggles punctuated the air as Billy dashed forward. 'Look out!' He made panicky leaps over clods and tufts but they were no match for a little body gathering momentum on a steep slope. He had no breath to yell as the other little body raced downhill to catch his sister and both boys hurtled forward on to a bush at the water's edge just as Sally plopped into the water and disappeared.

Tim clung on to the bush wailing as Billy waded straight in and found himself up to his stomach yelling with cold and shock. He flailed around among stones and weeds, lost his footing and went under. He came up again yanking Sally's arm, and yelled to someone, anyone, 'I can't swim.'

Even in the urgency and terror of the moment, he registered a movement high above him on the bank as Alan. He bent again to get hold of Sally's face, went under again but came up holding her by her chin and her arm. She was lifeless. He looked wildly up at the bank but only Timmy was there, gasping and hanging on to a branch, looking very tiny and in danger of falling in too.

Amazingly, Tim bent down, picked up a decent-sized branch, and threw it forward into the water. Billy looped both of Sally's arms over it and pushed her towards the bank. There was no good purchase for his feet, which were slopping about in slime. He'd lost both shoes and he could only just manage to keep Sally's face above water while he coughed and spluttered out all the water he'd swallowed. Timmy hovered on the bank, one arm vainly held out towards Billy who was still waist deep. It was a struggle to stay upright and hang on to the icy little body swathed in weeds.

Billy was too cold to feel any part of himself. He could almost hear himself think, 'I mustn't fall,' even while the water was pulling at him to lie down. He pressed his feet down and apart to keep his balance, while two eddies swirled around him. His arms were locked around Sally but he couldn't get her upright. This was going to last forever and he'd never get Sally on to land.

At last shouts approached the bank and there was Alan with two men. They almost slid down to the water's edge carrying a rope between them. One of them waded in and put Sally over his shoulder, while Billy grasped the rope. His hands were so frozen they kept slipping as the other man pulled them into the bank. He just saw it was the baker, then he doubled up coughing and coughing out all the water he'd swallowed. The baker got hold of his shirt collar and pulled him the last stretch up on to dry land. He ripped off all the clothes on his top half, put his big jumper on Billy and wrapped his coat round Sally where she lay, a wet slimy bundle, under the large hands of the first man, who was pressing her chest getting the water out of her.

Alan took hold of Timmy and pulled him to a safer position but Tim kept trying to kneel by Sally, wailing loudly.

'Is she dead, is she dead?' was all Billy could whisper in a shuddering voice to the men. They didn't answer, their hands both at work on her tiny back.

Finally they got a breath from her, Sally was turned over to make her cough everything up. Billy's knees buckled under him. The first man stood up and wrapped his clothes round Billy.

He said they must all get back to the village as quickly as possible.

'Here's my jumper,' Alan said, pulling it over his head, and the baker put it on Sally with his own jacket on top. The he lifted her up to his shoulder, where she hung, completely limp.

Billy felt himself put on Alan's bicycle and pushed along by the first man. He couldn't talk for the huge shudders that kept racking his body and he kept his eyes on Sally the whole time to make sure she was still breathing. Her face was a horrible colour like cabbage water. Alan's wasn't a whole lot better under his freckles. He only had a shirt on now, and he was shivering. He kept a tight hold of the whimpering Timmy and kept looking at Billy in a frightened way, his eyes goggling.

Timmy's wailing got louder as he lost sight of Sally's face, hidden in the baker's shoulder. The baker looked down at him. 'Come on, laddie, your sister's going to be all right. We just have to hurry along to get you all dry and warm.'

Billy's feet were freezing, the sodden socks hanging off his toes as he was pushed along on Alan's bike. His bottom half was soaking, water dripping over the bike wheels and great shudders kept rushing through his body. All the time he was thinking, *Sally might die.*

Timmy needs carrying. I was in charge of them. It was my fault.

He was going to get into the most awful trouble, the worst, worst Billy had ever been in. He'd have to tell Mother he'd lost his shoes, and when she saw Sally, Mrs Youldon would hate him and no one would ever trust him again.

When they got out of the leafy paths, the bike ran more smoothly. He heard the baker tell the other man to call at Fern Cottage where the midwife lived so that she could see what was best for Sally.

'I'll take Timmy home and fetch his mother,' Alan said.

Billy shut his eyes again and only opened them again when he felt strong arms deliver his drenched body to the waiting Mr Pawsey. 'Oh, lawks. Come quickly, Missus. Here he is, but in a state.'

Mrs Pawsey came straight out and led them to the settee in the sitting room. The baker said what had happened. 'I'd better not put him down, look.'

'Oh, Billy, our lad! You're like ice, and dripping wet. Heavens above, I better run a hot bath.' Mrs Pawsey sounded as if she was almost crying.

Mr Pawsey peeled off the rest of Billy's clothes and wrapped him in blankets straight away. 'Must get you'm warmed up. Time for a bath later. The Missus'll do you hot food and tea. That's what you need.'

'Tea. Right and I must find some sugar for it.' Mrs Pawsey hurried down the passage to the kitchen.

Mr Pawsey kept hold of Billy so tight that the blanket roughened his skin.

Billy squeezed his eyes shut while Mr Pawsey dried him and laid him bundled on the settee. 'You rest there now, till your tea comes, stay still.'

Mrs Pawsey brought hot sweet tea and held it while he drank and then he lay back again.

There were sounds of the baker being taken to the kitchen, the telephone, grown-ups talking, whispering, then exclaiming. Perhaps he dropped off to sleep, but it felt like a long, long worrying, a shivering and aching all over his body.

When he realised that Mr Pawsey was sitting beside him, he jerked upright. 'Mr Pawsey? Sally – is she still nearly dead?'

'Now, now. Not so. She's been taken up the cottage hospital just to get warmed through. She'll probably be up and about in a day or so, don't you fret.'

A cold wind blew in as the front door was shoved open. A man's voice called, 'It's Denson, *Sirius* reporter, Mr Pawsey. Can you give us the situation with the lad?'

Mr Pawsey shooed him off. 'He's resting. He's doing all right.'

'We need the story.'

'It's too soon.'

'I want it in the next edition, Mr Pawsey. I've just been up to the cottage hospital. The lassie is doing fine, considering. Not in danger.'

'We know that, thanks. We're in touch.'

'Rightie ho. So, see you in the morning.' The front door slammed shut.

'Huh. Local reporter thinks he can butt in everywhere.' Mr Pawsey lay Billy back on the baggy settee and tucked him in. 'You stay comfy here, my lad, and I'll see you're not disturbed again.'

Billy snuggled lower under his blanket. He felt easier now a stranger said Sally was doing fine. His eyes felt heavy. It was so good to be warm, even if there was going to be trouble later.

'You'll be in all the papers, Billy,' Mrs Pawsey said as she brought him a hot meal.

He struggled up a short way. Everyone would know it was his fault! 'Will I get t-told off?'

'Goodness no, my dear. People will say you're a hero. Here, eat this up.'

He looked at the plateful. It wasn't long since he'd been sicking up green water. 'Not sure I'm hungry.'

The Pawseys were always on his side, but they couldn't stop what other people would say. Worst of all, what would Mrs Youldon say? She'd trusted him to keep her little ones safe.

'It was my f-fault. I was in charge.'

'You pulled the little lass out. You were very brave, and now she's getting better with nice nurses to look after her. So eat this up, will you.'

'Is she really all right?'

'She really is, and it's thanks to you. She just needs a day or two to get to rights.'

He sat up and took hold of the dinner plate. It was stew and tasted super.

Even though he'd been told and even seen the newspaper saying that Sally was fully recovered, Billy was scared to go back to school. He'd been away for a whole week.

'We shall come too, and it'll be a special day.' Mrs Pawsey put out his best clothes as if it was a Sunday, but she insisted he get dressed in them.

She and Mr Pawsey followed him out of the house. 'Are you coming all the way with me?'

'We are. You'll see why.' She looked smart in her tweedy jacket that she'd worn to the pictures, and Mr Pawsey was in a proper suit with shoes. Would the teachers mind Mr and Mrs Pawsey coming to school?

At the end of the lane, they turned a corner and up ahead there seemed to be a line of people at the square, and not in a queue. 'What's all that?'

'You'll see soon enough, lad.'

As they walked nearer, Billy saw there was a platform in the square. On it stood the newspaper man, the Mayor with his big chain on his chest, and the head teacher. In front sat all the school children in rows. Everyone watched the Pawseys bring Billy near.

A cheer went up.

Mr Pawsey pushed him forward. 'Go on, our Billy. That's for you.'

What they'd said was true! It was a special gathering. Alan was already there with his mother, standing near the platform and he was in his best clothes too. He grinned at Billy and put his thumb up.

Mr Pawsey helped Billy up on to a big wooden box at the front of the platform. Alan followed. There were so many people looking at them! Was the whole village there? Mrs Youldon was at the front of the crowd. He didn't look at her face in case she was angry with him. Further back he saw Mother waving and smiling. Mother had come, and she looked pleased! When a lady in front of her moved Billy saw that Aunty and Kenneth were beside her. That was worrying. Kenneth would be bound to sneer or say something to get him into trouble.

It felt wrong to be standing up high in front of everyone. His face was hot and his hands were sweaty.

Alan nudged him and told him to stand straight. 'It's for you all this, Billy.'

He looked down at Mr and Mrs Pawsey. They were nodding to everyone around them.

'They're proud because you're their evacuee,' Alan said.

The Mayor rang his hand bell and everything went quiet. He talked about the local soldiers at war, about how there could be bravery at home as well as abroad. He told everyone what had happened down at the stream, the whole story. All the people in the audience clapped hard, nodding and smiling, 'Good for you, son.'

The Mayor bent to put a shiny medal round Billy's neck. The reporter passed him two whole boxes of sweets, one for Billy and another for Alan, because he was part of the rescue, fetching help.

The medal felt heavy against his chest as Billy's hands gripped the box of sweets. A whole box! That was so unbelievable it was difficult to get a thank you out. He and Alan looked at each other making big eyes while the three cheers sounded. The children in the front leapt up and down and shouted out, 'Give us a sweet, give us one,' but Mr Finlay waved them to stop.

'Sweeties are for the heroes, children. The school is proud of you, Wilson and Firbank. Responsibility and prompt action to help others in trouble, facing danger for the common good, putting urgent need before your own comfort. That's what Great Britain is all about. So you two take your sweets home and don't open them yet.'

Mrs Youldon came forward at the end of the speeches but could hardly speak, patting herself on her front.

He tried to mutter, 'I'm ever so sorry,' but she squeezed him round the shoulders lots of times.

'My Sally, you saved her. If she'd drowned . . . oh—' She shuddered. 'You're a good, good boy. If I had any treasure, I'd give it to you, Billy. And you, Alan.'

It was happy and it was embarrassing. He wanted it all to stop, but to be there too. He felt like running away. He felt like leaping high, high in the air. But he had to stay, standing straight.

After it was all over and the local head teacher had sent everyone back to school, Billy muttered to Alan. 'You should have a medal. It wasn't just me. You went for help and everything.'

'The thing is, I can swim, Billy. You can't. And it was you went in and saved her.'

The two mothers were walking over to collect them, Kenneth jogging in front. As he came up to them Billy whispered, 'Look out, Alan. Kenneth.' He waited for a sneer, or worse. But Kenneth only leant forward to finger the medal. 'I'm going to show people this when you come to the Vicarage.'

For once, Kenneth looked ordinary, nice, as if he even liked Billy. 'It was brave to go in after the girl when you can't swim.' He nodded twice, looking rather like Dad. 'That was brave.' He turned to the people nearby. 'He's my cousin.'

Alan muttered, 'Kenneth seems all right, Billy.'

The shock of Kenneth being nice made him wonder if everything had changed. He had a moment of imagining the three of them, Kenneth, Alan, himself, running through the grass beside the horse's field, playing chase. But no, that couldn't happen.

Aunty came up and hugged him. 'So proud of you, dearie.'

Mother stood beside her with a pleased smile, 'Well done, Billy. Your father will be proud.'

It was nice, of course it was really nice, but all of everyone's praise didn't take the guilty feeling away. Going into the water to rescue Sally didn't count. He should have been at the little ones' sides the whole time, not talking to Alan or climbing a tree.

He knew what he could do. He had something special to give Mrs Youldon on Christmas Day, a real treat, a real surprise. He tucked his box of sweets under his arm. When they all got home, he'd put it on Mrs Pawsey's high larder shelf until Christmas, wrapped up with a sheet of her draught paper. That hadn't been brought out since Uncle Frank's funeral.

CHAPTER ELEVEN

8th December 1941

Japan makes massive attack upon United States

They were all in the kitchen when the news announcer told about the bombing at Pearl Harbour. Mrs Pawsey gasped and let a dish slip back into the washing up water.

A section of Mr Churchill's speech followed the announcement. Mr Pawsey gave a sort of groan. 'They must have done that bombing even before they properly declared war. Now this situation is bigger than anything we've had before.'

Billy's stomach lurched. 'Will it be hundreds and thousands dead in that harbour?'

'Dreadful, dreadful. More like thousands and thousands.' Mrs Pawsey wrapped her dishcloth round her hand like a bandage. They were all quiet for some minutes.

'So we'll be at war with Japan now,' said Mr Pawsey at last.

Japan. Japanese people had slit eyes and bobble feet. He remembered that doll Angela had on her bedroom shelf. They'd probably be meaner than Kenneth ever was. Suppose they came over here! Angela had better throw that doll on to the fire.

Mr Pawsey got to his feet. 'Now there'll be action. The Yanks'll have to jump in with us at last.' He put his hand on Billy's shoulder. 'This could be a good thing.

They'll be backing us up like they should have done in the beginning.'

The kitchen looked just the same, the blue and white striped dishes stacked up for Mrs Pawsey to wash, the tea towel ready in Billy's hand, the tin bucket with the scrapings waiting to be taken to the pigs. Mr and Mrs Pawsey were there. Things must still be all right. And if they weren't, the Americans would have to help.

Everyone had been saying for so long that the war couldn't be won until the Americans came, that now they were coming it felt as if war should stop immediately. Christmas was over and there had been a party at the Manor with jelly and iced biscuits. Now there were GIs to look forward to.

The biggest boys stood in the playground with their arms folded across their chests, looking important, while everyone else huddled around to listen. 'See – now that they've been attacked themselves, the States are sending soldiers over here to be trained.'

'—and some of them are at a camp right near.'

'Two miles,'

'Very near.'

Billy knew something about America. It was where film stars came from. He'd seen some at the Picture Palace, and in old magazines of Mother's. The women had fur coats, and wore bright red lipstick and the men drove big black cars. America was a huge place. The nine- and ten-year-olds had had a lesson with Mr Finlay's globe. America's proper name was The United States and it was an ally.

It wasn't a brave thing to say, but Billy couldn't help thinking that such a huge country would be full of men for the government to use as soldiers, so they wouldn't need to enlist English boys.

He was at the shop with the ration books queuing for sugar when he first saw some of the GIs pass. They jerked their heads toward the queue with wide grins saying 'Hi there' or 'Howdy, folks.' Everything stopped and everyone stared. There was even a chink of blue in the thick white sky. The American soldiers were sort of glowing, their faces smooth and cheerful, really cheerful. Their uniforms were different, crisp and smart. Best of all, one of them threw sweets into the queue saying, 'Have some candy, buddies.'

Billy wasn't near enough to catch a sweetie, but he took home the shopping at a run. 'It's true about the Americans, Mrs Pawsey. American soldiers! I saw them. They threw sweets called candy.'

He went over to the pigsties to tell Mr Pawsey, the dogs running beside him as if they knew of the excitement.

Mr Pawsey rubbed his hands. 'So they'm at their training camp now? Let's hope it's a good thing, having 'em here.'

'I'm just going up to the Manor to see if Alan knows and we can tell Mrs Youldon. She needs to look out for Americans. They throw candy, and the little ones might get some.'

'Right you are, young-un, but pick all they titchy turnips from the side patch first.'

He worked as quickly as he could. Mr Pawsey gave him some turnips to take to the Youldons, a string bag full.

He called for Alan who said, 'Yes, saw them, saw them. They paraded past here, and we all lined up to watch.' He acted it out, the way the GIs marched and Billy tried to copy. Then they both ran down the lanes. They found Mrs Youldon had her sister indoors. They were nattering together and giggling.

'Hello my big boys,' she said, hardly looking at them.

'I brought these turnips for you, Mrs Youldon,' Billy said. He held the string bag near to her to make her see. 'Mr Pawsey said I could bring you the small ones. It's to make soups, you know.'

'You're a kind boy. Thank you,' she said, smiling quickly at him before returning to her very, very interesting chat with her sister. 'I don't know, Mary. I shouldn't, really. And what'll I wear?'

'You've got that pretty blue dress if you're going anywhere special,' Billy interrupted. He wasn't having Mary take over his place in Mrs Youldon's life. 'Is there a fête on?'

Mary burst out into a peal of giggles. 'A fête! Ooh, I want to be fêted, Joan. Don't know about you.' She did a twiddle in the middle of the floor, holding the edge of her skirt. 'Nylons, the Yanks have got. No kidding.'

Mrs Youldon's face was a little pink. 'All right for you, Mary. I've got the nippers.'

'Get them sat for, go on.' Mary turned her back on the children. 'The Yanks' bus will come at seven by the congregational church, Joan. See you there, we will. So get a minder.'

'Oh, Mary. I don't know . . Mrs Youldon scurried into the scullery without looking at Billy. He knelt down and brought out his knuckle stones to play with Alan and Timmy.

Sally, sitting beside them, had her tongue at one side of her mouth while she struggled to put a needle in and out of a piece of cloth without losing the thread. Billy got ready to rescue it.

There was banging from the scullery as the pans were hung up and a lot more chatter.

Alan made a face at Billy. 'Yanks'll be arranging socials with the locals.' He pulled some conkers from his pocket to add to Tim's collection and they started sorting them in size. Sally leant on Billy's knee with her sewing square. She was managing to do most of it.

The boys played with the little ones for quite a while without Mrs Youldon coming into the main room.

Alan said, 'She's no time for us with Mary here.' He stood up and stretched. 'Anyway, teatime. Got to go now.' He put his head round the scullery door, and the chattering stopped. 'Goodbye Mrs Youldon.' He gave Billy a nudge and went out of the door.

Billy played on for longer, folding the sewing square with the needle safely inside it and then helping Sally make a row of conkers from smallest to biggest. His tummy reminded him it was teatime. He stood and put his head round the scullery door. 'Should I go back now, Mrs Youldon?' This should bring the chatting to an end and Mrs Youldon back into play.

She turned to him looking rather shy. 'O h – you could have some tea with us. I was wondering – do you think Mrs Pawsey would let you mind the children tonight while I go out?

'But I've brought my dominoes and Happy Families. I thought we could all play together. I've been waiting till you're ready.'

Mary laughed and ruffled his hair as she squeezed past. 'All right then, Joan. I'm off. See you later, eh?'

She'd gone now. He pulled out his games and searched Mrs Youldon's face.

'Another time, Billy. I'd really like to go to that dance. Can't remember when the village last had one. You could bunk down by the hearth and go back in the morning.'

'A dance? You mean dance with men?' He and Alan had never asked about Mr Youldon, but they'd always assumed he was away at war like all the other men. She surely couldn't dance with anyone else.

Her cheeks went red but her eyes sparkled. 'Why not? I'd be going with Mary.'

'But she's not married. You're a mother!'

Her chin went up. 'Mothers can dance too.'

He stopped himself answering. Mother could dance. She'd done one at Uncle Frank's that time when he'd decided they do an 'entertainment'. It was a horrible time. Uncle had forced Billy to recite a rhyme, then was cruel about the stutter. He'd loved Mother's dance. Billy remembered back to when he was really little. Mother used to go to dances with lady friends who sometimes came to tea and had fancy cakes. In those days he'd thought of them all dancing together in a ring, like he did in infant school. How silly. Now he was older he knew what dances were for. They were where men met women and then took them out.

He said sternly, as perhaps Dad might, 'Dances. That's for young people.'

Mrs Youldon bent towards him. 'How old do you think I am, Billy?'

'I – hadn't thought. Just, a mother, really. A young one.'

'I'm twenty-one. Twenty-one. And I haven't been out since Sally was born. Think of that.'

Twenty-one. That was when you got the key of the door. Mrs Youldon had two children. He looked at Timmy catching the knuckle stones. He was nearly six. So she'd only been a girl when Timmy was born. The same as Angela, almost. Angela certainly wouldn't get married when she finished school, years before she'd had the key of the door.

When Mother went to dances, the lady next door used to look in on him every hour or so, she didn't really babysit. Those evenings hadn't been very nice. He muttered, 'I do want to look after the little ones but Mrs Pawsey wouldn't like it if I stayed out all night. I could go next door and ask big Ronnie's mother to sit for you.'

'It's all right Billy. I was going to go and ask her anyway before you turned up. I just thought – well, the kiddies would like it better if it was you. But you could ask at the Pawseys' if it would be all right for another time.'

He twisted one foot round the other. '*Another* time?'

He felt very cross inside. Cross that he hadn't thought about how old – how young she was, and cross that she wanted to go out and dance with men instead of staying in with him and the little ones playing dominoes or even Happy Families. If she'd asked him over for the evening he'd have let her collect the Bun family even though they were his favourite.

He looked at Sally and Tim. He didn't want them to be on their own, just having Ronnie's mother popping in to check on them. It would be far better if Mrs Youldon didn't go out. He didn't want her to, even though it was a shame for her never going out and being only just grown up. What could be done about it? He couldn't do dancing, or be a man for her. He frowned and shuffled his feet. Should Mrs Youldon go out? It was rotten, being only ten. You couldn't just do what you thought was best, even if you knew.

He slouched off home. She'd be popping next door and arranging things with big Ronnie's mother. He thought all evening about it. If Angela was sixteen, Mr and Mrs Durban would never give her permission to marry. She hadn't finished doing Shakespeare yet.

At breakfast, he took the risk of asking Mr and Mrs Pawsey. 'If I was sixteen and wanted to get married, you wouldn't give permission, would you?'

Mr Pawsey grinned. 'And have to find my own glasses and get stuck on my crosswords? Not likely.'

Mrs Pawsey said quietly. 'It wouldn't be for us to give permission, dear, would it? It would be your parents.'

'Oh! Oh, yes,' said Billy. 'Course.' He'd only ever thought of asking the Pawseys, the people he lived with. When he thought about being back at home, he couldn't imagine asking Mother and Dad such a thing. He said quickly, 'Anyway, it'll be years and years before I want to be married'.

'That's good,' said Mr Pawsey. 'Then let's go up the back field and fix that fence afore you do.'

When they got outside and found the wire, he left lots of time for Mr Pawsey to forget his earlier question, before he said as casually as he could, 'I wonder when Mr Youldon will be home from the war. Leave, you know. He hasn't had any.'

Mr Pawsey put down his pliers and looked at Billy. 'You's a doing some guessing, young fella-me-lad. Aren't you?'

Billy hung his head and nodded.

'Well now, no one's seen that Mr Youldon since the little'un was born. Before that even, if I remember rightly. So those kiddies haven't ever known their father. That's her tragedy, poor young woman, struggling on her own. There's those knew her as a girlie, they feel for her.'

'I do too.' Billy worked on twisting wire for the fence while Mr Pawsey talked about the news in Europe, but Mrs Youldon's age, the whereabouts of Mr Youldon and whether she should be going to dances seemed much more important than the progress of the war.

CHAPTER TWELVE

February 15 1942

Our stronghold, Singapore, surrenders to the Japanese

It was an awful day. All the grown-ups Billy saw from home to school and the village square had very long faces. Mr and Mrs Pawsey said that Great Britain had suffered a terrible blow. He couldn't imagine it. Surely, going to war was the worst?

He went to collect wood with the little ones at the end of their lane.

Timmy whispered, 'My aunty's walking out with a GI. She gets nylons, chocolate.'

That was only Mary. It didn't mean Mrs Youldon would do the same. He thought of Jiminy Cricket and whistled, *Always let your conscience be your guide* as he thrashed the bushes with a stick.

Timmy tugged his hand, 'Mummy says it'll be the end of Aunty's problems.'

He didn't answer, but took the children home, holding Sally's hand very tightly. Inside their home, he looked up on the shelf to see if there were goodies, presents from some GI, but everything looked normal.

Mrs Youldon was folding the sheets from the Grange. She looked the same as usual.

'Did you go to your dance the other week, Mrs Youldon?'

She chucked him under the chin. 'My little guardian, aren't you? Yes, I went to the dance and had the best time of my life. And I'm going again, if I can get a sitter. No good asking you, then, Mr Straight-and-Narrow?'

He shrugged, and thought about what Mr Pawsey had told him. He looked at Timmy and Sally, playing quietly in the corner with the conkers. He knew in a way what it was like not to have a father, Dad being at work so much when he was little and now being away altogether, and the shock of Kenneth not having a father any more. But he and Kenneth were big and knew what their fathers looked like. Timmy and Sally didn't.

'I'll have to ask Mrs Pawsey about staying over,' he said.

'That'd be so nice, Billy. If you can.'

When he got back home, he saw to the pigs and spent a few moments looking at their clever faces with those know-all eyes. Then he went indoors.

'Mrs Pawsey?'

She was knitting, not like Aunty knitted with a neat, quick clicky-click, slim needles darting, lengths of smooth fabric, green, pink, grey appearing – but on thick wooden needles with a shove, a poke and her tongue stuck to one side of her mouth. Her knitting was all colours, left-overs and unravelled jumpers from the last village jumble sale. She saw him watching.

'It's a blanket. We've all got to do what we can for our poor soldiers out in the field, even if we're no good at it, like me.' She chuckled. 'I got in trouble for it in school. The teacher said I wasn't trying, but I was! I was just no good at that sort of thing. And now look at me.'

'Mother says she's no good at it either. She doesn't do any.' He thought of Kenneth unravelling the old jumpers for Aunty's knitting. Billy supposed he should that too, but perhaps he was no good at that sort of thing 'Mrs Pawsey?'

'You're still muddy, off and wash now.'

'I will.'

'But?'

'If Mrs Youldon was going to a dance, would it be right for me to stay over and look after the little ones?'

She put her needles down, criss-cross on her lap and sighed. 'Lots of our girls are walking out with strangers now there are dances. Americans.'

'Yes. Mrs Youldon's sister is. She wants Mrs Youldon to.'

'It goes to their heads. The excitement. The money those American boys have got! And when our poor boys get back from the trenches, worn out and ready for fun, all the best girls will be gone.'

All the best girls! Would it be like that for Uncle Ted, none of the best girls left for him? He was already worn out two years ago after Dunkirk. If he was fighting in the trenches his hair might be *all* white by the end of the war, and then who would marry him? 'So should the ladies here go out to those dances?'

'Well. I don't know. With all these hardships young people do need some fun. Joan Youldon, she deserves some sunshine in her life.' She picked up her green and pink and purple knitting mess. 'You can sit for her, Billy. Stay over, as long as you call next door if anything goes wrong.'

It was the third time he'd stopped over and now Billy was meeting a real American face-to-face.

'This is GI Joe, Billy,' Mrs Youldon said.

'Howdy,' Joe said. His legs were as long as tent poles and Billy had to tip his head right back to look at his face. It was a nice one, freckled like Alan's, with a great wide smile. 'I hear you're a football player. Good goalie, eh?'

'I'm quite good, but I'd be better if I had boots and studs.'

Joe laughed. 'What do you play in?'

'Just wellies or shoes.'

'Our game's different in the States, but I'll kick-around with you and your mates, some time.' He squeezed further into the room together with his friend Dwaine, who was much older and had a black moustache and eyes as dark as the gypsies'. They'd brought their own mugs and a tin of condensed milk for their tea and some candy bars. Timmy and Sally couldn't take their eyes off those, and it wasn't long before they had some in their mouths.

'You're older, Billy. You try this,' and Joe pushed some fat sweets wrapped in twisted yellow and blue paper. 'Bubble gum. You chew it, then blow bubbles. Look!' and out of Joe's mouth came a bright pink bubble as high as his nose.

The little ones giggled until their faces went red. Billy thought he might need to practise doing that so he put them in his pocket for later. 'Thank you very much, Joe.'

The Americans laughed and looked at each other. 'Neat! Get that real English voice.' They leant forward on the bench, arms on their thighs. Joe was next to Mrs Youldon, his trunk arms by her sticks. Her legs in socks and canvas shoes would probably go three times into one of those shiny black boots.

'You know it's great to be in an English home, lady.'

Probably this was very different from what Americans had. Did Joe and Dwaine have a proper bathroom and were they shocked when they found the privy outside, just as Billy had been when he was first evacuated?

The two men totally filled the little room but sat respectfully as Mrs Youldon chatted to them in a high voice.

Timmy and Sally were squatting on the floor. They nudged each other while they listened, their faces lifted to the visitors. Billy stood beside them like a guard. It was exciting to hear the funny way the Yanks spoke, but he felt anxious too. The men didn't belong here.

After they'd gone, the small room was suddenly lighter and bleaker. Mrs Youldon went back to her work with quick steps, chatting over her shoulder to Billy.

'That Joe's a young regular soldier, but Dwaine only wanted to join up when the Jerries started bombing the supply ships. He thinks it's awful, all our food being wasted in the sea and all of us going without decent food. He joined up then, but because he was older, he was put on administration jobs. He's the one who helps organise the dances so he's very popular.' She laughed. 'We girls had the time of our lives at the dance, the best way of cheering us all up in these dreary old times.'

Billy thought of Aunty. She badly needed cheering up. She worked all hours at the WVS to take her mind off losing Uncle Frank, and never had any fun. She could do with some dances.

In the kitchen, the range fire was spitting out sparks because the wood had got wet. He and Mr Pawsey hadn't managed to fix the leak in the wood store. He moved the tea towels off the rail in case a spark caught them.

'That's right, Billy, thank you.'

'Mrs Pawsey?' he started. 'When you telephone Mother next, please can you ask if my Aunty can get free to visit on Saturday?'

'Yes, dearie, I will. You miss her?'

'Mm. Aunty's nice, and does kind things. When Baby was new she taught me about babies having different cries, and how to hold her. She put the pear drops in my pocket when they were all leaving me alone to go to their billet.'

He looked at the floor remembering the awful funeral day, and how she'd saved him from having to go back right then with all the misery and crossness about his behaviour. He wanted to be kind back. 'Mrs Pawsey?'

She was packing up Red Cross parcels for soldiers, and he was cutting the string.

'You know last Sunday, when the sermon was about families taking GIs into their homes for Sunday lunch?'

'Ye-es . . .'

He could act out the Vicar, he often did it with Alan. The Vicar here was very, very old, and sometimes his voice was quavery. Often he wagged a finger at the congregation. He acted the Vicar for Mrs Pawsey: 'You may think Americans are different, but these are homesick boys. Giving hospitality to them is next to having your own Tommies at your tables.'

She laughed. 'You're a case, Billy. What are you asking?'

'Can we give hospitality to Dwaine and Joe, please? They visited Mrs Youldon but she hasn't got a table for them to sit at.'

'I'm sure as we can squeeze in two more round ours.'

He grinned and as soon as the lengths of string were laid out beside the parcels, he ran off. Time to tell Alan. GIs were bound to go to the Manor where there were huge tables and it would be super if he, Billy, was the first one who invited Americans.

On the Sunday, the two men marched into the front yard smiling. After they'd shaken hands all round, they hitched up their sleeves. Joe said, 'We're goin' ter make ourselves real useful before we eat.'

Mr Pawsey looked glad, and took them down to the field. Joe picked the apples from the high branches. When he climbed up the ladder, his long arms reached to the top of the furthest fruit.

Dwaine helped with fixing the barn door and the broken wall behind the pig pen. It was embarrassing that these were things Billy hadn't been able to do. He was Mr Pawsey's proper helper. He watched carefully so that he could have a stab at the jobs next time. The leak in the wood store roof would take much longer to fix. Perhaps Dwaine would come again.

Indoors, Dwaine opened a haversack and pulled out goodies. He and Joe half-filled Mrs Pawsey's store shelf with tins of meat and tinned fruit. They finished with two brown oblong packets. 'Heath bars, you folks. They're everyone's favourite. Chocolate in them.'

Billy twirled in a circle. 'Mm. Mm. *Love* chocolate! We'll have to make these last, won't we, Mrs Pawsey?'

'We? Are you thinking Mr Pawsey and I would share something like that with you, Billy?' she teased him. 'Thank you from the bottom of our hearts, boys. These'll certainly boost our spirits.'

'You guys got nothing in good ol' England,' Joe said. 'Now we're here an' we gonna win you back your world.'

'Good Lor',' muttered Mr Pawsey, fiddling with his glasses. 'So mebbe you'll give me back full sight and be done with it.'

Mrs Pawsey got the food out of the oven, and everyone helped get it to the table.

It was a jolly meal, having the GIs around the table. They said they'd never had rabbit pie before, or mashed carrots so nice.

Billy hardly said a word, because of listening to all they said about America. Their stories of Iowa and Minnesota showed how foreign they were. They seemed to have a lot of parties and picnics and fancy times out. They didn't even call pavements 'pavements' but 'sidewalks' and said their trousers were 'pants', which seemed very, very funny.

Joe was nice, but Dwaine was quieter and safer. His hair gleamed and his trousers – or pants – had creases. What's more, he drove a jeep. Aunty would like that.

Billy went in the yard with him when it was time to go. He stood by Dwaine, watching Joe jog down to Mrs Youldon's.

'Can you come over next Saturday, Dwaine? My family are coming for their visit, my mother and my aunty.' Kenneth would be coming too, but he wasn't going to announce that.

'Say, that'd be darn good. It'll be swell to meet your folks, buddy.'

'Good.' He took a breath. Better let Dwaine know who was married. 'My father's a soldier now. Mother doesn't like that and I don't, because he was in a retained occupation and I think he's too old to fight. My uncle didn't get to be a soldier because he got killed first. He was on a bus that went down a hole when the underground station was bombed.'

'Shucks. That's too bad. Real hard on your aunty.'

'Yes, she does war work to take her mind off her loss.'

'Say, I guess that's all anyone can do,' said Dwaine.

'She doesn't have any fun, really,' Billy added, in case Dwaine didn't think about the dances himself.

'You don't say? You people sure have it tough.'

After the GIs had both gone, Billy had a run round the garden to think things out. When Mrs Pawsey came out with the pig swill he took the bucket off her. 'Dwaine is going to come over on Saturday so I can introduce him to my family.'

'That's nice, Billy. I see as you've taken a special liking to him.'

He hadn't particularly thought of that. It was what Aunty might like about Dwaine that mattered. Aunty would surely like Dwaine. He was big like Uncle, but jolly, and he didn't say nasty things or make people arm wrestle. It was exciting to think of having a grown-up to introduce when Mother visited. Annoyingly, Kenneth would be there too. Billy needed a proper plan so that neither Mother nor Kenneth got in the way of Dwaine meeting Aunty.

On Saturday, Billy did all his chores extra fast, then he went to where Mrs Pawsey was bringing in the washing. He collected the pegs and started putting them in the peg bag, which meant he didn't have to look at her.

'Mrs Pawsey?'

'Mm . . .'

'Could you specially chat to Aunty today when they all come, because the last time she visited here was the awful funeral time, and if Mother's there when Dwaine comes, she'll do all the talking.'

'The things you think of, Billy boy! But I'll be glad to see your aunty and enjoy a chat with her if you're taking your mother off on your own.'

As soon as footsteps sounded on the gravel outside, Billy ran out to take charge. The weather was cold and breezy so it didn't seem odd to be hurrying the women inside. He handed Jill and Kenneth the kite Mr Pawsey had recently made him, so that they'd go in the field, then took Aunty to the sitting room. Mrs Pawsey took Aunty's arm and started asking her how she was.

'I've got some shabby clothes up here, Mother.' Billy pulled her upstairs to check all his clothes for mending and outgrowing. He'd worry her with tales of sagging socks and buttonless shirts to keep her busy in his bedroom. Aunty was safely drinking tea and chatting to Mrs Pawsey when Dwaine arrived.

As Billy heard Mrs Pawsey doing the introductions, he ran downstairs, shutting the door quietly on Mother and her folding-up of clothes.

'Delighted, ma'am,' Dwaine was saying, and he bowed his head. Aunty blushed. Billy remembered her praising Dad's manners but Dad had never bowed.

Dwaine passed four tins of Spam and some fruit juice across the side table between them. 'I thought you'd like these, ma'am, back in your billet. I've got more for you, Mrs Pawsey.' He nodded to where he'd placed them ready. Dad had never brought things, even for Mother, so it wasn't likely that Uncle Frank had. Aunty should be impressed.

Billy worked quietly at the back of the room piling up the logs ready for banking up the fire. Things were working well. He knew his arrangements were exactly right. It was all in a love story book *Time and Together* he'd found in the vicarage charity box a month ago. The next thing, after a man had been introduced to the lady, was to leave them alone to talk.

It was time. He arranged the last log on the pile and stood up. 'Mrs Pawsey, can I help you take those tins to the kitchen?'

She let him pick up the tins and followed him out there. She put her hands on his shoulders, looking deep into his eyes. 'Not yet eleven, and you're acting the man of the world, Billy.'

He didn't answer. So she knew what he was up to. He didn't care.

Mother soon came downstairs but because Mrs Pawsey was already in the kitchen and there were new tins to put away, she spent some time exclaiming and discussing all the benefits that Americans brought with them. By the time she got to the sitting room to meet the visitor, Dwaine and Aunty were well into their conversation. Mother was the newcomer and had to join in as best she could. Billy followed her in, absorbing his pleased feeling. He was able to look useful, feeding the fire with firewood.

The front door opened, bringing a draught of freezing wind. Kenneth came in to dump the kite. Billy went to the hall to divert him.

'Did it fly well?'

'It was okay. I've finished with this. Jill got fed up with holding the string. She's still out there making a wood house so I'll get my paint box.'

Bother. That was in the sitting-room. He couldn't stop Kenneth going in for it and the roll of lining paper that Mr Pawsey had given him. He stood against the door. 'We've got a visitor, a G.I.'

Kenneth raised his eyebrows and pushed Billy to one side.

'This is my son,' Aunty said as he walked in, 'Kenneth.'

Billy stayed at the door watching in case he stayed too long. Kenneth hesitated looking Dwaine up and down, then leant forward to shake hands with the tips of his fingers.

'Good to meet you, sonny.' Dwaine smiled at him, then went on talking to Aunty.

Kenneth would hate the 'Sonny'.

Billy moved to the sideboard and picked up the paint box. 'Here you are, Kenneth.'

Kenneth took it without looking, watching his mother chatting for a moment or two. Then he collected his roll of paper and went out to paint in the kitchen, his bottom lip pushed forward.

Billy followed him out and shut the door behind them both. He should have realised that Kenneth wouldn't be pleased.

'And who's that supposed to be?'

'It's a GI. We had two for Sunday dinner. It was fun.'

Kenneth closed his eyes, briefly, as though it would have been terrible to be there. He took a jam jar from the draining board and filled it with water. He took it to the table and dipped in his paintbrush, twisting the end over and over to make a fine point.

Mother was helping Mrs Pawsey bring plates from the kitchen to the dining room. 'You're able to put a lovely tea on the table with the extra stores you've been given.'

Mrs Pawsey nodded, as though she didn't realise Mother wanted her to put some in her going home bag. 'We are lucky, aren't we? It's so cheering to have these little treats. Billy deserves some.'

'Billy! I hope your mouth isn't full of chewing gum. I don't want you to spoil your tea.'

He shook his head. Mother thought chewing gum was common, so he and Kenneth would be the only boys for miles around that weren't allowed it. His bubble gum was still in his other trousers, ready for trying out the bubble blowing when no one was watching.

At teatime, the grown-ups were very jolly but Kenneth was quiet all through the bread and butter, Spam, carrot cake and even the tinned peaches.

'So tasty this Spam, Dwaine. More evap, Kenneth? It'll fill out those cheeks,' Mrs Pawsey encouraged him.

'No thank you.' Kenneth sat with his hands folded on his lap.

When Billy finished his last peach slice, nibbling as slowly as he could to make the taste last, Aunty said. 'Go and spend some time with Billy, dear. You've almost been ignoring him.'

Billy stood. 'Coming, Kenneth?' Horrible though it was to spend time with him, it would keep Kenneth out of the way.

Kenneth picked up his paper, paints and brushes and elbowed Billy upstairs to his room, kicking the door shut behind him. 'Damned Eyetie,' he said. 'Don't even like Spam.'

'He's not an Eyetie! He's a GI.'

'An Eyetie GI then. Look at that greasy black hair and gypsy face.'

'Shut up. GIs and Eyeties are nice. I like them. I like Dwaine, and Mr and Mrs Pawsey like him – and Aunty likes him.'

'She's just being polite. You don't know a thing, you're just a football twerp.' Kenneth picked up his paintbrush with a flick of his head, then turned his back. Billy wanted to hit him so badly, but as Kenneth bent to his painting, the back of his stringy neck looked weak, like something that shouldn't be hit.

'If I'm a football twerp then you won't want my company,' Billy said and stomped downstairs. He scooted out of the back door and made for the field. 'Huh, meanie!' he said now that no one could hear. It was cold enough for his breath to come out in little clouds, which was very satisfying, like being a fearful dragon. All the fence posts had sparkly white tips and spiders webs laced across the long grass. Beyond the horse's field he could see Aunty and Dwaine walking in deep conversation. Apart from Kenneth, it was all going very satisfactorily.

He leant on the pigs' wall, keeping out of the way. He hadn't given them names, because Mrs Pawsey said that way he wouldn't feel so upset when they had to go to market. He did so like them, though, especially the tubby little one they called the runt.

'Well!' said Mother, coming up behind him holding Mrs Pawsey's egg basket. 'A bit of company is certainly doing your aunty some good. I gather Dwaine's invited her to a dance. Perhaps he'll bring some friends next time I visit you, then I can go.'

Billy swung round fiercely. 'You can't. Dad's away somewhere being a soldier. *He* can't go to dances.'

Mother looked almost alarmed. 'You're going to be – eleven, soon. Growing up, and I hadn't been noticing. I must ask about the secondary school. Mrs Pawsey might know if it's any good. You can't stay where you are until you're fourteen, given there's no sign of this infernal war ending.'

Billy stood upright, firmly. Surely, Mother would see he was worth the same as Kenneth?

She went on, 'Or fifteen, it's said the school leaving age is going to be. I wonder if there's a technical school. Your father would want to know the reputation, the discipline. So important. Kenneth's school makes them into little gentlemen. Too far away for you to go, unfortunately, even if you were accepted.'

Billy was going to say, 'Unless you got me a billet near you,' and then thought of how truly awful it would be to leave this place, to leave Mr and Mrs Pawsey. He walked beside her, silent until they reached the chickens.

'Oh there's no eggs,' she said, looking at an empty pile of straw.

'Wait.' He scrabbled in the hedge and in a patch of tangled dandelions. 'Here's two, Mother. And there's another one under Sparky, that gingery hen.'

She looked at him rather sadly. 'I can see you're going to be rather a useful boy to have around.' Then with a strange switch of subject, which Billy fully understood, 'Anyway, not much football at Kenneth's school. They don't pride themselves on their sports. It's all literature, Latin and algorithms.'

'And art,' said Aunty coming up behind them, 'if you're talking about Kenneth's grammar school. I was just telling Dwaine about it.'

'Quite an artist, I hear, ma'am, that young man. I guess we don't go in for that culture stuff too great in the States. Some say we should. No opportunity to partake in culture at the present time, of course.' He laughed, but not bitterly.

'But you do have time for football,' Billy put in. He wasn't sure whether that counted as culture.

Dwaine winked at him. 'Too right, buddy.'

Aunty's eyes were bright as she said, 'Well if you're short of culture, and if your – unit – will let you, you could come to Kenneth's art exhibition. It's before the end of the summer. You'll come, Billy dear, won't you?'

'At Kenneth's school?' he said. It would be interesting to see it. 'Yes. If someone can take me over, I'll come and see Kenneth's paintings.'

And if he went, surely Dwaine would want to go with Aunty?

CHAPTER THIRTEEN

May 1942

Rommel readies for a new offensive

Billy was the biggest boy amongst the evacuees now. Even the twins and all the farm food they had every day hadn't made them grow as tall. His muscles were the sort that Uncle Frank couldn't have scoffed about. But you needed more than muscles and speed to play football really well, you needed proper football boots with studs.

Alan's mother had managed to get Alan some. Billy stared at the studs as Alan ran. They made a smashing pattern of holes in the mud. 'Flipping heck, you're so lucky, Alan.'

'I know. It's that job she has in Piccadilly. There always seems to be a visiting officer that can put his hand on something special. Or even stuff from abroad. There's people working there who go secretly to other countries and no one's supposed to know. But these are English boots.'

'I don't think you can get them anywhere near here, can you?'

'Ask your mother for some. She gets to the town. Say it's for an early birthday present.'

'Five months early? Bet she won't.'

Jill had come with Mother, looking smart in a little skirt cut-down from a woman's tweed one, and with shiny strap shoes. Kenneth held her hand. He always

183

looked smart, like a boy on a knitting pattern or a Persil advertisement.

As soon as he could choose the right moment, Billy said, 'Mother, my shoes pinch my toes. If I could have new boots, they'd last longer than shoes. And if you don't mind it being so early, they could be my birthday present if they had studs on.'

'Studs!'

Mrs Pawsey looked the other way and took some cups and saucers from the dresser, putting them quietly on a tray.

Mother sighed, a loud sigh. She looked at Billy, then Kenneth, then Jill and then back at Mrs Pawsey and rolled her eyes.

'Just when the rationing's got even worse. Always something more to get for children, isn't there, Mrs Pawsey?'

Kenneth had hold of Jill's hand. 'Looks as if you'll have to wait a bit longer for your coat, Jilly. There won't be enough rations. You won't cry now, will you?'

Mrs Pawsey stood in front of Kenneth. 'I'll get Billy's ration book.' She came back into the room and showed how many rations were left. 'Here you are, Mrs Wilson. You should be able to get him some boots. We've not used many for him, not really.' Then she took the tray out to get tea.

Mother squeezed the toes at the end of Billy's shoes and counted the points left in his ration book again. Billy waited, watching her face. Did this mean she would be getting boots or not?

Kenneth sat on the low padded chair, his legs stretched out before him. It looked as if he was showing off his shoes. They looked newly polished and shiny. 'Do you polish all the shoes, Kenneth?' Billy asked.

Kenneth didn't answer, and Mother, with her back to him, mouthed to Billy, 'Prisoners of war.'

There were buns for tea and some butter too. It was a proud moment. Mrs Pawsey had swapped her extra eggs for it. Billy helped look after the hens, so if they laid more than the quota for collection, it was partly thanks to him. And he'd done the swap deal with the twins' farm.

'You have such treats, Billy,' Mother said as she spread a sliver of butter reverently on the half of her bun which didn't have currants. 'I wish things weren't so hard for Jill. And Kenneth, of course. But at the Vicarage, we're aware of how much we need to help others.'

'We get by, don't we, Jill?' said Kenneth, smiling at Mrs Pawsey with his sad head on one side.

Mother leant towards her, 'Kenneth draws pictures that his mother puts in the Red Cross parcels, and he unravels the old jumpers people give in to the Vicarage. Then Doreen knits scarves and socks with the wool.'

'And it's all wriggly, not nearly as good as new wool, Mummy says.'

Everyone started as Jill spoke. She spoke so rarely that Billy had hardly taken in that she could talk properly now. She probably had done for ages when he wasn't around.

Mother went on, directing her conversation at Mrs Pawsey. 'I don't knit, of course. Doreen's tried to teach me, but it's not my sort of thing. I was taught deportment and elocution at school, not much help to the war effort.'

Mrs Pawsey bent her head to her tea cup. 'No, it wouldn't be, that.'

'I help in other ways, don't I, children?'

Kenneth said, 'Yes, Aunty. You're a tower of strength.' He looked at Mrs Pawsey so that she could encourage Mother.

Mrs Pawsey said, 'You mustn't grow old before your time, Kenneth. How about popping into the yard for a game of football with Billy?'

'I think I'll say *No* to that, thank you very much, Mrs Pawsey. Falling about in the mud is more Billy's thing than mine. I can clear the table for you.'

'Such a help,' said Mother.

'No thank you, Kenneth. I'll see to it,' said Mrs Pawsey. 'But you should try to play football, even if Billy's a much stronger player. He does so well, even without boots.'

Mother leant forward to take the half-bun off Kenneth's plate. 'Can't waste this, if you're leaving it, dear. Such a treat, Mrs Pawsey.'

It was hopeless. Even with Mrs Pawsey mentioning football, Mother wasn't remembering about the boots.

Mrs Pawsey handed Billy his freshly ironed best clothes; a cream shirt, a green v-neck, and his jacket that he only wore on Sundays. 'I's'll want you to look just as good as all those grammar boys, won't I?' she said, as she walked down the lane with him to meet Dwaine. He couldn't help skipping along. Even if visiting Kenneth's school turned out to be boring, it would be topping to turn up in a jeep.

At the road, you could hear immediately it was coming. It was going at a slow pace because of boys running alongside.

Billy put his thumbs up to them. 'I'm going to ride in that!'

He sat in the front all the way to the Vicarage, where Mother and Aunty were waiting in the front garden. They'd both done their hair in waves and had curls with Kirby grips. Aunty's plum-coloured dress made him look twice, and then he remembered her wearing it that Christmas Day they'd spent at her house, when Uncle Frank dressed up like Father Christmas. Dad had asked Aunty if her arms were cold because they were bare. But today was quite hot, and Mother was wearing the blue spotted dress she liked best.

He hopped out and into the back seat, still high above the ground and the ladies slid gracefully into the front as if they always travelled that way.

'Marvellous you can get the fuel, Dwaine.'

'For reconnaissance,' he said, grinning.

Billy didn't know quite what he'd expected of a grammar school. Probably a great brick building like his Wandsworth school, doubled or trebled in size. But Friary Court was more like the Grange, a great drive up to the front and an archway to one side. As they got near, they could see through the arch that there were vehicles of all kinds parked, including some army trucks. Kenneth had told him that upstairs there were dormitories and because of the war, some boys were boarding.

'Boy, this is quite something,' said Dwaine, as they walked to the huge open doors. 'A lot different to my high school, I'll say.'

'It is impressive,' said Mother, adjusting the feather in her little hat.

Aunty grabbed hold of Billy's hand. He held it limp, so that she would realise he was too old for her to do that. She dropped it, and held his elbow instead.

'This is exciting, isn't it, Billy? Kenneth's going to be quite a star. His paintings were chosen although he's one of the youngest in the school.'

Billy was interested to see the many people, especially servicemen on leave. All were rather quiet, rather like a crowd going into church. Yes, it was exciting. Mother led the way, Dwaine held Aunty's arm and she was still holding Billy's elbow. Once inside, they were ushered into the great hall. Lots of screens on feet surrounded the walls and people had to step between them and look at drawings, written work and designs pinned on each one.

Dwaine gave a running commentary as they admired each display until finally they passed the last screen to face the back wall of the best paintings. Beside it stood Kenneth.

Aunty breathed out. 'Kenneth, dear, here we are!'

'Well, I say,' said Mother.

Billy looked up at a scene of soldiers parading past the local church. It looked as if he could see them for real through a window. Then there was a smaller drawing of a man working at a desk. There was one of a huge vase of flowers and another of a pile of vegetables, a painting of the church and children coming out of it, and two which were just like patterns, all sorts of colours and shapes swirling about. Kenneth smoothed his hair and grinned as they gazed at the colourful paintings. Billy had never seen him look like that.

'These really yours, Buddy?' Dwaine was saying. Kenneth nodded but didn't reply.

'Cor, Kenneth, they're ever so, ever so good,' Billy said.

Kenneth looked surprised. 'Do you like them?'

Billy nodded very hard. He didn't like Kenneth, but his paintings were super. 'They're like a real artist's.' It was true what Uncle Frank had said back in Wandsworth. Kenneth was going to be famous.

'Herbert would so love to see these,' Mother said to Aunty who stood, glowing and silent. 'He'd be so proud – he always wanted to paint himself.'

Aunty's face tightened. 'And don't you think Frank would've loved to have seen his son's work? If I was lucky enough to still have a husband like you?'

Mother fluttered her hands. 'Sorry, Doreen. Of course. I suppose I rather forgot, what with Herbert taking Kenneth on as another son and you now having . . .'

Dwaine interrupted Aunty's gasp. 'Ladies! I gotta thank you for showing me this fine school. It's time to admire some scientific work now.' He took the arm of Aunty and marched her off to look at the science laboratories. Mother gazed after them, nodding to herself. One of her eyebrows twitched. She wandered to the nearest table to look at some sketch books.

Kenneth leant down towards Billy and muttered, 'Let that be the last time we have to set eyes on him! You won't invite Yanks round any more, will you? Don't you hate them?'

Billy shook his head. He really liked them and the more Dwaine came round, the better he liked it. Of course, Kenneth wouldn't know how often that was, or that he played football with Joe and Dwaine and other GIs at the Manor whenever they could get free.

He gazed at each of the paintings again and again. It was amazing that a cousin of his had done them. There were other super drawings and paintings around, but they were by much older boys.

The hall was enormous. Two large corridors led off it, as well as a square area with several doors. He'd never find his way around if he had to go to school here. 'Can we go to where those big maps are and then to the biology labs?' He knew there'd be animals in jars from what Kenneth had talked about before.

'In a bit. There's tea and cakes.'

'That will be welcome, Kenneth.' Mother followed him to the dining hall at the end of the first corridor.

They sat with their tea and rock cakes until Aunty and Dwaine re-joined them. It was good hearing other people around commenting on the paintings, and saying admiring things about Kenneth's. Aunty got pink and breathy. Billy saw Dwaine take her hand. Perhaps he was going to love her.

A bearded teacher with a caved-in chest stepped beside them. Kenneth stood up. 'Sir, my mother, my aunt, my cousin and a – an American.'

'Delighted. I'm Kenneth's art teacher, so naturally feeling very proud. And are you another budding artist, Kenneth's cousin?' the teacher asked Billy, hope in his eyes.

'No, sir. I'm rotten at drawing.'

'Shame,' said the teacher, turning away. Then he took the adults off to see round the rest of the school. Billy was left with Kenneth.

'Brilliant teacher, Mr Woodhead. Did you see his chest? Some boys say he had consumption, all his lungs eaten away. Don't know if it's true, but it's good that he doesn't have to go to war and can stay teaching us, isn't it?' He stood up, away from the crumbs on the table. 'Come on. There's lots of subjects on display. We'll go and see the interesting bits. Bit different from your little school, isn't it?'

Billy nodded. He'd never imagined a school like this. The inside was larger than the Manor. He grew quieter and quieter as they went from the maps to the gymnasium with its leather horse and wooden bars all up one side, then the science laboratories full of instruments that he'd never seen before, and lastly the art room. That was only to look at the materials because all the decent work was on display.

They ended up in a cloakroom area that looked on to a playing field. It was the sports area. There were changing rooms with basins for washing, and a small office by the rear doors. Kenneth knocked on the door and went in. Billy could see shelves of clothes and shoes inside.

'Look!' said Kenneth, coming out again. 'Lost property.' He led Billy out of the sports area. 'Here you are, right size.' He passed over a pair of nearly perfect football boots. And they had studs.

'I thought there wasn't football here.'

'Well, there is for some. We're not forced to do it. I don't, of course. Here you are.' Kenneth pushed the boots into his middle.

Billy felt as if his eyes were falling out of his head.

'Take them, then.'

Billy hadn't even put his hands out, not daring to think they were for him.

'I can't – they're not mine.'

'They are now. The teacher in there will think they're for me, but I'm not going to use them, am I? I do extra art when it's footer. Go on. They're what you wanted, aren't they?'

Billy looked hard at Kenneth's expression in case this was some cruel trick, but Kenneth's face didn't look mean.

'I-I do want them. They're smashing,' he said, stroking the leather, 'Thank you. Thanks ever so much.' He hugged them to his middle, hard, in case they disappeared into thin air.

Kenneth found a piece of newspaper on the changing bench. 'Here, you'd better wrap them up. Let's go and find the grown-ups. I've had enough touring now.'

Billy followed, clutching the boots. They were better than any birthday or Christmas present he'd ever had and it was *Kenneth* who'd given him them. It was almost too difficult to speak. Now he couldn't wait to get back to the Pawseys to put them on and try them out.

Dwaine and Aunty were deep in conversation so didn't notice him holding anything as they walked back down the drive, but Mother did.

'What's that messy bundle, Billy?'

'Football boots,' his voice was jerky. 'A present from Kenneth.'

Aunty turned round. 'You found boots for him.'

'They were in Lost Property. No one wanted them.'

She looked across at Mother. 'Heart of gold.'

Mother was looking into the distance and muttering, 'Of course, I do remember you once saying something about wanting boots, Billy. Well, now you have some. Lucky boy. Make sure you thank Kenneth.'

Dwaine had a little smile round his mouth. 'How you goin' to make that up to him, Billy?'

Kenneth marched ahead as if not hearing.

Billy started. 'I – d-don't know.' He grabbed the boots tighter to him. Whatever was coming, he wasn't going to part with them now.

CHAPTER FOURTEEN

June 25th 1942

British RAF make 1,000 bomb raid on Bremen

The second-hand boots were actually quite worn at the heels, but it didn't matter. They had studs. They were proper football boots and they were his. He'd already put his name inside by the ankle, using a laundry pencil of Mrs Pawsey's. She understood how important football boots were for someone like Billy.

'See? You thought Kenneth all bad and he's seen to it that you've got exactly what you need.'

At the first opportunity he raced down to the Manor. There was the whole story of the grammar school visit to tell Alan, but most importantly about how he'd got the boots.

Alan was impressed. 'That was really decent of Kenneth.'

'Yes! I thought he was sneering and not at all on my side when I was asking Mother for boots, but all the time he must have been thinking how much I wanted them, and then how he could get me some from his school.'

He and Alan compared boots and studs and played an even longer game than usual, so that Alan was called away for yard sweeping duty before Billy was due home.

Now he just had to tell the Youldons about the boots. They felt deliciously heavy on his feet as he ran down to their lane.

When he reached their open doorway, Timmy met him with big eyes. 'She's crying.'

Sally was hanging on to her mother's skirt while Mrs Youldon tried to mangle some sheets. The airer was low enough for her to spread them on but she was making heavy weather of the mangling. Billy stepped forward and took the handle. 'Hello'. He saw her red eyes, but it wouldn't be polite to mention it.

She sent the children to play out.

'But Mu-ummy . . .'

'No, Sally. Play out. Go with Timmy.'

Timmy looked at Billy trustingly as he took Sally's hand and slipped through the doorway. Sometimes, Billy felt like a dad here.

Mrs Youldon took the handle from him. 'We'll take turns,' she said in a wavering voice.

He breathed out. 'What's wrong, Mrs Youldon?' But he wasn't sure he wanted to know. He looked at the chipped enamel bucket with its steamy soda smell. Would she have to tell him? He didn't want to say, 'I'm sorry for your loss' again.

'It's Mary.' She began to sniff and her eyes dripped more wet on to the sheets as they pulled the next one flat between them. 'I should be happy for her. She's going to marry him, that Chuck. And that means going to America with him after the war.' She smothered a sob as she lifted another heavy sheet. 'She'll have a machine for doing all this. A washing machine. Imagine! Joe showed me a picture in a magazine. It's like a small train carriage with a lid. You put the clothes in, then a hose for the water, add the soap stuff and press the electric switch. It swills round and round does all the wash for you, even getting the water out! That's what they have in America.'

'It's a long way to go to do washing.'

'Oh, you!' She nudged him in the ribs. 'What'll I do without her? Why can't I have someone to look after me?'

'You've got me and Alan.'

She started crying again. 'I mean a man. It's so far away. If she goes, I'll never see her. Grrr, this sheet just won't go through the mangle.'

Billy grasped one end of the sheet and twisted. He knew the drill. Mrs Youldon grasped the other and they held the middle over the wooden sink. His hands stung as he struggled with the steamy linen. Her hands didn't seem much bigger than his, although they were bright red with doing this so often.

'Why do the Grange people need such thick sheets?' he said when they'd flattened sufficiently for the mangle.

'They lie more, I suppose.' She cried and laughed a bitter laugh at the same time. 'I know one of them that does. Not that Timmy'll ever know him.'

Billy carried on turning the handle. He supposed it was because she was upset she was saying nonsense things. Wasn't Mr Youldon ever going to come back?

She pulled out the sheet. 'I shouldn't be saying those things. Especially not to a child. You forget what I said, mind.'

'About Mary going to America?'

'No, not that, she's telling everyone. Anyway, she'll have to wait for the war to be over before she goes with him. What I said about the Grange people. Don't repeat that.' She passed Billy one end of the wet sheet. 'Can you fold? Joe's off soon, he thinks. It might be to Africa. Fancy that, fighting the war over there in jungles and that!'

Africa, America. It was all very far away.

'Then, when it's all over, Chuck will send for her and they'll get married out there so his folks can give them a proper do.' Her voice crumpled into a choke.

'I'm sorry she's going. But Joe hasn't told you to go has he? I don't want you to go to America. Or the little ones.'

She laughed. 'No, Billy. He's a lovely boy and a good dancer, but still a boy. I do worry about how he'll cope with Africa, boiling sun and natives.'

Billy had a sudden thought. 'What about Dwaine? Is he going too?'

'I suppose so. Same regiment.'

He dumped his end of the screwed up sheet in the second bucket, the dry one. Now Aunty would be sad again.

It was time to fold the mangled sheets ready for hanging out. He said in jerks between turning them, 'Please stop crying. Cheer up. Mary hasn't gone yet. Perhaps Chuck will like Africa so much he'll find a black lady to marry.' He felt in his satchel. 'Look, I've got biscuits. I saved them for you and the little ones. So don't cry any more.'

He hadn't had much time to talk about his boots with Timmy and Sally before it was time to run home. There was a worried feeling in his stomach about Dwaine.

He rushed indoors to ask Mrs Pawsey if he could telephone the Vicarage. She looked at him closely.

'Something up, Billy?'

'No. I just wanted Aunty to come on Saturday. Mr Pawsey's going to invite Joe and Dwaine again. Aunty had fun last time and I think Dwaine's called for her, down at the WVS centre.'

'Ho, ho. Aren't you doing a bit of match-making?' She chuckled.

'I think the GIs are having to go away, that's the thing.' He picked up the egg basket to start his evening chores.

She nodded several times so that her under-chin shook, 'All right, my dear. We need to give them a good send-off, if that's the case.'

'No Kenneth?' Mrs Pawsey asked as Billy's family arrived on the Saturday.

'No. He made some excuse – and after all he's mature enough now to have his own friends and pastimes.' Mother sounded more than happy about that. 'Although I was a bit surprised. He's normally so keen to be round you, Billy. You haven't fallen out, have you?'

He shook his head.

Aunty said, 'Of course they haven't fallen out. Kenneth's just so busy with his art assignments. He's even sent him a note. Here you are, Billy.'

The envelope was closely sealed with a blob of pink sealing wax on the V.

Billy went upstairs with it, sensing trouble. He took out the folded sheet. It had skulls and crossbones all over the bottom of it.

Billy

_You're a measly rat. I told you at my
show I didn't want that Eyetie around
again. You said No, and so I got you the
boots. I heard Aunty Marcia on the
phone to Mrs Pawsey so I know it was
all your idea to have the Eyetie round
and get Mummy to visit you._

You better watch out.

Kenneth

Billy put his hands on his middle, which suddenly
felt very cold. Even the underlining looked sinister. He
remembered shaking his head when Kenneth said
didn't he hate Eyeties, and wouldn't he stop inviting
them over, but he'd meant, No, he didn't hate them.
Explaining wouldn't help. It would make it worse if
Kenneth knew he'd planned for Aunty to go out with
Dwaine.

How could he keep the boots safe? Suppose
Kenneth pretended he needed them himself for
school? Mother and Aunty would insist Kenneth had
them back.

Loud barking below announced the GIs' arrival so
he ran downstairs. Noah and Japhet wound
themselves in and out of his legs as he waited for
Dwaine to come up the path.

Dwaine had brought sugar, which made Mrs
Pawsey throw up her hands and hug him. He also had
cookies and two Heath bars. Without Kenneth, there

was more to go round, but Billy couldn't enjoy his share. He put them in the cutlery drawer until he could take it to the Youldons.

While Mr Pawsey was talking shipping routes and war strategies with Joe, Aunty and Dwaine sat down together. Billy hovered near. They soon started chatting with smiles on their faces. They were getting on ever so well. Kenneth would hate it if he could see.

It was only after tea, when the men were lolling back smoking, that Dwaine told everyone they were being sent off to war, the two regiments together.

Everyone clucked and sighed. Billy's sigh was long – sad, but relieved too. He didn't want Dwaine to go and Aunty to lose her new friend, but if they weren't to be together, the problem of Kenneth doing something awful to the football boots was gone. He tried not to look at Aunty's doleful expression.

Dwaine's was rather serious too.

Joe said, 'I'm all for it. Shucks, we didn't come all this way to see no action. And how else would someone like us see North Africa, huh?'

'Had to happen, Dwaine,' Mr Pawsey said. 'You'se trained up now, ready for action, baint that so?'

'You bet,' said Dwaine, 'although we sure were having a darned good time here.'

'Super-duper,' said Joe.

'Do you know what you'll be doing?' Mrs Pawsey asked.

Joe laughed. 'Making it darned hot for the enemy, in a place where it's already darned hot.'

Billy thought of his Tarzan pictures. 'Is it jungle?'

Dwaine said, 'North Africa's more desert, so the nobs say. He tapped his nose. 'Seems I'll be driving a jeep for some colonel across those distant sands.' Then he looked at Aunty. 'But I'll be hoping to get back to jolly old England for someone more important, once we've won the war.'

Auntie blushed, and Billy rubbed his hands under the table. It was lucky Kenneth wasn't around to see that blush. Would he change his mind about Dwaine by the time the war was over? How could everyone stop Aunty being sad until then?

When Joe went down to the pigs with Mr Pawsey, Billy said, 'Can you stand by the gate, Dwaine? I'm going to take a photo of you. I've been saving my film for special things.'

'You want a snap of me! Gee, I'm bucked to think there'll be a record of me in Ol' England. Let me fasten my jacket and put my cap on for this.'

Billy collected his camera from the sideboard. Even though Aunty couldn't have Dwaine nearby for a few years, she'd feel a bit happier with a photograph of him.

'Reckon you'se a hit with our Billy, Dwaine, if he's using one of his precious snaps on you,' said Mr Pawsey.

'It's for his Aunty he wants it,' Mrs Pawsey whispered. It was embarrassing that she knew what he was thinking.

Billy got Dwaine to go outside the garden gate and into exactly the right position for the light.

'Well darn it, you're like a pro, Billy. Guess I'm like a film star now!'

They both were, great tall Joe and handsome Dwaine, with their wide smiles, corn cob smell and neat collars. They were like the green and red Sunny Jim pictures on the corn flake boxes, promising something much more special than plain, unsugared flakes.

He decided to put his camera away in the dark of the wardrobe until another special occasion. That might be Mr Finlay getting the football team together, or new piglets arriving or, if the war did ever end, Uncle Ted doing handstands on the garden path.

In any case, this was going to be a good photo of Dwaine in his cap, the summer sky blue behind him. He could fold a piece of cardboard to fit round it, like real photographers did. That way Aunty could hide it in her bag and then Kenneth wouldn't see it.

Mr Pawsey winked at him. 'Yes, my laddo. It might be a long time these Yanks are away. As well your Aunty has a photo.'

It was just a photo, but Billy had a very guilty feeling about the whole Dwaine thing. He was the one who had made it happen. He'd only wanted Aunty to be happy and go to dances like the other ladies, but he'd sort of cheated Kenneth. And he still had the boots.

CHAPTER FIFTEEN

November 1942

Oran, Algeria falls to US troops

He was with Alan standing behind the chicken coops ready to play, but the ball was still under Alan's arm. Billy looked down at his boots, so perfect for tipping the ball right to the edge of the lane. Alan stayed where he was.

'Come on.' Billy dropped on to one foot then the other. He rocked on his feet to and fro so that he could feel the studs under them. He and the boots were ready for action. 'Alan, come on. We haven't got long before my mother gets here.'

He peered at Alan's face. Working in the fields had made his freckles so close together he'd soon have a brown face instead of a pink one, and he was frowning. He grumbled, 'It's not the same without any of the GIs.'

'They gave us a smashing party, though, didn't they? All that singing, the grub and the hokey-cokey. I had two coca-colas. I *love* that drink.'

'So do I, but it's months since we had one.' Alan scuffed one foot into the dried dust of the chicken run. 'And I haven't had a letter from my father since September the second, and my mother hasn't either. She thinks he's in Asia.'

Billy thought of something cheery to say. 'Asia's the desert. He might meet our GIs there because it's very empty. I've got a picture of the desert in my *Best Boys'*

Stories. I got it at the party. It's the first book I've had since I was eight and it's got airmen in it, too.'

'Has it?'

'Yes. You got *Marvel* with Captain America, didn't you? We can swap if you've finished it.'

'Okay.' His hair needed cutting and a lock trailed miserably over one eye.

'Listen, Alan.' He linked arms. Alan was his best friend. They told each other everything, like having to eat tripe, or being bullied, or worrying about whether their fathers were being shot. Even Alan's mother was right in the thick of it, because of her secret work in the Piccadilly office and Alan hadn't had a visit for ages. Billy jerked at his arm. 'You're coming to my place. There's sponge for tea with red jam. It's because Dwaine left a big bag of sugar for us so Mrs Pawsey could bake stuff. We'll play football a bit later, won't we?' He took the ball from Alan and toed it to and fro.

Voices sounded from down the lane.

'Hey, the bus must have been early. That's Jill's voice.'

Mother's sounded soon after. He pulled Alan to go and meet them. Aunty wasn't with them this time, but Kenneth was. He wore a pale blue shirt with short sleeves and it was too large for him, mostly round the chest, so that it bagged and flapped as he sauntered along, holding a notebook under one arm. Mrs Shawditch must have had another pile of jumble to share out.

Alan stood smartly, feet together, pushing his hair into better order while Billy ran forward.

Mother bent down to look at his knees. 'Not too bad.'

He opened his mouth to tell her all his latest news but she held up a hand. 'I'll tell you our news in a bit, Billy. I must get indoors and take the weight off my feet first. Hello, Alan. What a nice, smart boy you always look. Thank goodness Billy has one decent contact in this place.'

Kenneth passed Billy then nodded to Alan. He followed Mother past the front gate and into the front yard but not through the front door. Once Mother was out of hearing range, he turned to Billy and Alan, putting a finger under his nose and cocking his chin up, 'I note, you two, few nasty smells here today. The company in this environment has improved.' His eyebrows raised a touch. 'Civilised without Yanks and especially Eyeties, isn't it?'

Alan scowled and clenched his fists. Billy nudged him to walk away a few steps. 'Typical.'

'He's talking about Dwaine.'

'I know. It's because of Aunty. I feel like bashing him.'

Alan nodded. 'Swine. But aren't you scared about him taking back your boots? Anyway, it wouldn't be right to bash him. Let's just ignore him.'

Alan always knew the right thing to do. Billy sighed. 'All right.' He pulled him towards the front door.

The dogs barked and ran around in circles claiming attention but Mother was striding down the hall with flushed cheeks, pulling Jill almost fiercely behind. Jill was getting a little bold these days and she rolled her eyes at Billy as Mother pressed forward into the kitchen.

'Mrs Pawsey, good afternoon. Listen to the latest government demand. Would you believe it! I've been sent to work at the garage to take calls and fill petrol tanks. It's two miles walk each way, too. As if what I do at the vicarage isn't work enough! I'm sure you're glad you're not a woman under fifty so that you can remain here at leisure with your dogs and chickens.'

'I dare say I shall keep busy enough,' said Mrs Pawsey. She'd been cooking since early that morning for a fundraising tea. Billy had done all the washing up. All the tea money was going to prisoners of war. And she had all her ordinary work on top.

Mother was an embarrassment. She turned to Billy. 'I have to warn you that I won't be able to visit so often, Billy. The weekends will be my only chance to do things for myself.'

'And I'm having to stay at school all day,' said Jill in a happy voice. Now that she was mixing with other children, Jill had stopped clinging to Mother and Kenneth. She smiled up at Billy and Alan. 'Shall we go in the room where the dogs are?'

Billy had a quick check around. Kenneth hadn't come inside yet. He was still outside sketching the doorway in his notebook.

Billy led Jill and Alan into the parlour. Japhet slid off the leather chair with a guilty expression. 'Naughty boy!' said Jill, then stroking and hugging him. When they'd played with the dogs for a while, Billy said, 'Let's play cards. Beggar your Neighbour?' He took out a pack of cards from the sideboard drawer and dealt.

They were playing a slow game for Jill's benefit when Kenneth came indoors to see what they were doing. Alan played a card, Jill followed.

'You have to pay me two for that, Jill.'

Kenneth butted in, 'For goodness' sake, teach her the suits first. She's a novice, remember.'

Jill put down two cards. Billy played on, remembering to ignore Kenneth, and his last move made him the winner. He put a thumb up at Alan.

Kenneth flicked the jokers across the table. 'Don't you aspire to something more than games of chance at your age?'

Kenneth's fancy words made Billy feel stupid. It would be jolly nice to kick his sarcasm away and leave a stud pattern on his skinny legs.

Alan stood up and stretched. He wouldn't like being told what to do. 'I've decided to go back to the Manor, Billy. We'll play later, right?'

'But there's jam sponge.'

'Still.' Alan jerked his head at the cards to show what he meant, and made off down the path.

Now Alan was out of the way, Kenneth turned mean and grouchy. He lifted the cards and tipped them all over the table.

'Hey! What's that for?'

'Mummy's getting airmail from that greasy Yank. Your fault.' He dug a finger into Billy's chest. 'Interfering dummy!' He stomped around the room, wagging his finger.

Jill tidied up the cards, watching carefully. Perhaps Kenneth was sometimes like this back in the Vicarage, perhaps even with Aunty. There wasn't anything Billy could say.

Kenneth did another round of the room, his stupid head wagging as if he was an old teacher telling the class off. 'Mummy needn't think *Doo Wayne*'s coming back from war to walk out with her again. When the war ends, they'll send the Yanks straight home to *Tha States*. I'll be an adult by then and then she'll have to listen to my advice.'

Billy pushed his chin forward. 'It's eight years till you're twenty-one. The war's never going to last that long.'

'Fat lot you know, twerp.'

Teatime interrupted Kenneth's rant and Jill ran into the dining room ahead of him. Billy played safe and moved his football boots from their usual place. He hid them with the cleaning cloths in the scullery. Kenneth wouldn't look for them there.

Mother dominated the conversation over the tea table. 'Wonderful to wash my hands in your bathroom. I never thought I'd appreciate something so simple as Lifebuoy soap. Oof! That petrol pump makes my hands so dirty and smelly that I can't wash them clean enough. There is *no* soap at the garage, although I've asked and asked, and we're reduced to a sliver of Sunlight at the Vicarage. Dwaine gave Doreen a lovely bar of soap, lucky thing, so she and Kenneth have that luxury at their billet all to themselves. All my headscarves positively stink of petrol now and by the time Friday comes, my poor hair is just desperate for its wash.'

Kenneth ate his bread and marge grimly, refusing the fish paste and only pushing it towards Billy after he'd been asked twice. The cake was jolly nice, but when everyone else said so, Kenneth just continued chewing silently.

As soon as tea finished, Billy made himself busy with his outside chores. That way he couldn't get into an argument.

After the family had gone home, his own words seemed to hang in the air. *The war won't last that long.* To say that might be like a jinx and make more war last even longer. It was like boasting you'd be best at something, and then finding you weren't. It was a very scary thought.

If the war did last until Kenneth was twenty-one, think of all the soldiers who wouldn't be coming home, the children at school crying and crying because it had been their father who'd bought it. Uncle Frank had bought it although he wasn't fighting, Dad had to fight although he didn't believe in war, and Uncle Ted had fought right from the beginning and must, must, must be safe.

In the parlour, Mr Pawsey was settled into his old leather chair with the newspaper. He didn't normally bother with one, now that wartime newspapers were so skinny. After reading Billy the headlines, he just grunted every now and then and didn't chat.

The headlines didn't made Billy feel any better about the end of war, even though the allies had won some battles as well as lost some. It was worrying to think whether people he knew were among the dead. He fetched his old heroes book from the top of the settle. Although he'd read it umpteen times already, he liked holding an old book, a book that came from Mr Durban's home, the home that held the shashka. Dad might be in danger, the GIs definitely were, Uncle might be lost in Belgium or Holland or France. They were all heroes. He hadn't thought he could ever be a hero himself, until that time Mrs Youldon said he was one. But being nearly drowned was as much as he could bear. He really didn't think he could manage being a British soldier under constant fire, like Mr Durban had been in Russia, like the soldiers were in Europe. He turned a page. Joan of Arc died in an actual fire, and there was a picture of her standing in it.

The only way to calm the wonky feeling inside of him was to imagine the shashka in his hands. It was what he always did when things were scary. He hurried up to his bedroom to pull it from its special place. He slid his hand under the mattress and into the gap of the wooden frame, but it wasn't there!

He sat down low, level with the mattress and peered all along the gap. He put his knee under the mattress edge to make sure there was no way the envelope could have dropped out. He felt around until his legs had cramp, squatting by his bed, one hand under the mattress. His shashka picture really had gone.

His chest hurt and he felt sick. No one knew this hiding place so it meant someone had been snooping around. The only people who ever came in were Alan, Mr and Mrs Pawsey, Kenneth and Mother. Kenneth was the obvious person to snoop, of course, but then he'd have taunted Billy with it, waved it around and sneered at Billy's keepsake. In fact, he'd gone off home quite politely, even praising Billy when Mrs Pawsey mentioned his latest football triumphs.

Alan was his best friend; he wasn't the sort of person who took things that didn't belong to him and he'd never, never take Billy's most special possession, even for fun.

Mother might take the photo, thinking a sabre wasn't the sort of thing he should look at, but then surely she would have said something critical like, 'It's disappointing that you want to spend your time looking at weapons.'

Mr Pawsey – if he'd been moving the bed or taking the mattress off – might not have realised the picture was special, might even have thrown it away! That would be dreadful, for then it would never come back. It would be truly lost.

Mrs Pawsey might have accidentally shifted something when she changed his sheets. But then why wouldn't she have given it to him? He thought back to the first time he'd hidden it there. It was after his first night at the Pawseys. Mrs Pawsey had asked if he had a comforter, a teddy or a blanket. He'd told her that he had something special and he might show her one day. But he never had! She'd shown him her special picture after Uncle Frank had died, she'd trusted him and shown him it in her bedroom, the picture of Gordon. He'd never shown her his picture in return although he had always trusted her really tremendously. There just hadn't been a time when the subject of sabres came up. Was Mrs Pawsey so disappointed that he hadn't shown her his secret that she'd taken it away to teach him a lesson?

Without the shashka to hold, he was alone against all enemies. He put his arms around his middle. His insides fluttered horribly. Everything felt very shaky, especially not knowing who had taken the picture away. He sidled downstairs. How best to ask?

In the parlour Mr Pawsey was fixing the shove-ha'penny board where the markers had come loose.

'Please, did you ever have to fix my bed, or move it?'

Mr Pawsey looked mystified. 'Your bed? Move it? No, my lad. Far as I'm concerned that bed's as fixed as my own. There for good, see.'

'I just wondered if anything had fallen out, any time?'

'Fallen out? What you on about, lad? Have you been jumping on the mattress and broken sommat on it?'

'No.' This was going wrong and it was obvious that Mr Pawsey knew nothing about any picture. It would be even more difficult asking Mrs Pawsey, especially as it was more likely her. He moved slowly into the sitting room where she was struggling with her knitting again.

'What's up, lovey?'

'I've lost something. I wondered if you'd found it? It was in a secret place in my room.'

'What sort of thing would that be?'

'A picture. A photo, in an envelope. I did mean to show you, but it isn't of a person, you see, and . . .'

'No, dear. I haven't seen any picture. Tuesday I cleaned your room and I haven't been in there since. When did you last see it?'

He hung his head. 'I look at it most days.'

The sick feeling was worse. He didn't want to think about what was obvious. Kenneth, so angry about Dwaine. Billy had stayed out in the garden after tea, and Kenneth had stayed in. He must have spent the time up here, searching for something to take or spoil. A photo of a sabre would be far more interesting to him then boots. He'd have lots of questions about it. Would he tear it up out of spite? Would he ever give it back? What could Billy do to persuade him?

Mrs Pawsey clicked her teeth. 'That's a shame your picture's missing, Billy. Perhaps it will turn up.'

'Was Kenneth in my room when I was feeding the chickens and collecting the pig swill?'

She kept on knitting. 'I reckon as he was. He wasn't down here with your mother.'

Billy didn't need to say any more. He knew it was Kenneth's punishment for bringing Dwaine into Aunty's life. He went to the scullery and sat by the dogs. Noah licked his knees and Japhet put his head against Billy's side.

He couldn't tell Mrs Pawsey how important the shashka was. A boy of eleven holding a photo to make himself feel safe! It would seem dreadfully silly. The only person he could complain to was Alan who knew the whole story and what the shashka meant. But how had Kenneth known that he had anything special or where to search for it? It couldn't just be luck. He'd never ever taken out the shashka when Kenneth was even in the house, had he?

Billy sat on the stairs, his head in his hands, thinking back through all the visits. Then he sat up with a jerk. There had been one time. The night Kenneth stayed, the night after Uncle Frank died. The time when there had been the terrible crying, Billy had pulled out the shashka and waved it to and fro, lending its power to Kenneth. Surely, Kenneth hadn't been watching him even then?

That night, Billy didn't find it easy to sleep. It was the first time that he'd had to sleep without his shashka on guard under his mattress. He'd had it from the very first day he arrived at the Pawseys'. Thank goodness he'd taken Mr Durban's letter out of the envelope when he'd found the hiding place to keep with other letters. At least Kenneth wouldn't have any hint about where he'd got the photograph, or who had given it to him.

When he got to school, he told Alan straight away. Alan was quite clear what had to be done. 'You must face him with it.'

'They're not even coming over much now because of Mother's job. It might be six weeks before their next visit, and even then he might decide not to come. He's got good reason not to! By now he could have binned it, or torn it up.'

'You could phone him. Phone your mother and get your Aunty to go through his things.'

'She wouldn't. Even if she did, how can I explain what I've lost? I'd have to say where I got it, and then Kenneth will know about Mr Durban and the whole thing. It'll be awful. As it is, when we're back in Wandsworth he's going to want to go where I go, and know who I know.'

Alan made a fist and crossed it over Billy's fist. 'Rotten business. I'll help if I can.'

Billy hunched his shoulders and followed Alan into school. There was no way round the problem. He'd have to wait until he saw Kenneth next. He'd get him away from the house and have the whole thing out. If only Kenneth was a German, he could kill him and no one would mind.

Meanwhile, he'd be like a soldier without armour, a Cossack without his horse, Kenneth without his art.

CHAPTER SIXTEEN

April 11th 1943

Cheese ration to be cut to 3oz per week

Alan and Billy had both learned to knit now and a hated job was easier if they did it together. They were as fast as Mrs Pawsey. They all sat in the parlour with the wireless on. There was pretty miserable stuff on the news. Just as the allies were getting some successes abroad, the rationing was getting worse.

Mr Pawsey seemed to mind it the most. 'This'll be the third cut this year. Goodness me, we thought as we were badly off in January when it was ten ounces, and worse in February when it was seven! Three ounces! Ha — one bite, an' it'll be gone!'

Mrs Pawsey always took things in her stride. 'They've let us have another pint of milk instead, so that'll be for making butter and cheese.'

'Curds and whey at the Manor, I bet,' Alan groaned. 'We already get it at school dinners and I hate it.'

'Now, now. We have to think - it's better than our boys are getting in the trenches.'

Billy started knitting faster at the thought. Soldiers needed socks more than anything.

Alan's father was an officer working in communications, but that didn't seem to help Alan. He hadn't had a letter for months. 'My father might be a prisoner of war and not get *anything* to eat.'

Mrs Pawsey put a comforting hand on his. 'No, Alan. You'd have heard if he was a POW. They're allowed to write letters home as long as they don't say where they are. Ronnie's brother is a POW and I know his mother gets letters.'

'An' even them as has become prisoners, there's that Geneva Convention. It's the rule - prisoners of war have to be treated right, see.' Mr Pawsey nodded at Alan.

Billy couldn't imagine Dad as a prisoner of war. It was easier to think of him in a Nissan hut, probably teaching the others what to do. 'My father doesn't write much and then he usually quotes things. *Best foot forward*, and that. He always quotes sayings by famous people, like dead writers or even Romans. I don't know what he means half the time. When I think I do, I get it wrong.'

Kenneth accompanied Mother to the Pawseys next visit. This time he came up the lane with a long decorated jacket and no sleeves that fitted over his ordinary clothes. It was very foreign-looking, and when Kenneth got near, the decorations turned out to be sewn flowers and leaves. He looked flipping stupid.

'Like my artist's jacket? Mrs Shawditch found it at the church fête and thought it would be just right for me.'

Billy didn't answer. Did Kenneth really think he'd forgotten about the missing picture?

'Shame about that American ship going down with all hands, isn't it? Full of GIs, it was.'

Kenneth was trying to rattle him. Dwaine's regiment had all been flown out, so they wouldn't be on any ship.

Mother breezed indoors with a case full of woollens and cast off clothes. 'Some woollies to unravel and some of these men's clothes will fit Billy, or can be altered, Mrs Pawsey. The rest will find good homes, I'm sure. I must say our vicarage is quite rich in clothing materials.'

She was flushed and cheerful, full of stories about her garage job.

'It seems to be suiting you well,' Mrs Pawsey remarked.

'Oh yes. Now that Kenneth can take himself to school and choir, and Jill is settled in nursery school, I'm much freer. Freer to work, don't you know?' and her laugh trilled down the hall.

Billy tried to get Mother to one side, but Kenneth kept picking up something for her, or sorting her piles of clothes so that his head was always between Billy's and Mother's. Billy's clenched fists itched to grasp hold of Kenneth and get some answers about his shaska picture. 'We'll go down to the field, Kenneth. There's something I need to show you.'

Kenneth looked pleased at first, as if Billy had made him a present, but then as Billy marched smartly down past the pig sty, the chicken house, the coops and towards the horse's field, his expression became wary.

It didn't matter. Billy wanted him to be uneasy, to wonder what was coming, a football challenge, a beautiful plant to paint or some baby animals.

There was a shed with old farming tools not far from the horse and this was the spot Billy had chosen in all the weeks he had been waiting for this moment. He leant against the door and crossed his arms, partly to stop himself hitting out.

'Is there something you need to tell me, Kenneth?'

Kenneth hesitated. There was nowhere for him to sit or lean without standing right close to Billy. His expression became sly. 'Are you sure you want me to tell you, old thing?'

Billy's muscles tensed from the top of him to his feet. Had the blighter torn his photo up? 'You'd better come out with it,' he said through his teeth.

Kenneth swept one foot over the other and rested it on its toe, his foreign jacket billowing out behind him in the wind. He put one hand over his chin as if he had a beard to stroke.

Billy leant forward and grasped Kenneth's shirt collar. 'You have something of mine, haven't you? Something that you took, stole, from my bedroom after snooping around last time you were over here.'

Kenneth raised an eyebrow and tried to shake his neck free of Billy's hold. 'Have I? And what might that be, pray?'

'Stop talking in that soppy voice with stupid choirboy words.'

'Then I can't answer your query if I'm not allowed to talk.' He tried again to wrest himself free.

Billy held on more firmly. 'I had a secret place in my bedroom, it's not secret now and I shan't use it again, but I had something hidden there and after your visit, it was gone.'

'Oh dear. Tragic. What was it now — a colouring page, a set of pretty scraps?'

'You know jolly well,' Billy gave a shake to each word.

'Remind me.'

'A photograph.'

'Ah yes. Let go and we'll discuss it.'

Billy let go, and strode a few paces to and fro in front of Kenneth, breathing heavily. Would the rotten beast have torn it up?

'Let's see, now. If I did have a little snap safely amongst my treasures, what might it be worth if you wanted it back? You do want it back, do you, or should I bin it with the other rubbish?'

'Why are you doing this, Kenneth? Why are you so beastly all the time? What's *wrong* with you?'

Kenneth's face lost its superior smirk and his eyes hardened. 'I think you know. People who interfere in other people's lives deserve to be punished.' He turned swiftly, pushing his face into Billy's, 'Don't they?'

Billy pushed first Kenneth's chest to move his face from his, then his back, just hard enough to unbalance his pose. Kenneth wobbled and couldn't prevent a couple of running steps. 'Oh, it's going to be fisticuffs, now, is it? All about a silly little sword. Shall we call Jill to be referee?'

Billy gave him another push and started striding back to the house. Firstly he needed to check with Mother about Uncle Ted and *mental problems*. Secondly, now that Kenneth had admitted stealing the photo, it should be possible to shame him into returning it.

Kenneth walked behind him. 'You could get it back by telling me where you got it and why it's important.'

Billy slowed his stride. Of course Kenneth would want to know that, and anything else he could get out of Billy. But if he told Kenneth, if he even told Mother what Kenneth had taken, he'd have to go on to explain why he had it. At the moment, Kenneth didn't know. That was obvious because he'd called it a *sword*. He gritted his teeth. Best to keep things that way. He strode on and left Kenneth to guess what he would do next.

Indoors, Kenneth took out his sketch book and began drawing the three Toby jugs on the dining room mantlepiece. Mother would still be in hearing distance.

Billy said loudly, 'So you admit stealing my picture, Kenneth?'

Kenneth outlined the handle of the fat coachman jug. 'Sorry?'

Billy said it again, more loudly.

'I've no idea what you're talking about. You've lost something, have you?'

'What is it you've lost, Billy?' Mother called.

Billy leant against the wall, outside the open dining room door. He'd looked forward to saying, *It's all right, Kenneth's admitted stealing my picture*, and then everyone exclaiming so that Kenneth had to hand it back, looking sheepish and guilty. But if he had to explain what the picture was, and whose it was, and why he'd been given it, was too high a price to pay.

The tomato-coloured jacket with its fancy stitching lay across the chair next to Kenneth. How would he like losing that? Suppose it went missing, stuffed behind the straw in the pig pen, given to the clothes collection at the church hall? But then he'd be as bad as Kenneth, a liar, a thief, or even worse, if he damaged it. And sure and sure, Kenneth would still have the photograph, ready to wave in Billy's face on the right occasion. He might even have the cheek to pretend he was just keeping it safe. He always kept himself looking as if he was in the right.

All in all, better to let Kenneth keep the photograph, not knowing what it truly was, until he forgot all about it.

Billy had been without his picture for so long, managed without it so long, that if he could just wait till the war ended, he could see the real shashka, and not just its picture. He strode on down to stroke the dogs, and then to the kitchen where he was due to peel potatoes.

If he was at home, he could at least go to Boots library to find pictures of sabres in one of the encyclopaedias. Here there was no library apart for the small private one in the town. The school had only a few battered books on the headmaster's bookcase, apart from the small pile of Beacon readers.

Billy found Alan in the lane next day struggling along pushing a pram overloaded with bags of paper for re-cycling.

'I'll help you with that.'

'Thanks. It'd help if this pram had four wheels!' It was Alan's turn to take all the scrap paper to the tin shed on Broad Street.

Billy took the corner of the pram hood, holding in the paper and keeping the pram from tipping to one side. It was a good chance to offload all he had to tell Alan about Kenneth's latest.

'I did confront him. I could've bashed him, but I didn't. He admitted it, you know, but indoors when Mother was listening, he pretended he didn't know what I was talking about.'

Alan nodded, listening sympathetically as Billy explained why he couldn't go further. 'Listen, I've found something super for you. It'll cheer you up. Come up to the Manor when we've finished this.'

Billy began to feel better. It was good having someone to tell who knew the whole story and understood. Perhaps Alan had some goodies to share out of a parcel from his mother.

They dumped the pram load in the shed and turned the high wooden catch so that little kids couldn't get inside.

'Race you to the Manor,' and Alan took off at speed.

They slowed down and caught their breath as they got to the Manor's side entrance.

'We have to wash our hands first, and then I'll show you why.'

Upstairs, but only on the first floor, the arched area that led to the huge mahogany door was empty of nuns and everyone else. 'I am allowed, don't worry.'

Alan led him through the door and up to another. When he pushed that open, Billy couldn't help gasping. It was full of books, up to the ceiling and around all four walls. A little staircase with a post stood beneath a pair of glass doors that someone had left open. For a few moments, they both walked round each wall in turning, looking up and down the millions of books.

Alan was proud. 'This is the Manor library, and only two of the nuns and the land girl are allowed in here, and that's because they look after it.'

'But who lets you?'

'It's only recent. Remember Rachel? She wasn't much good at the farming work, but Mr Partington senior who owns the Manor and lives in this private wing, heard that she had a degree in history. He said she could look after the books and just do the packing of fruit and veg.'

'So she lets you come in and read all the books? Whee. Why just you?'

'Rachel's specially nice to me. It's because my mother's office did something that helped her father. It was to do with hiding him or getting him away from one place and off to do war work. I don't know, I'm not allowed to know. I just know he's alive and she didn't expect him to be. When Kenneth took your sabre picture, I asked her to see if there was one in here so I could show you.'

Billy grasped Alan's arm. 'Really, truly? Did she find one?'

'No, but she kept on looking and last week she did find this.' He pointed to his right. 'Now you see why we had to have clean hands. This is valuable.' A book with faded maroon covers lay closed on one of the padded seats that surrounded the room beneath the bookcases. 'Look at this! *Classic stories from the Russian Empire*. Shame there aren't any pictures.' He picked up the book and carefully opened it where a cardboard strip marked the place.

Billy saw small print on yellowing paper, a line drawing halfway down the page. He started reading, and perched with Alan on the seat, the book placed between them.

The new Cossack, strong and dark, mounted his horse, ready to embark on a raid in a distant land. Beneath him, the kazachii ybraynii sedlo, a saddle decorated with the booty of Grandfather's previous raids and pillages. Now his old life of idle freedom was behind him together with his adolescence and he must accept his responsibilities as a member of the group. Thus he would be identified as a man.

Last night, the songs round the campfire had described the possibilities of death and glorified the brutality of war. Death would be an honour! He threw out his chest. He was young, death just could not happen. A sword that managed to kill him would be honoured with the name Shashka lixodaika, the name which identified it as legendary for downing an invincible Cossack warrior.

He already had a shashka himself. He put one hand on its hilt as the sun hinted a presence on the horizon. He sniffed the air, fresh with the scent of feral cat, ripe for the hunt.

If he was the grandson of a rabble-rouser, one of the motley escapees of the political and penal systems of Polish Ukraine seeking the freer frontier, he was, above all, a Cossack. His grandfather's generation had developed military prowess to defend themselves against raids, and thus his father had been raised. Like other Cossacks, Father had learned a nomadic lifestyle to avoid enemies. He lived in a constant readiness to fight. So impossible was it to settle, farm and feed themselves this way, they depended on fishing, hunting but mostly pillage. The spoils displayed on Grandfather's saddle symbolized the honour of a Cossack warrior.

He had only known his father part-time, for Cossacks must leave their wives and children the moment duty called to embark on raids. But during those times at home before his honourable death, Father was memorable. He starred in all aspects of Cossack culture – the haunting folk songs, wild athletic dancing and dramatic, aggressive horse-riding.

Eventually the Tsar employed the fearless Cossacks to defend Russia's borderlands and it was in such a way that Father died. His compatriots brought

*him to the family for his final hours, enough time for
him to croak his wish to his only son.*

*'Take this shashka, son of mine, and let it only
leave your hands in those of your son, or in death, of
a noble warrior as brave as you must become. Mind
its path, protect it well. It will inflict the most terrible
wounds.'*

*After his father's death, he put it to one side, had
wild times, passionate times, ruined his mother's
hopes of his heroism then sped back to renew them.*

*And now, the camp fires dead and his comrades
mounted beside him, it was time to ride forth. Ahead
of him, twenty years and many skirmishes on, would
be the Great War. But for the Shashka, a much longer
history awaited its terrible potential.*

When he reached the last words, Billy's eyes
stretched wide as he looked at Alan. 'Whoa!'

'See. The story's like Mr Durban's, except it wasn't
his father who gave him the shaska.'

'Isn't there any more to the story? I want to know
what happens next.'

'Rachel says these are extracts.'

'Oh. Can I borrow the book?'

'Course not. We can only look at it here. No-one's
allowed to take anything out of the library. They trust
me to come in and not touch anything behind glass. I
think it's only because of Rachel, and Mr Partington
being at the ceremony when we got rewarded for
saving Sally.'

'But I saved Sally, so I'd be allowed in.'

'You're not a Manor vaccie, though.'

It was a difficult book to read, and Billy hadn't understood all the words, couldn't even read one or two of them. 'But I need to read it again. Well, lots of times.'

'When I'm with you, it's probably all right. Anyway, does it make up, a bit, for losing your photograph?'

'Rather. It was spiffing of you to find it. Well, of Rachel too. And I'm glad about her father, if that was really true about Jews.' He sat further back on the seat and read right the way through again. He didn't need a picture of a shaska so much now. He could just think over this story as many times as he liked.

'Look here. *On into the Great War,* Alan. Hey, that means this story's before the time of the Cossack who gave it to Mr Durban! Suppose it was the same shashka!'

Alan gave a little shudder. 'If it was . . . it says it has a longer terrible history after that.'

CHAPTER SEVENTEEN

12th June 1944

US troops liberate Rome

It was jolly hot. Billy plodded beside Alan as they made their three-mile walk home from the secondary school. He pulled his satchel off his shoulder. 'Phew. I'm flipping well going to rest in a minute.'

At the grassy hill-top leading down to the village, they flopped down and chucked their heavy satchels to one side. They lay on their backs in the sunshine watching the buzzards wheel. The four fields around and below them shone blue, baby blue, Mother would call it.

'You see all that flax? It's the same colour as an awful buster suit I had to wear when I was small. It made me itch all over.'

'Flax? I wondered what it was. Those fields weren't all blue last year.' He pulled a dandelion out of the ground beside him and chewed the end.

'Mr Pawsey says the farmers will be glad when they're allowed to change crops, flax needs so many workers. They haven't got enough land girls. They need us boys. You don't even go up to the farm although you're *sinewy and spry.*' He laughed and poked Alan in the ribs. That's what Mr Finlay called you, and it's about right.'

'You're a head taller. I'm better delivering the groceries. It's hard enough work.' Alan blew dandelion seeds to the wind. He said, 'We won't be doing any of that stuff when we get home. How long've we been here now?'

Billy thought a moment. 'We got here August '40 the second time, wasn't it? Or was it before?'

'End of July, I think. No, I'd just started junior school, so it was early September. That makes it - nearly four years. And if we add the first time, 1939, when we were at Mrs Youldon's, we've spent a good third of our lives here.'

'You reckon? It feels like half of it.'

'It was my father pointed it out when he wrote. Now he's safely back in his regiment, he says he really resents how much the war has cost him in time, let alone anything else. I bet he can't wait to get home.'

'I can't imagine living in London now; here feels like home.'

'Not for me. I can't wait for the war to end. It's more like a boarding school, lined up in camp beds in that attic room. I'll be flipping glad to get my own room back and all to myself.'

'Yeah, lucky blighter.' Billy sighed. 'Think of me sharing mine with Kenneth.'

'It's only fair. You've been lucky these years up at the Pawseys, a room to yourself.'

Billy lay back and looked at the plain blue sky. He had been lucky. Now that the allies had some successes, war might end. There'd be no bombing, no killings, no sending soldiers to foreign lands — but without war, he'd lose this life. There'd be no farmhouse, no dogs, no pigs, no Pawseys. No Alan.

He sat up, slowly. 'When this lot's all over, you and me'll still be able to get together, won't we? It's not that far from Wandsworth to Thornton Heath.'

'You can bus it. I remember going to Wandsworth when the new council building opened. It's a 109 isn't it?'

A couple of terrier dogs appeared, barking and leaping at each other. Billy whipped out his camera from his satchel. He lay down and snapped upwards. 'I'm going to need an album soon, I've got so many photos now — thanks to your mother getting those 120s.'

'Thanks to those Belgians working with her. Can't you ask for an album for your birthday?'

'I didn't get far with her over the boots, did I? If Kenneth hadn't got me some, Mother would never have got round to the idea.'

'You're going to grow out of those boots soon.'

'Already have. Mr Pawsey split the backs for me so I can still wear them. They do hurt a bit, but not as much as playing in plimsolls.'

Alan grinned, 'So a hard choice, chum, new boots or album.'

'Won't get either. Mother won't see the need for a photograph album. She thinks photos are for the mantelpiece in silver frames.' Screwing up his eyes, he could visualise the ones at home in Wandsworth. They were on the bookcase in the garden room; himself as a toddler, two of Jill in frills, and the wedding photo. Both Mother and Dad looked stern, almost as if they knew a war would start a few years later.

'Those aren't the sort of photographs I'm interested in taking. I want real life action, people doing things, not just standing and looking. If I can get photos of exciting or interesting things like . . .'

Alan was lying full length, his head on his satchel.

'...like one of yourself pulling Sally from the water that time!'

Billy grinned. 'Yes, you bet.' That would be good, just so that people always know he'd really done that, so that he'd know himself.

A droning in the distance made them both jump up.

Alan shouted upwards, 'Hey - yippee! A heck of a lot of 'em.' A lead plane came into view through a sliver of cloud and then the whole formation. 'There must be a hundred, two hundred!'

They whooped and leapt up, waving, watching the vast bank of planes come over then fade into the distance.

'What about that!' Alan peered at the white trails. 'Some German town is going to cop it tonight.'

Billy shivered. 'Suppose all the people there want revenge? They'd put iron helmets on and pour over the Channel, all up the beaches and along the lanes, coming for us.'

'Daft! You know what happens to people when there's bombing. No chance of them going anywhere.'

Billy gave him a push. 'So! Just saying, *suppose* . . . '

They watched till sound of the planes had faded to a murmur. Billy said, 'Your mother'll come for you one day soon, and then we'll know war's nearly over.'

Alan punched the air. 'We'll have toys and sweets and lights in the street at night and meat and ice-cream and no queuing.'

Billy shrugged, blinking hard. That seemed far away. 'Can't think what it'll be like now in Wandsworth. Angela said there's loads of it bombed.' He kicked a pile of pebbles into a straight line.

Alan leant over and lined them all up into the formation all the planes had just made. There was no sight of them now. He jumped to his feet and shouldered his satchel. 'Come on, forward to the downward path!'

This was their usual game. Billy took the hill at a run and they reached the bottom, and the edge of the village side by side. 'Come to mine, then we'll go to the Youldons after tea, okay?'

When they got as far as the horse's field, they saw Mr and Mrs Pawsey pulling rhubarb. Billy shouted, 'Did you see all those planes? Alan'n me saw them, hundreds of them.'

'No missing'em, was there?' Mr Pawsey said slowly. 'We're on the offensive, no doubt about that. We's'll have to wait and see what happens now.'

They were eating bread and dripping and Mrs Pawsey was topping up the tea-pot when the telephone rang. She wasn't in the hall long.

'There's news for you, Billy. Your mother's had a telegram from your Nanny. Your Uncle Ted has been invalided home. He's in a military hospital, recuperating.'

All the crumbs fell off Billy's lap as he leapt up. 'Uncle Ted! He's my favourite person. Recuperating? That means getting better, doesn't it?' He whooped and whistled around the room.

'It's wonderful news to know he's safe, dear, even though he's injured. The receiver's still off. Do you want to talk to Kenneth? It's him who's phoned.'

Kenneth. All these weeks since the business of the shaska and Kenneth had only come that once, probably to avoid trouble. Now something wonderful was happening it was Kenneth giving the news. *Billy's* news. He rushed into the hall. His hand felt damp on the telephone receiver as he squeezed it tight. 'Kenneth?'

'Long time, eh, Billy? Aunty Marcia though't you'd be pleased to hear this, so I said I'd phone. Your Uncle's back - in a hospital, in Sussex.'

Was it true? Kenneth wouldn't dare make that up. That very thing he'd been aching for, Uncle Ted safe in England. *Hospital.* What sort of injured? He jolly well wasn't going to ask Kenneth. It was too bad how he always knew everything first.

And there was the secret matter of the shaska between them. Did Kenneth really think that a gap in visits could make Billy forget?

'Pass me over to Mother, Kenneth,' he said, trying not to let the quiver in his voice sound.

'But . . .'

'I need to speak to her.' He couldn't let Kenneth be top dog.

Mother came to the phone. 'Hello dear. Yes, good news. Nanny was informed yesterday. She says that Uncle Ted is quite safe and in a military hospital.'

'But what's his injuries? Will he be better soon?'

'I don't have much information, Billy. We'll see. The main thing is, he's home.'

Alan stood up and clapped him on the shoulder. 'See, chums stick together. News from my father last month, from your Uncle Ted today.'

Sickeningly, just when Billy wanted Mother to himself to find out all possible details about Uncle Ted, Kenneth decided to visit with her. This time, he had his science exercises under his arm. Each page held a different topic, diagrams and notes in tiny neat writing.

'Science, old thing. Even if they get you to a secondary school, I doubt if you'll do much of that. It won't be for proper studying, more for teaching you how to hold a block of wood or metal, I expect. That place probably doesn't even own a bunsen burner!'

Billy put one hand in the centre of Kenneth's bony chest and pushed him firmly backwards into the yard. 'Stay there with your rotten pieces of science notes. I'm going to talk to Mother.'

Kenneth stepped forward again. 'I shouldn't.'

'Why?' Billy crossed his arms over his chest.

'Well, you see,' Kenneth leant forward as if he was explaining something basic to Jill, 'Aunty Marcia hasn't told you, Billy, but your uncle's got mental problems and he'll be in hospital for some time.'

Billy's arms uncrossed and fell down to his sides.

Kenneth had his superior expression, although he hadn't even GOT a second uncle and if Dad was really now 'Dad' to him, Kenneth hadn't even got *one* uncle. 'Sad, isn't it? Mental problems. I wonder if it will run in the family.'

Billy took the four steps that separated him from Kenneth. From here, he could actually look down on him, and he did. 'I shall check with Mother.'

'Do. Although, that's less than kind. Madness of her brother? An embarrassment to her, probably.'

Billy's need for his precious support surged back. *Take this shaska son of mine, never let it leave your hands.* 'Never mind that. If *you* had an Uncle Ted, you'd be proud of his army service.' It wasn't a kind thing to say, reminding Kenneth that his father hadn't served, and Billy's father had, as well as Uncle Ted. It

233

stopped Kenneth saying any more so Billy strode to the parlour and asked Mother straight for news of Uncle Ted.

She swallowed. 'Yes, dear, that is true. Uncle Ted needs treatment for his nerves.'

'What nerves, if he's not in the war? Why can't he go home to Nanny's and be looked after there?'

'It takes time and — doctors' help.'

Kenneth had followed behind, close enough for his breath to stream warm on the back of Billy's neck. 'You can't rush these things, Billy,' he said in a kind voice, as though he was a nurse and Billy was small and ignorant.

'No. But we don't need to worry. Ted only had minor injuries otherwise. He might be to rights in time for the end of the war. Who knows.'

Billy left Kenneth in the parlour and dragged along the hall, sliding his fingers along the dado rail. There never seemed to be any good news that didn't have bad behind it. He took refuge in the kitchen.

'Let's not have that long face, Billy lad. Be thankful your Uncle is in one piece,' comforted Mrs Pawsey. 'Many aren't.'

Billy nodded. It was far better to have Uncle Ted with mental problems than in many pieces, like soldiers who were blown up by cannons and bombs.

'Be proud of your Uncle Ted. He'm just a wounded soldier. Minor injuries.' Mr Pawsey said.

It was time to feed the pigs. Billy went to the back lobby, picked up the swill bucket and started off across the yard. He wouldn't let Kenneth's sneers get to him. He started marching, just as Uncle Ted had taught him before the war even started. He hummed to the marching rhythm, *Pack up your troubles in your old kit bag and smile, smile, smile.* He imagined Uncle Ted, smiling, his kit bag holding his few minor injuries.

There would be lots of football matches during the next months and when Uncle Ted got out of hospital, he'd tell him about all of them, and with Uncle Ted around, no-one would be listening or caring about Kenneth.

CHAPTER EIGHTEEN

May 7th 1945

Germany surrenders to the Russians

Billy was lying on his stomach trying to get a good picture of the pigs feeding through a hole in their wall. He'd learned a lot about photography since having his first film. As well as talking with Mr Pawsey about photographs in some books which sat on the shelves upstairs, the science teacher had offered to help him on Tuesdays after detentions. He knew how photographs were developed and how different degrees of light changed your snaps. He'd given Billy a fat book full of information. The Pawseys made a special place on their bookshelf to keep it safe until Billy went back to London.

And that was near, not just a hope like in the hymns they'd been singing in school. All the victories and the wild events, like Mussolini's capture had made everyone very jolly. They'd had a wonderful May Day with a full maypole, and the very next day just as Big Ben sounded on the wireless, the church bells rang out nearly drowning the announcer's voice, 'London calling. Here is a news flash. The German radio has just announced that Hitler is dead. I repeat that. Hitler is dead.' It was a moment Billy couldn't ever forget. Mrs Pawsey whooped, Mr Pawsey whooped and they grabbed each other round the waist and danced around.

Billy almost couldn't move with shock. Dead! He'd wished for it, and even German officers had wished for it. They'd tried to assassinate him but failed, so it seemed as if Hitler could never die and now he was really, really gone for ever. He'd looked at Mr and Mrs Pawseys' beaming faces and said, 'We haven't got an enemy now, have we?'

On the street everyone was cheering, but then he heard jeers too. Not far behind him was Des on his crutches, both feet blown off in Belgium, his mother and two old men next to him in a small crowd.

'Yeah, who believes the German report "Died fighting bravely to the last", what? Not me, for one.'

The huddle around him shouted agreement. 'Too right. Wish I'd been the one to stick a rifle down his throat.'

Billy turned round to stare. Those people looked horrible, their noses turned nostrils upwards, all the lines deepening round their mouths, their worst teeth showing. Everyone hated Hitler. Billy did too. Hitler was the one who'd started all the fighting but when people wanted to punish, they were very ugly. This was the face you would wear when you felt like killing someone.

He hurried across the square to the group who were cheering. A lady gave him a little union jack on a stick and he jogged with it to the Manor. The side garden was full of bobbing heads where all the children were outside jumping and leaping around. Billy saw Alan and joined in. They clapped each other on the back, yelling, 'Told you, told you.' No one did much work for they had to get ready for a victory day.

Mother had been too busy to visit for a month, so another of Kenneth's phone calls updated Billy. His voice sounded grating.

'We're having a splendid do here for VE day.'

'So are we.' Billy was going on thirteen. He'd dealt with elementary school toughs, he'd starred on the football field. He could talk back to Kenneth. 'The Grange will do something super and we lot are going to go up there soon to get everything ready. You can stay at the Vicarage and say prayers with the vicar.'

'I'll tell them you said that.'

'I bet there's something about *sneaking* in the Bible, so you'll cop it if you do.' Billy put the telephone down and swaggered down the hall. It was good to have the last word.

He put the camera back around his neck and scuffed his shoes down the path towards the chickens. One of them was about to transfer from being fed to being food. He wanted to give it a good last meal.

'Reckon as it's a one-time event.' MrPawsey commented. It would be criminal to be had up for it. Roast chicken, tomorrow night, Missus if you please.'

'I'm glad I'm here for VE Day.'

Mr Pawsey took the pipe from his mouth. 'So are we. So are we. Got to be truthful, our Billy, we're dreading the day when you have to go back home.'

'Now, now, what a silly thing to say,' Mrs Pawsey corrected him. 'Aren't we very happy the country's safe enough for Billy and all the evacuees to go back home. His family should be together again, you dotty old man. Billy, it's only right you should be at home where you belong.'

He didn't answer. Gordon couldn't be here, where he belonged. Billy was here now, had been here for ages. Didn't he belong here now? It was something he didn't like thinking about.

When he went to Mrs Youldon's, she said the same sort of thing as Mr Pawsey had. 'I know I've got to be glad about the end of war, but, you know, Mary going to America, you going to London, me staying here without either of you.' She looked very small, as if the piles of extra laundry would swallow her up.

Billy looked at the children. How would Timmy feel? He'd been following everything Billy did for the last four years, and Sally had been his shadow since her rescue. He felt the pull of her wherever he went. He felt the pull of his wish to stay, whichever of the Youldons or Pawseys he thought of.

He had to be glad. It wasn't just *Keep your sunny side up, up.* 'It's the party tomorrow, Mrs Youldon. The Manor's got jellies and iced biscuits and all the nuns are making hundreds of sandwiches. You'll have lots to eat. Alan and I have got to help putting out all the tables and chairs and the land girls are putting up streamers.'

If war was over, people wouldn't be killed, Dad would come home and help with Uncle Ted. They'd be able to eat proper meat, sweets and get things like pencils and 120 film. The end of war would be a good thing.

There was dog barking from the back of the house.
'Best shut 'em in with all this excitement,' Mr Pawsey said.

'Come on, Billy! Time to go.' Alan was calling up from the yard.

Billy ran to the front door. Mrs Pawsey, dressed all in red, white and blue, almost pushed him out of the door. 'Go on ahead. We're coming after you.'

Alan raced him up to the main street where everyone was gathering. A horde of boys pulled them towards the line of trestle tables Billy had earlier helped to lay. They were covered with white sheets and red and blue streamers with Union Jacks fastened to the table legs at each corner.

After a lot of shouting and laughing and cheering, everyone was in their chosen seats. John sat on one side of him, Alan the other and the noisy twins opposite. There were some speeches and a lot more cheering, then the feast began.

'Sandwiches first, you lot,' ordered a large woman presiding over the food. 'Cakes and jellies after. Hold out your cups and I'll pour your drink.'

A hundred hands wavered over the pile of food and like the rest, Billy filled his mouth. Someone put a silly paper hat on his head, someone else waved a rattle in his face. A young woman filled his beaker with weak orange squash.

For this moment all that mattered was the thrill of knowing the war really was over and sharing that wonderful fact with all the village.

The twins had their mouths full, but open as usual. John passed the biscuits and said, 'No more war! You realise we're now witnessing the end to all that beastliness.'

Billy stared at John, who looked almost old enough to be called up. He was talking rather like Kenneth.

The noise of the celebrations went on long after dark. Everyone had shouted and sung themselves so hoarse that, despite himself, Billy fell into bed, too tired to dwell on what was going to happen next.

In the next weeks Billy ran round the village snapping everything he thought might change, taking people in their daily tasks as though they might disappear in a cloud of smoke.

He took the camera to school and photographed, from underneath, all the closed desks with their Union Jacks poking up. The helpful science teacher let him photograph in peace. He was marking test papers. They were on eighth-of-a-page slips written both sides (bad luck if your handwriting was large). He had the sort of cough that echoes like a church organ before the tune comes. He was an old man, far too old to be a soldier and probably too old to be a teacher.

'You'll be off to London soon, Wilson. You and your talent. Shame. I warn you, you may not get much attention there – schools'll be so crowded, I predict. Now, I'll find you some photo corners. Place all your best photos in your album carefully. Keep old envelopes for the other snaps – you never know if they're important. Then, when you're ready to leave school, you can take them to show important people what you can do. It's like your evidence, you see. People might book you to photograph their weddings, christenings, family celebrations, that sort of thing. You'll be able to make a living, I'm sure. Better than being a teacher anyway.' He gave a wry smile.

He was too old to keep proper discipline in class. But the boys had some respect for his knowledge.

Billy said, 'It would be good to get respect for my photographs.'

'Indeed, you should, Wilson.'

He could almost see a life ahead. That made a difference. When he ached at the thought of leaving the Pawseys and the Youldons, it helped to look far into the future, beyond life in Wandsworth, which would now be shared with Kenneth and which would be for good. It was very scary. He was needed here, everyone liked him here and they wouldn't have a proper football team in the village without him. It wasn't even as if he would be going back to his Wandsworth school with Miss Johnson and Mr Finlay. Thirteen was too old, so he'd have to go to some secondary or technical school.

His time was going to end here. Name plates were going up on roads, signs were already back on the signposts. He could see how many miles he was from Brighton, from Salisbury, even from London.

Billy went back to his bedroom and sat on the bed, thrusting his hands deep into his quilt. In Wandsworth there would be no dogs to greet him every time he got home from school. There wouldn't be any pigs or hens or fields to hear outside the windows, and he'd be too far away to ever visit Mrs Youldon and the children. His parents just thought of the Pawseys as elderly fosterers and the Youldons as poor folk to avoid. They wouldn't understand that he needed to come back to visit. They wouldn't bring him. When he left here, it would be so very long before he was twenty-one and could decide to catch trains by himself without permission.

When they saw his long face, Mr and Mrs Pawsey told him to think about seeing Nanny and Granddad again. He had to think back four years. He hadn't seen them since the very first night of bombing. He could just remember helping Granddad in the garden and shed, stomping around in his wellies after him, trying to make things with little bits of wood and a tiny hammer that Granddad had given him. He could almost smell the lovely roasts Nanny had made, and nearly remembered her hugs.

'And your Uncle Ted. I expect he'll be out of hospital soon, Billy. Think of that.'

He whistled a few of his cheery tunes, but they didn't seem to work as well as when he was younger. He tried to imagine the hospital helping Uncle so that he could do handstands again and go home to Nanny's and Granddad's. Then they'd all be laughing around their dining table like long ago. Now he was big, Billy might be more nearly one of the men, and let into their conversations. Then of course there was Angela and Mr Durban to see. They'd be pleased he was back, and at last he could hold the shashka once more. Kenneth could keep the photograph, still not knowing what it was. Billy could take his own photographs of the shashka and everything else.

It was best to think of all these things directly the sad feelings came on. It was going to have to happen, this going away. He went to his bedroom. He was going to have to deal with it. It was going to happen tomorrow. His suitcase was packed and stood beside the wardrobe, all ready.

He looked all around. When he was gone and the sheets were taken off his bed, he needed something of himself to stay behind. So he made a guilty cross with his penknife under the mat. He put presents on his bedside table: his first photo of Mr and Mrs Pawsey, his best essay and a bar of chocolate from Dwaine that he'd been saving.

In the morning, Mr and Mrs Pawsey were rather quiet, although determinedly cheerful. Billy could hardly look at them at breakfast. He knew they didn't want him to go. It was best not to say anything because he might start crying. There were three more hours before he was collected for the journey.

He went to the scullery and hid his head in the dogs' backs, pretending to find clumps in their fur. He walked them all around the village for a last look at the familiar lanes and cottages.

A crowd of the lads from the village school were kicking a ball in the middle of the road.

'Billy! C'mon, be goalie.'

But for once he didn't want to. It wasn't worth getting into a game he couldn't continue.

'I'm off back to London soon. Got to get ready,' he said, practising for more difficult goodbyes.

'Yaw, we'll lose our best player. Not fair. Can't you ask your folks if you can stay put?'

He shook his head.

It was time to go down to the Youldons for the very last time. He'd spent his half-crown that Granddad had given him at the very beginning of war. He bought frames for the three prints of his photos for Mrs Youldon, so now she could put them properly on the shelf. He'd bought a skipping rope for Sally, a toy tank for Tim.

He saw them in the distance, talking to Big Ronnie's mother, Sally on one side of Mrs Youldon, Timmy on the other. Suddenly he couldn't face the goodbyes. He could hardly manage his own sadness, the children's would be awful. He went back round the corner to the newsagents and asked for a pen and paper. He wrote his note and left it there with the presents for Mrs Youldon to collect, then he went round to Alan's.

'I've already been down there,' Alan said, smart in a new shirt and slipover with damp, combed hair. 'You can't not go. She's always on about you saving Sally. It's all right for me, Mum's said she'll bring me down here sometimes if I want. But if your mother won't, you've got to say a proper goodbye. Mrs Y. will be sad and she'll think you can't be bothered.' He walked Billy back down the lane. 'Go on.'

Billy walked as slowly as he could. He would just say goodbye and then go. As he went inside the familiar cramped space, he saw with relief that the little ones were out playing with friends. Their mother was piling the ironing up like a wall, while the two side irons heated on the stove. Billy sat hunched on the bench as Mrs Youldon twisted her apron.

'Billy, you're really off then. Oh my, this is awful. I knew it would be.'

'I've left stuff for you at the newsagents.'

She came and gave him a hug. 'You're such a dear.'

He held on to her until he could trust his voice. 'Will you go to America if they ask you?'

She shook her head. 'I'm staying right here until Sally and Timmy are grown, husband or no husband.'

He looked at her. 'But Joe, or someone, might come and ask you.'

'No, Billy. Listen. When the GIs were here I wanted to go out, have some fun, but I'll tell you a secret. I keep thinking Mr Youldon will come back for me. Now the war's over, he'll find out that things he thought he knew – the fine gent up at the Grange – wasn't anything to me. That gent just used to pester me and I couldn't do a thing because I was only an under-maid. I couldn't complain. But Mr Youldon thought I wanted to be with him and waltzed right off before our Sally was born, never even clapped eyes on her. So Timmy lost his Daddy 'n all. Mr Youldon had it wrong. So I'm going to wait right here like I always have, and hope he'll come back.'

Billy leant towards her. 'I hope he does too. Really soon.' He tried to take in her story, but Mr Youldon had never seemed very real. 'When I'm a photographer I'll earn money. Then I'll come down here on the train. I will see you all again, I have to.'

She hugged him again. Her head only came to his shoulder now, although he was the child. 'It's such a long time.'

He didn't ask whether she meant he had been in her life a long time, or would be away a long time. Both were true.

'You'll be too fine to come back. Up there in London.'

He shook his head, wordless, and looked straight at her for the last time. 'Never.' Then he forced himself out of the tiny room into the cloudy light of his last day of evacuation.

Slowly, he meandered back to the Pawseys', now no longer 'home'. Mother had arranged to collect him early afternoon. That was not far off now.

Instead of gloom, Mr and Mrs Pawsey met him with what seemed genuine smiles.

'Billy! You're not going on the train now. Your aunty has gone on it with Kenneth to see his relatives. You'll never guess who's going to come to collect you! Your uncle.'

At first Billy felt a sick thump inside, and then shook his stupid thoughts away. People couldn't come back from the dead. When Mrs Pawsey said 'Uncle', he'd had a sudden image of Uncle Frank rising up in the middle of the front room, showing his arm muscles.

'Your Uncle Ted! Isn't that lovely? He's got a car, don't ask me how, and collected your mother and sister and after their dinner they're coming over for you.'

'He's out of hospital?'

'Yes, all ready to go home and soon he'll be here.'

'Really? Wheeee.' He whizzed round several times, all his sadness mixed with relief.

'You are packed and ready, Billy, aren't you?'

He nodded, then went upstairs to look at his already packed suitcase. Last time he'd used it was when he arrived here on Jed's cart. He slung his precious camera round his neck. Uncle Ted. After all this time and all that longing to see him and then hospital and now he really would see him. He'd see Uncle Ted just as he had to leave the Pawseys. It was like leaping into a pool of marshmallow and ice, sweet and thrilling but chilling and shocking. He so wanted to see Uncle Ted. He so wanted to stay here. Silly fantasies came to his mind like Uncle Ted moving into the Pawseys' home and telling everyone that Billy had to stay there too.

Mrs Pawsey looked at him dithering on the stairs. 'Well, our Billy, no good us being sad. You have to think of all the people, all the things you've missed in Wandsworth, so you'll set off from here looking forward, not looking back.'

He nodded and tried to stop thinking how much he wanted to stay. He'd be seeing Mr Durban. Angela. The shashka would be there in its scabbard just waiting to be drawn out, shining. If it could be magic, waved in the air, brandished, he could make everything, everyone just as he wanted. He'd stay right here and all of them could visit.

'Now, we've a while till your family get here. We'll have some dinner first.'

'I . . . couldn't.'

But when Mrs Pawsey pushed him gently into dinner, he saw that she'd somehow found some of his favourite foods to put on the table: sausage pancakes, cauliflower cheese, apple pie. So he had to eat.

'Had these saved in the back of the larder, specially for you, Billy.'

'But your rations, Mrs Pawsey!'

Mr Pawsey waved a paw. 'You'll be queasy in the car if you don't fill that stomach of yours. Now I've left my specs in the other room so pass me the right things so I don't end up eating the salt and pepper instead of my dinner.'

Billy almost laughed. Then the very last meal, those dreaded last moments with the Pawseys, were filled by Mrs Pawsey talking about Uncle Ted and how the military hospital had put him almost to rights. A soldier friend had lent him a car and someone on the staff had found him some petrol from their own ration. Now he was coming hot foot to take up with all his family where he'd left off.

Hot foot? He must be better.

Billy said, 'Nanny and Granddad will be ever so glad.'

'Reckon they'll be over the moon,' said Mr Pawsey. 'Their only son. Lots haven't been so lucky.'

It was a terrible thought. Mr and Mrs Pawsey hadn't been so lucky. They had lost Gordon and now they were losing Billy, at least until he was grown up.

He thought of his grandparents standing at the door, their welcoming arms out saying, 'Ted!' And then 'Billy!' But would they recognise him now he was the size of a man?

If there was more talk, Bill didn't take it in. It seemed only seconds between his last wonderful mouthful of Mrs Pawsey's food and the barking of the dogs announcing that his family were at the door.

Jill, newly bold, led Uncle Ted in by the hand, a grey-clad Uncle Ted, unsmiling, blinking.

Mother busily talked and greeted, while she organised Billy's belongings.

He tried to take in the reality of Uncle Ted. It was as if he was back from the dead. He was nodding to the Pawseys, standing in the hall with loose trousers and bony wrists. He stared at Billy, the white block of hair highlighting his forehead. He was thin, pale, serious.

Billy stared back, longing for the grin. 'Hello Uncle Ted.'

Mother stepped forward. 'Told you Billy was huge, Ted. Look at him, how am I supposed to look after a boy like him?'

'I'm sure you'll manage a lot better than old folks like us,' Mrs Pawsey bit in, 'and we loved every minute.' She turned away quickly.

Mr Pawsey's glasses were firmly on his nose as he strode forward to Ted with a large outstretched hand. 'So this is one of our heroes? Welcome back, soldier. Here's as hoping you'll settle back home, happy to be with your folks.'

Ted's handshake was listless. 'Hello. Thank you. Hello.' He nodded to left, right and straight ahead, as though trying to take in everyone. He kept blinking as if the lights were too strong, but they weren't even on.

Billy risked an approach. 'You sent me a top that first Christmas of the war, Uncle Ted. It was super. Thanks ever so much.'

Uncle Ted frowned. 'A long time ago. I – yes – I did send that. You're a bit big for tops now?' His voice sounded funny, sort of strangled and perhaps something had happened to his teeth. 'I am trying to get used to everyone, but you all look so different. Baby's a little girl, and you're growing into a man.'

There was a silence while everyone thought what to say.

Uncle Ted was trying hard. 'Do you still like football?'

Billy nodded hard. Would Uncle Ted ever kick a ball to him again or was he too weak? He looked it.

Mrs Pawsey said, 'Oh, he's a wonderful football player. Quite the star of the team here. Have you packed your bravery medal and your newspaper picture, Billy? You must show them to your Uncle Ted. He will be proud.'

Uncle Ted looked confused.

Mrs Pawsey explained. 'He saved a little girl from drowning three years ago. Very brave.'

'You're a hero, then, Billy. More than I am.' Uncle Ted's forehead puckered.

Mother stepped in hurriedly, 'Right everyone, we must be off. Billy – have you said thank you? And of course I must thank you both, Mr and Mrs Pawsey, for having my son. We none of us knew it would be for so long.'

'Not long enough,' Mr Pawsey muttered, but Billy heard.

He nodded to show Mother he had said his thanks. The adults' to-and-fro of thanks and goodbyes, reminders and checks washed over his head as he concentrated on getting his suitcase into the boot of the car. This couldn't be happening, he couldn't be going.

He spotted the bin for the pig swill. 'Just a minute.' He ran to the pig sty for a last look, ignoring Mother's aggrieved call, the 'Billy!' fading as he ran further from the house. The dogs were loose and ran after him, pushing their bodies against his, nosing at his hands for a stroke.

'Look I've got to go,' he whispered. 'Noah, Japhet, I've just got to. I don't want to. Just don't forget me, right?'

He turned to the piglets. 'You'll be pork before long anyway. It's we-have-no-choice for you, too.'

He walked back towards the house treading his boots hard into the mud, so as to leave a set of clear imprints, the dogs at his heels. Mother's complaints filled the silence in his head as she prodded him forwards to the car. 'What are you doing? You've had oodles of time for all that.'

He could hardly look at the Pawseys now the leave-taking was upon him.

'Don't lose your glasses,' he said to one, and 'Your dinners are super,' to the other. He wanted to say how much he'd miss them but no more words would come out and he found himself hustled into the back seat with Jill who was bouncing happily on the folded blankets.

251

'You've been the best young lad we could have wished for, and I hope you find your way back here just as soon as you're old enough,' said Mrs Pawsey in a wobbly voice as she pushed a basket of goodies into his hands.

Mr Pawsey said something too, but it was drowned in the noise of Uncle Ted cranking the starter handle. The engine coughed into life. Uncle Ted slid into the driving seat and slammed the car door. He raised a hand to the waving Pawseys. The car rolled forward and away. A belch of petrol vapour was all Billy saw and smelled as he knelt on the seat to hold the Pawseys and their home in his vision for as long as he possibly could.

The car turned left out of the lane and all sight of the homestead had gone.

'Phew!' said Mother. 'The wretched evacuation is finally over. Can you believe it?'

'Ov-er, ov-er. Off to London town,' Jill sang. She bounced up and down on the seat jogging Billy's knees. Each bounce caused a miserable squelch of his skin against the leatherette car seat.

'I know how it feels, not trusting that a terrible time has really come to an end.' Uncle Ted said, fingers twitching through his white forelock. He turned round to Billy. 'Now you can put your evacuation right behind you.'

'Running wild amongst pigs and chickens. It certainly wasn't good for him, Ted.'

'No, and on your own there. Can't have been good for you, Billy. Rotten war, rotten for all of us.'

As they passed the road with the congregational church, Billy saw a group of little girls. They turned to see the car. There was Sally. She started running wildly after the car, waving and waving, her little arms high above her head. 'Bill-eeeee.' It seemed as if she was drowning and he wasn't staying to save her this time. He pressed his face to the window until she was a tiny spot in the distance.

'Don't kneel up like that, Billy,' said Mother. 'It's not good for you.'

The windows were steamed up already. Billy wrote where they couldn't see, 'I will come back. It *was* good for me.'

END OF BOOK TWO

If you have enjoyed Infiltration, please consider leaving a review on Amazon and Goodreads. Reviews are extremely helpful to authors and to potential readers

If you haven't yet read Book One of the trilogy, it is Intrusion. http://www.amazon/dp/B00UN1433G
It tells how Billy's story begins in 1937 when war is threatening and Kenneth is first introduced.

Book Three, Impact, set in postwar London with Billy and Kenneth in adolescence, will come out towards the end of 2015.

Other work by Rosalind Minett can be found on Amazon.

Me-Time Tales: tea breaks for mature women and curious men. A set of ironic short stories.
www.amazon.co.uk/dp/B00RO8RJPU

Crime Shorts
No. 1 Oyster, a boy with potential
www.amazon.com/dp/B00OQTA1FK

No. 2 Homed, who is guilty child or adult?
www.amazon.com/dp/B00VAVQ1DS

Blogs:

www.characterfulwriter.com

www.fictionalcharacterswriting.blogspot.com

Lightning Source UK Ltd.
Milton Keynes UK
UKOW06f1808070416

271760UK00016B/370/P